RUNNING
FOR
SHELTER

Also by Michelle Spring

Every Breath You Take

Published by POCKET BOOKS

RUNNING FOR SHELTER

A LAURA PRINCIPAL MYSTERY

MICHELLE SPRING

POCKET BOOKS

New York London Toronto Sydney Tokyo Singapore

POCKET BOOKS, a division of Simon & Schuster Inc.
1230 Avenue of the Americas, New York, NY 10020

Library of Congress Cataloging-in-Publication Data

Spring, Michelle.
    Running for shelter / by Michelle Spring
        p.   cm.
    ISBN 0-671-87093-9
    I. Title.
    PR6069.P73R86   1996
    823'.914—dc20   95-35499
                                                              CIP

First Pocket Books hardcover printing August 1996

10   9   8   7   6   5   4   3   2   1

*For Mack Spring
and
Bernice Spring*

ACKNOWLEDGMENTS

The people who helped me to shape this book through their comments on the manuscript were Felicity Bryan, Michele Topham, Cathy Douglas, Brigid Mellon, my wonderfully supportive editors—Yvette Goulden of Orion and Jane Chelius of Pocket Books—and my even more wonderfully supportive partner, David Held.

For sharing advice and expertise, thanks to Inspector Chris Bainbridge of the Essex Constabulary, to Hilary Coulby and her colleagues at the Manila office of Oxfam, and to Hamit Dardigan, Carol Gilligan, Lizbeth Goodman, Diana Held, Peter Held, Veronica Held, Rosa Stanworth Held, Ashley King, Gill Motley, Henrietta Moore, Frances Pine, and Meghan Vaughan.

I am grateful to Mrs. Widad for arranging my visit to the Kuwaiti embassy and to the ambassador of the Republic of Kuwait and the counselor and their staffs for making me welcome.

I am grateful also to the late Graham Davies, whose intelligence and care made a difference.

But I would like to acknowledge most of all the help of people from Kalayaan and from the Commission for Filipino Migrant Workers. Sister Margaret Healey combines clearheaded analysis with passionate commitment; if domestic workers from the Philippines receive just treatment, it will at least in part be due to her efforts. Fe Balotabot, Alma Laranjo, and Joy are private household workers who were generous enough to share with me their experiences; they have lived the stories that most of us merely read.

The inquiry into the conditions of domestic service has been conducted by means of two series of questions circulated respectively among mistresses and maids. . . . The answers so far received provide an unequivocal condemnation of our whole system of household organization. . . . From these varying social levels the answer returned is clear, decisive, and for the most part, reasoned: the profession is felt to be undesirable, if not repulsive, under its present conditions.

—*The Guardian*, May 27, 1913
(repeated on May 27, 1994)

RUNNING
FOR
SHELTER

1

If it hadn't been for my promise to Helen, I would never have risked the roads on such a drenching day. Rainwater sheeted across the windscreen, creating gaps in vision. The Saab might sometimes have been a semisubmersible for all I could see of the route. And more than once during the journey, I had to slow to a snail's pace where Norfolk topsoil, under pressure of the deluge, had surged out of one field and relocated in another, pressing the road into temporary service as a riverbed. I wondered what it would be like to have to abandon my car here in the dark in the middle of nowhere. I felt vulnerable—as if the cultivated Norfolk countryside might be nothing more than a veneer over a wilder and less hospitable core.

But the sense of abandonment among the elements was a fleeting phenomenon, and I had little time to savor the

sensation of exposure. With a 'nuff-said suddenness—
as if it had already proved its point—the downpour
ceased.

Burnham St. Stephens came into view. In the village
high street, an elderly couple, umbrellas stolidly furled,
sauntered along the pathway behind their dogs, and all
was calm. The puddles by the roadside were placid. The
row of terraced houses that adjoined the churchyard,
their lights shimmering through thin curtains, looked as
cozy as kittens, and the wilderness retreated into my
unconscious again.

It was good to be back. As soon as the car rolled to a
halt outside Wildfell Cottage, I opened the window and
breathed deeply of the moist night air. The sounds of
the engine died away. Gradually I tuned in to the under-
tones that pricked the silence of the countryside. Even,
after a moment, the snuffling of a hedgehog, working her
way around the patch of meadow that we refer to as
a lawn.

The door to the cottage opened, and Helen stood
framed in the glow of light. "It's just me, Helen," I
called softly.

"Laura!" Helen stepped forward into the dark. Her
voice was round with pleasure, and her welcome
brought me ease. She ushered me inside, unlaced my
damp boots, shooed away the neighbor's cat, and settled
me on the sofa, plumping the downy cushions behind
my back. She poured me a glass of red wine from the
bottle that was breathing on the hearth.

"Cheers," she said with a smile, snuggling down in
the armchair. When she lifted her wine in my direction,
the reflection from the fire made rainbows in the glass.
For the first time, I regretted all the weekends at Wildfell
Cottage I had recently missed. Best friends need to be

sometimes together, and Helen and I had a lot of catching up to do.

"To you, Helen. And," I added, as her eleven-year-old daughter came in from the kitchen with a tray of hors d'oeuvres, "to the chef. Ginny, these phyllo pastry parcels are wonderful. Don't tell me you learned this at school." In my day, cookery classes rarely went beyond the white sauce.

Helen took that as a cue for an old joke. Our shared history, Helen's and mine, goes all the way back to our undergraduate days, when we lived in rooms on the same corridor in Newnham. Even then, a passion for shopping was one of the qualities by which you could tell us apart. My rooms were plain and comfortable and none too neat; Helen's, by contrast, were bursting with treasures from bric-a-brac sales. Today, when I want excitement, I head anywhere but for the high street. Helen's idea of adventure is to stalk the shops and the market stalls until she captures a party frock or an early edition of Stendhal at a knockdown price.

"If you spent more time in Marks and Spencers," she teased, "you would realize that the best hors d'oeuvres come out of a freezer."

"Wrong, Helen," I said, pulling a face that wouldn't look amiss in bedlam. "If I spent more time in Marks and Spencers, I'd go mad."

I shifted my legs so that Ginny could squeeze onto the sofa beside me. "It must be two months since you've been to the cottage, Laura," she declared, making herself comfortable and offering me another savory. "What's the story?"

I tried to pass it off. "You know what it's like, Ginny. In my business, things seldom go according to plan. A little case here, a little case there . . ."

"Here a case, there a case, everywhere a case, case . . ." Ginny intoned, picking up the refrain. She's growing up.

"I am in the extraordinary position—extraordinary, that is, for a woman who's not an heiress—of having three separate locations where I can warm my toes. The house in Cambridge is the official residence, the address to which the Inland Revenue writes and the place where I store my bits and pieces. The flat in Camden Town is where I often stay when I am working in London; my partner, Sonny, calls it "our home," but I am not so sure. For one thing, Sonny created it—the blinds, the tiles in the kitchen, and the stain on the bathroom ceiling are all down to him. For another, the title deeds are actually in his name.

And here in North Norfolk, just five minutes' drive from Holkham Bay, is Wildfell Cottage. The cottage is really a converted barn—though those bald words hardly convey its beauty—and it is set in the wooded corner of what was once a farm, on three graceful acres of land bisected by a stream. Helen is my co-owner, our friend Stevie is a tenant, and Wildfell is my favorite place of all.

We come here often in summer. In the mild evenings, we sit in the garden until dark, breathing in the heady scent of honeysuckle. And even in the winter, when our visits are more sporadic, the cottage remains a fine place to catch up on your reading or your sleep, to warm yourself on friendship or simply to wash away the tensions of the town.

But life and work had kept me on a London treadmill for many weeks past, and at Wildfell I had made myself conspicuous by my absence.

"What have you been up to then?" I asked Ginny. Changing the subject.

"We've got a new maths teacher at school. *Mr.* Stephenson."

"Are you trying to tell me that he's a little on the formal side?"

"A little!" Ginny exclaimed. "You should have been there yesterday—" and she was off, on a tale of pupil derring-do and teacher-don't. She peppered her account with exclamations designed to convey how *monstrously* unfair it all was. Within a minute, her enthusiasm kindling mine, Ginny had me giggling.

When Helen Cochrane and I first took over Wildfell Cottage, little Ginny was just a big-headed baby with a foolish grin. The week after we pocketed the keys, the Cochrane household fell apart; Helen's husband went to work one morning and simply disappeared, shedding in one fell swoop the frightening responsibilities of fatherhood and marriage. It was at Wildfell that Helen and I huddled together waiting for news, while the police scoured the southern counties and reporters vied for the story. One of the most searing memories I carry from that time is the sound of Ginny's sorrow. The slightest noise—a footfall upstairs, the wind in the garden— would set her off again. "Da-da-da-da-da," she would intone for minutes on end, until Helen or I, unable to bear her song of loss, would succeed in rocking her to sleep. James Cochrane turned up again, of course. He made a new life for himself, and with Helen's help— generous for her daughter's sake—he repaired his relationship with Ginny. But Wildfell has never ceased to represent a place of safety for Helen and Ginny and me, a kind of spiritual center—living proof that home is where you make it.

Suddenly, Ginny looked at her watch. "Ten o'clock!" she exclaimed, and she bounced off the sofa and up the stairs like Cinderella with an early curfew. I raised an eyebrow at Helen, lowered it again as I remembered that the long-running skirmish over television had at last been resolved. Ginny's campaign had grown more vociferous over the years, but Helen and I had been adamant: we refused to share our evenings by the fire with *The Gladiators*. Stevie, our new tenant, had presented Ginny with a portable telly, on condition that it not be allowed to wander beyond Ginny's bedroom.

So when Helen and I settled to the serious swapping of news, savoring the ups and downs of each other's life, we started with Stevie. Stevie is my right-hand woman at Aardvark Investigations. She is bold and resourceful and formidably self-contained, and I've always regarded it as a mark of good fortune that she is for us, not against us. Our search the year before for a congenial tenant to share the pleasures of Wildfell—and the costs—had proved complicated to say the least, but Helen and I had agreed in the end that Stevie fitted the bill.

"It was the spoons that persuaded me that we had done the right thing," Helen recalled, referring to our first weekend all together at Wildfell. The rain had been heavy for days, forcing us—again—to stay indoors. Stevie transformed necessity into pleasure. She had a casserole bubbling in the oven when the rest of us tumbled in on Friday evening. She fed us. Then—using subtle suggestion where nothing stronger would have worked—she arranged us around the fireplace, adjusted the piano stool, and launched Helen off on a thumping rendition of "My Baby Just Cares for Me." I unpacked the saxophone and joined in. Ginny sang, her voice promisingly throaty for one so young. And though Stevie had claimed to have no musical talents, she established, to our astonishment and delight, a jaunty rhythm on the spoons. *Spoons?* we asked. Evidence, Stevie winked, of a misspent youth.

Now our conversation moved on to Helen's new job. Helen works at Eastern University in Cambridge, but I can't any longer describe her as a librarian. She has confounded those acquaintances who labored under the illusion that you have to be either pompous or aggressive—preferably both—to whiz your way up the management ladder. As of February, with the retirement of old Evans, Helen had taken over the top job in library services. Her first months involved some pretty radical reshaping of policy, but she didn't seem fazed; getting there, she insisted, is half the fun.

I looked Helen over carefully. "There's more of the executive about you now," I said with as straight a face as I could muster. This wasn't, I well knew, Helen's idea of a compliment.

"Sure," she replied, laughing. "It's the slipper socks. They reek with authority." And then she switched the subject. "What's Sonny been up to lately?" she asked, referring to the man I love.

"I've hardly seen him for the past two weeks. My dear partner"—I use that term in the professional and the personal sense, since Sonny shares my business as well as my life—"has been jetting around like a European commissioner, for a no-expenses-spared client."

"And Stevie's in Texas for the moment." Helen smiled pointedly. "So, Laura Principal, that just leaves *you*."

I knew immediately what she meant and couldn't prevent myself from shifting to the defensive. Explained that I'd been oh-so-busy. That work in London had been piling up, so that I'd found myself sometimes with two or three cases on the go at once. "There's a problem of time," I concluded, "since the business really took off. I have less time for myself, less time to be in Cambridge, less time for breaks at Wildfell. Less time, period."

Helen didn't disagree. "Yes," she said dryly, "we've noticed." She poured me another glass of wine and waited for me to continue.

It was a fair cop. "What can I say, Helen? You know as well as I do that Sonny and I have always aimed for separate but parallel lives. A shared life, during the week, when Dominic and Daniel are at their mother's. And lots of separate time around weekends and vacations, when Sonny fulfills his fatherly commitments and I hang out with my friends. It's worked well up till now."

"But it's getting harder?"

I shot Helen a grateful look. Helen was looking not to quarrel, but to understand. "Much harder," I agreed. "I used to be able to draw the boundaries firmly, but you know what these things are like. Our lives are becoming almost impossible to disentangle."

I gave Helen a recent for-instance: how Dominic and Daniel's latest interest was competitive swimming. How, accordingly, Sonny had been doing evening duty at the pool. And how, while Sonny was flitting from one European capital to another, I'd been left holding the towels. I sighed. Even I didn't know to what extent I wanted this new domesticity.

Helen smiled as if to say: It's not that big a deal. "Give yourself time," she advised. And then she caught my eye. "But one thing you owe us, Laura. If you are going to redraw the boundaries, do it openly. Don't drift away."

"Drift away? That's the last thing I'd want."

The embers in the fire flickered low. If we were going to stay up later, one of us would have to fetch logs from the shed. Helen took the decision into her hands. "Don't know about you"—she stood up and stretched—"but I could do with an early night." Helen won the toss for the first shower, moved the cat from her chair to mine, and ambled off to bed. At the foot of the stairs, she turned back and smiled.

" 'Night," she said. "Nice to have you here."

" 'Night, Helen," I whispered.

I unlatched the back door. The neighbor's cat snuggled his face into my neck, unwilling to be put out just yet. With one hand supporting the heavy base of his soft, smooth spine, I stepped out into the night. The moon had been hidden by clouds when I drove up to Wildfell Cottage, but now it beamed down, illuminating the apple tree with a silver sliver of light. John lifted his head and left me at last, his ears alert, padding purposefully off toward the meadow. I made my way happily to bed.

Saturday morning I was up early enough to startle the village postman. He was scrunching his way along the gravel drive as I stepped out into the dew. "Good morning," I said.

He handed me a letter addressed to Laura Principal. "Don't get much post around here," he observed. It was intended as a question.

"No," I agreed, my attention taken by the envelope. Who would write to me at Wildfell? I looked curiously at the Canadian stamp, the handwriting, the indecipherable postmark. My mother grew up in Saskatchewan, before my father—dashing in his Air Force uniform—

whisked her away to England. But the address wasn't written in a round, straightforward style, like my mother's; this was an upright British hand, and the self-conscious flourish on the capitals looked distantly familiar.

Inside was a single sheet of plain white Basildon Bond. And a few lines, amounting to little more, in effect, than a telephone number and *Hello, remember me?* There was no return address.

I swallowed hard. Padded back inside the house to make a pot of coffee.

Remember me? I boiled the kettle and ground the beans and splashed the water into the *cafetière,* thinking all the while of Claire. Yes, friend of my youth, I remember you. I burdened the plunger and poured hot coffee into my favorite mug. I fetched logs from the shed. The rough scratch of the bark on my hands was comfortingly here and now, but it didn't staunch the flow of memory. I carried the logs into the sitting room, swept the grate, laid the fire, and lit it. Quietly, so as not to wake the others. I put on a recording from Berlin in the 1960s. Finally, I rummaged through the oak sideboard, found the photo of Claire that had been tucked away long ago, and—as the air filled with the voice of Ella Fitzgerald at her expressive best—I settled into the armchair and just let it come.

When Claire and I met, we were eleven years old. My father, Paul, was a long-distance lorry driver, half his life or more spent in transit between Bristol and the Continent. My mother, Dorothy, ran—still does—a hairdressing business from the back of the house. They were thrilled when I passed the examination for entry to grammar school. I was apprehensive. I didn't know whether I could hold my own in a big school, full of girls whom the neighborhood kids would call toffee-nosed. Didn't know how much the differences mattered, the little things that could set me apart: that I alone of my classmates helped my mother in the shop; that I didn't own a dressing gown; that I had never been to the theater in London—indeed (would I dare to say so?) had never been to the theater at all.

Claire's father was an architect. Claire had a dressing gown—two in fact—and her family went on regular expeditions to London, theater and all. But from the moment that she offered me a butterscotch behind Mme. Perrault's back, taking the sting out of the French teacher's mimicry of my poor pronunciation, I knew that—against the odds—we would be friends.

I studied the photo. Nine years had passed since I'd last seen Claire, and many more since this picture had been recorded. And still, there was nothing unfamiliar to me in the features of her face. I recognized the composure, above all: that look that said, "Try me. I won't be surprised." The eyes, berry bright behind wire-framed spectacles. The neat row of teeth, the imperturbable mouth, and the heart-shaped face: all so precisely, so poignantly Claire. All twelve years of her, perched on the granite balustrade of the railway bridge, until her mother in a voice rising toward panic ordered her down, and her father—always more interested in aesthetic possibilities than practical ones—lifted his camera and captured this image.

He had presented a copy to me. I don't know why Oliver Atkinson liked me, but he did. He recognized, perhaps, that I had no need of him and would make no demands. Oliver Atkinson was charming and irresponsible. He wasn't made for demands. Years later, when he killed himself, people whispered, "What a terrible thing, how unhappy he must have been." Not me. I loathed him for it. For the way Claire's eyes went out of focus: bright as berries they remained, but they never seemed again to look directly at me or anyone else. For the fact that Claire left, soon after, for Canada. For the fact that I had not heard from her since. Until today.

Helen emerged, her face scrubbed and shining. She peeped over my shoulder at the photograph. "Claire," she said at once. "What made you think of her?" So I passed her the letter and waited for her reaction. "But that's great news," she said. "Claire's coming back to England at last."

"Only for two days," I demurred. "And she doesn't give a home adress, so I still can't contact her in Canada."

"But she has given you a telephone number where you can reach her while she's in London. So," Helen insisted, "the important thing is, you can reestablish contact." She patted my shoulder to show how pleased she was and headed for the kitchen.

When Helen returned with a fresh pot of coffee and a tray of scones, she indulged me. Or maybe she was genuinely curious, having met Claire only once. "Were you alike?" Helen asked. "When you were at school?"

"No. No, not really." For one thing, I explained, Claire was the beautiful one. The extraordinary look of her is part of many of my memories. Stretched side by side across her bed, playing cards and eating (unthinkable delicacy) cucumber sandwiches, with real butter and the crusts cut off. Riding our bikes up and down the lane behind my house: chasing, whooping, daring, Claire's silvery plait swinging over her shoulder as she bounced her front wheels over the ridges that rutted the center of the path. These flashbacks still make me smile with pleasure.

But, as so often happens, Claire's beauty kept people at arm's length. When we went to our first dance together—me overdressed in what my mum thought of as party clothes, Claire far more sophisticated—I shuffled around the dance floor with several of the local boys, while Claire remained on the sidelines, exquisitely aloof. In the presence of boys, her composure froze into icy disdain; the more nervous they were about bridging the distance between her alarming good looks and their own adolescent scruffiness, the frostier she became.

I could comfort Claire in those days. I knew how to draw out the sting of rejection for her, as she did for me. But then, her father died, and with him went the possibility of comfort.

This part Helen already knew, but I told her again. How father and daughter had a row one weekend and parted on bad terms. How Mr. Atkinson, always teetering on the edge of depression, tipped over, drove to Norfolk and hanged himself from the highest beam of Wildfell Cottage. How at one stroke he denied Claire the father she adored and turned their holiday home into the instrument of his death. Soon after, Claire, of course, sold Wildfell Cottage to Helen and me for a pittance and disappeared overseas.

"Oh, the shark bites . . ." Ella Fitzgerald was still singing, with a roughness that suited my mood. I went in search of a pullover. My roomy cashmere warmed me, a little. And Helen's friendship warmed me more. She let me reminisce the morning away. She asked me questions and listened to my answers. And then she persuaded me to put on a jacket and to accompany her and

Ginny for a long cleansing walk along the headland of Holkham Bay.

Helen, with the courage of a true friend, even broached the subject of why it mattered to me still: she made me confess—perhaps made me realize—that Claire was my link with childhood. When Claire left, I put away childish things. And sometimes, most powerfully, I want them back.

I have no doubt that—for me at least—Norfolk is the perfect place to unwind. It has everything: surging seafronts, peaceful harbors, nonstop clean air, and fresh seafood without the prices or the pretensions of big-city restaurants. Best of all, these delights can be mine within two hours of leaving the office—no hanging around airports, no haggling for a taxi, no last-minute discovery that my beachside hotel is now fronted by a motorway.

I had planned on staying over in Norfolk after Helen left on Sunday. An extra day or two—wandering around Wells-next-the-Sea, taking a boat out to Blakeney Sands to watch the seals—would have suited me to a T. But Sonny had other ideas. He rang from London to entice me back, wanted me to see a theatrical producer—a very big deal in the arts world, he said—on Monday.

"You made the appointment," I protested. "Shouldn't you be the one to keep it?"

He played the busy card. "I'm still tied up tracking Dr. Jamieson—"

"That cosmetic so-called surgeon who ran off with his liposuction assistant?"

"That's the one. Mrs. Jamieson's silicone has slipped. She is understandably outraged to find that hubby has abandoned her for a new experimental object."

"So you're busy. What else?" Sonny had several other reasons up his sleeve. Obligation, for one: I owed him, he reminded me, for the time he returned early from Manchester to help me with a case. Prudence, for another: even with lots of work on the books, he insisted, we shouldn't ignore a client with as much clout as producer-extraordinaire Thomas Butler. Finally, and most persuasively, Sonny made me an offer I couldn't refuse: a night at the theater, his treat, as soon as his current case was complete.

The deal was struck. I set aside my reservations, packed my bag, and schlepped through the puddles back to London. I passed the journey by anticipating some of the ways that Sonny and I might celebrate our reunion.

But when I tiptoed into the flat in Camden, I found Sonny settled into the sofa, his body padded by holiday brochures, locked into anticipation of quite a different kind.

"What's all this?" I asked, planting a kiss on his forehead. As if I didn't know.

"Time to get cracking," Sonny declared, smoothing my hair for me where it had been ruffled by the wind. "If I don't book up soon, the boys and I will be spending the summer at Butlin's."

I knew from experience, it wasn't concern about booking arrangements that propelled Sonny into the search for a vacation site, it was pleasure. At the whiff of winter's end, he likes to launch himself into the first phase of holiday hunting. In round one, no destination is out of bounds; Sonny weighs the merits of Bournemouth and Blackpool alongside those of Bali. Then, gradually, the range narrows down until he has the perfect holiday in his sights. He shows the same single-mindedness and attention to detail—and the same enthusiasm—that make him a successful private investigator.

As for me, I am usually content to keep tabs from the sidelines, and then, when his plans are laid, to wave him fondly on his way. But this evening I had a different agenda. I snuggled in alongside Sonny on the sofa. He scarcely noticed. His long, lean legs brushed against mine, but his mind was somewhere in the south of France. My question—"Do you fancy somethng to eat?"—met with no reply.

I traced the line of thick, fair hair that fell across Sonny's forehead, the curve of his eyebrows, the sweep of his cheek. Even with stubble on his chin—by omission, not design—he was well worth a look. Disconcerted at last by my gaze, Sonny shook the hair back off his forehead, but it was a few seconds more before he could wrench his eyes away from the travel guide and focus them on me. Even then, a determined finger marked his place in the book.

"Say something?" he asked.

I smiled and laced the fingers of his left hand through the fingers of my right. "Why don't we slip out and have a curry?"

The smile was returned, but I could tell, a tandoori wasn't top of his agenda. "Sure, if you like," he said, kissing my fingers before freeing his own. "Say in an hour, sweetie? I'll probably be finished with these brochures by then."

Then he reopened the Michelin guide, and without so much as an au revoir, he bolted back to France.

Probably wasn't good enough. I slipped my jacket back on and skipped out. Past the first Indian restaurant. On to the second, where the *nan* bread was fresher and the spices more subtle. Returned half an hour later with a feast, which I spread in front of him.

At last the brochures were abandoned. Sonny loaded his plate diligently, leaving no chicken, no *bhaji,* untouched. And then—after we had eaten, after he had finally properly acknowledged my sacrifice in returning early to London—we said to hell with housekeeping and cozied off to bed, leaving the dirty dishes to make their own way home.

2

A deal's a deal, so midway through Monday morning, I met Thomas Butler at his Mayfair club. Sonny, leaving nothing to chance, had issued me a brief résumé of Butler's career. I passed it over, letting memory serve instead.

Thomas Butler was one of the most powerful figures in the West End. He had produced a string of successful shows, beginning in the eighties with *Highwayman's Revenge*, but his move to mega-status hinged on a spectacular financial gamble. Butler's proposal for a musical drama about death row had received unanimous thumbs-down from major theatrical backers. *Without Windows* eventually became a hit, launched largely from Butler's own funds, and his fortune and formidable reputation were established. He was shrewd, he was intelligent and he was very rich. He was also known as the liberal conscience of the West End. Even in the instrumental eighties, his productions didn't eschew issues of social justice, and Butler was the name most often brandished aloft by anyone determined to demonstrate that commercial needn't mean crass.

At first meeting, I found it difficult to link these facts with the face of the man I joined for coffee. Thomas Butler looked (appropriately, as it turned out) like a child's-eye image of Frair Tuck. He was roly-poly, pale-skinned, and plain, with deep-set hazel eyes, and he was a pleasure to talk to. Had his manner, I inquired when we had warmed up a bit, won over reluctant actors to his team?

"It doesn't work like that," Butler explained, while waiting to order peppermint tea and nothing else for himself. Probably a sensible course of action, in view of the approaching lunch hour and the size of his waistline. "The names—the television stars who bring in the coachloads of visitors—need constant flattery. But the real professionals, the ones who make a production work, don't need to be persuaded. They know a good production when they come up against it. And all my productions," he added with a glint, "are good."

Butler noticed that I lingered over the menu. "Go on, don't be put off by my peppermint tea. The BLT in this club is the best in London. Not to be missed."

Feeling relaxed in Butler's company and, alongside him, slimmer than usual, I broke my customary injunction against eating with clients. It turned out Butler was right. The sandwich was extraordinary, the thin slices of bacon piled high, the mayonnaise made by an expert hand, and the tomato fresh and sweet.

With the arrival of our order, we got down to business.

"The matter is delicate," Butler warned, as the waiter glided away.

"The matter often is." I held my sandwich with both hands, intent on preventing the slippery tomato from making a dash for freedom. "If it weren't delicate, you would probably go directly to the police, and Aardvaark Investigations would be the loser. That's why it is in my interest to be discreet, and in your interest to be frank."

"All right, I'll be frank." Butler's smile suggested that he was as aware as I of that old joke. "Do you know the Duke of Leicester?"

"On Curzon Street?" We exchanged confirmatory nods. "Where *Hope Fulfilled* is playing? Is that one of yours?"

Butler rejected this suggestion with a shudder of distaste. "No. Nothing to do with me. But my *Inside Sherwood Forest*, a contemporary fable on the theme of Robin Hood, is next on schedule. We began work in the Leicester's rehearsal rooms a month ago." His speech gave me a chance to make serious headway with my BLT. "You're enjoying that," Butler observed. The smile of amusement lightened his face.

"Delicious." I grinned back. "So what's going on in Sherwood Forest that requires investigation?"

"I'm afraid someone connected with the production has taken the theme too much to heart. We've had a spate of thefts, beginning with a cigarette case taken from Hannah Humphries on the day rehearsals began, and continuing up to the present. Saturday morning one of the backstage crew found his leather jacket missing. His pride and joy, apparently. It was all I could do to stop him going straight round to the police."

I finished the BLT and shifted into a more comfortable position in the deeply cushioned chair. "So you suspect someone from the cast? Or the crew?"

"Precisely," Butler replied, relieved at this ready understanding. "Like all theater companies, we have a security regime that prevents outsiders getting wind of the way rehearsals are going before we're ready for the world—or more particularly, for the tabloids. It also forestalls compensation claims from wandering tourists who might tumble off the proscenium."

"You have a doorman?"

"From a private security firm. He opens the rehearsal rooms, stays behind until everyone's gone. And he keeps a comprehensive record of comings and goings."

"And when the cigarette case, and the leather pride-and-joy, went missing, the only entries on the doorman's record were members of cast and crew. Right?"

"Right. That is why I need your help. The team is getting jumpy. It's not good for concentration to know that someone is rummaging through your things while you're rehearsing. And when one of your workmates walks off with another's prized possessions, it's bad for group morale. People are beginning to look at each other with mistrust."

"You have a theory?"

"Everyone has a theory. Maid Marian suspects Little John; the chief stagehand puts the blame on the Sheriff of Nottingham; Nottingham himself, a notorious anticleric, has fingered Friar Tuck."

"And just whom do you suspect?"

"I haven't got a clue. If you ask me"—and here Butler paused, looking around as if for confirmation that we couldn't be overheard—"the whole lot of them are a bit shifty." He laughed, his little eyes crinkling with delight. "But you must promise to keep that confidence to yourself!"

"Mum's the word." I refrained from adding the childhood follow-up, "Keep it under your armpit," and mentally slapped my own wrist. There's such a thing as being *too* relaxed. "And you can't go to the police because you don't want the cast further upset by formal investigations?"

"It goest deeper than that." Butler lowered his voice, glanced quickly around the room again. This time he was serious. "What if the person responsible should turn out to be one of my key players?"

"Liam O'Laughlin, for instance?"

"Oh, so you've heard? I didn't know that private investigators kept their noses to the grindstone of celebrity gossip."

"Let's just say I have my sources." Ginny is an assiduous fan of Australian soaps. She had mentioned Liam O'Laughlin only yesterday at the cottage.

"Liam's contract cost me a fortune. O'Laughlin plays Will Scarlett—badly, I fear—but his mere presence will guarantee full houses for months. It could be disastrous for the production if he turns out to be the thief. However," Butler added, forestalling my next question, "there is no reason to suspect him. Liam may not be the brightest boy on the London stage, but his behavior is, as far as I know, aboveboard."

"But if your faith in O'Laughlin should turn out to be misplaced, I assume that you wouldn't want him hauled up before the magistrates and transported back to Sydney?"

"Precisely. What I do want is for you to find out who's doing it—and quickly. Put a stop to it without involving the police. Keep it in-house, so to speak. Is that too much to ask?" He suddenly looked uncertain. It was hard to tell whether his doubts turned on the ethics of the brief or on my personal capabilities.

"For the man who introduced me to the best BLT I've had this side of New York, nothing's too much. I'll give it my best shot."

We shook on it and then got down to details. I filled three pages of my notebook with background on the theater world, and names and numbers of contacts. I spun a plan of action off the top of my head and set a date the following week on which to provide Butler with a progress report.

There was only one more thing to do. But before we could do it, the waiter presented a telephone to Butler. Although I tried to look absorbed in the contents of my briefcase, I couldn't fail to notice that Butler listened attentively, and that when he hung up, his pudgy face was creased with concern.

"Not another theft?"

Butler shook his head. "Nothing so simple." There was no trace of the former openness. Butler signed the bill, collected his briefcase, and with the curtest of farewells was gone.

Back in the office, I filled Sonny in on my meeting. He leaned against the doorframe, very much at ease, and assumed a thoughtful look.

"What's up?" I asked, as I was obviously intended to do.

"I've got a problem. I don't feel relaxed"—he *looked* completely relaxed, I noticed—"about you hanging around with the great and the good in the acting world. Rumor has it that some of these actors could charm the trunk off an elephant. And what will you do," he asked with exaggerated concern, "if you happen to come across one who's even better looking than me?"

"Give me a break," I groaned. "The only actor in this

production with a reputation for good looks—and I use the word *actor* advisedly—is at least ten years too young for me. Liam O'Laughlin is definitely not my cup of Horlick's. As you know," I said sidling up to Sonny in a Mae West imitation. "I go for the older, more sophisticated type." I rubbed my shoulder slowly up and down his arm.

"So do I." Sonny laughed, pulling me toward him. "So I'm your only toy boy, am I?" Sonny is younger than me, and he teases me about the age gap a little too often. I resolved to take it up with him sometime soon, preferably after trouncing him at a game of squash. For now, I was considering other games.

"In the office?" Sonny asked with a raised eyebrow.

But as luck would have it, just then the office door opened and Stevie strolled in. For such a muscular woman, Stevie is astonishingly light on her feet. I rarely hear her coming up the stairs—unless, that is, she happens to be wearing her biker boots, in which case you might imagine that the Hell's Angels, Oakland chapter, were moving toward us en masse. Today, she was wearing suede slip-ons and entered as demurely as Giselle. She wasn't in the least nonplussed to find Sonny and I wrapped up in each other's arms.

"Hi, kids," she called, flinging a wide-brimmed hat onto the arm of the coatrack with a flick of her wrist.

"Terrific aim!" This in breathless admiration, simultaneously, from Sonny and me.

"And a terrific hat," I added, drawing away from Sonny to run a finger around the leather brim. "How was Texas?"

"More to the point," Sonny interjected, "how was Old Macdonald?"

Old Macdonald is the name we use for a rich American rancher who has become, much to the benefit of our annual accounts, a regular client. A few years back, he came to us for help with a problem with the European end of his business. Stevie handled the case. She finished in no time flat, dotted the i's and crossed the t's. But then Macdonald tried to help her with her spelling, and she responded with an unambiguous no.

Macdonald has never met a woman like Stevie before—or so he tells us, every time we see him. Her indifference drives him wild. He tried to impress Stevie by showing off—and even *I* have to admit, the guy's got a few things to boast about. But Stevie had other things on her mind. Then he tried to undermine her self-confidence, challenging the way she did things, running her down. But Stevie's self-esteem comes from some place that Macdonald couldn't touch; she just shrugged and walked away. In desperation, Macdonald tried to buy her off, offering a hard-to-resist salary if she'd base herself in Texas. But body guarding for an autocratic rancher is not Stevie's idea of a good career move. Besides, having just found her feet at Wildfell Cottage with Helen and me, she had no intention of abandoning the Norfolk coast for the Lone Star State.

Poor Macdonald. "That girl just looks right through me," he had complained recently, in a doomed bid for the sympathy vote. I was listening with half an ear while going over some paperwork with Dee, one of the freelancers who works with us in the long gaps that are the staple of her acting career.

Dee hadn't even bothered to tell Macdonald off. She looked at me instead. "That *boy,*" she declared with an impressive Texan drawl, "just hasn't learned a thing from twenty years of feminism." Not for nothing does Dee aspire to a career on the stage.

"Woman." Macdonald had corrected sourly.

To make a long story short, Macdonald doesn't give up and Stevie doesn't give in. Once or twice a year, he finds some excuse to apply for her services. You can refuse if you want, Sonny and I remind her.

"I can handle Macdonald," Stevie insists. We believe her. If you saw her in action, you'd believe her too. When Stevie says, "Back off," not many people hang around to argue.

Still, we were surprised when she agreed to spend two weeks in Texas advising on security for Macdonald's ranch. What I hadn't realized, until I waved her on her way, kitted out with new boots, was that Stevie is a passionate rider. And here she was back from her fortnight, looking slimmer, browner, and distinctly happier.

"So?" I asked, intrigued.

"So," Stevie answered wryly, a smile playing around the corners of her lips. I badgered her all afternoon, quite shamelessly, but I didn't get a word about the source of that smile. She deflected questions like a cabinet minister with a second family to hide. All she would say about Texas was that the sky at night was big and bright. I reckoned I'd heard that song before.

"Library issues desk," a voice croaked into the telephone.

"Put me through to Helen Cochrane, please." I gave my name and resisted the impulse to recommend a throat lozenge.

Helen's first words brought relief. "Laura? What a ninny you are! Do you realize that you forgot Claire's letter at the cottage? I was just about to put it in the post for you." Helen chuckled, and I could hear the mischief in her voice. "Sign of a secret ambivalence, maybe, about meeting up with Claire again after all these years?"

"Drop the fake Freudian stuff, Helen, I can't afford your fees. And," I said airily, "I don't need the letter anyway. Toss it away. All I need is the number where Claire can be reached when she gets to London." Helen read it slowly to me and repeated it just to be sure; I noted it down in pencil on the back of Claire's photo. "And thanks," I said after a few more moments, signing off. "It was a lovely weekend. See you soon."

Being a private investigator is only 50 percent inquiry. The other half consists of business routines, scarcely distinguishable from everyday procedures in the plumbing and heating trade. And the first principle of buiness, drummed into me by Sonny when negotiating our partnership, is that clients should agree to the terms of en gagement *before* you run up your phone bill, your petrol account, and your adrenaline levels on their behalf. So much for my business acumen. When Thomas Butler dashed away from our Mayfair meeting, I had let him go without even alluding to anything as vulgar as a contract.

The most tedious sort of slog follows from the things you should have done when you had the chance, but didn't. I had slipped up, and I now had no choice but to chase Butler. I drafted a letter of explanation to him, typed it with my own fair hand, and popped it into an envelope with a copy of our standard contract. From his secretary, I learned that Butler was not expected back in the office until the following week. My progress report was also due next week, but without Butler's signature on a contract, I would be unable to make any progress at all. The secretary was moved by my dilemma. She revealed that Mr. Butler would touch base briefly at his home in Palace Gardens Terrace, Kensington, before departing for New York.

I started out the office door, then pulled up short. "Stevie?" I called. Leaving Claire's letter behind at the cottage had been careless, and I wasn't going to be caught out again. "Stevie? Where's that photo you were looking at? With the phone number on the back?" But no need to worry. Stevie, my practical pal, said she had slipped it into my briefcase.

Butler's house in Palace Gardens Terrace was not the biggest I had seen by a long chalk, nor the most elegant, but it had an unpretentious prettiness that took my breath away. The first two floors had substantial bay windows of a pleasing shape, their rounded arches framed by a stipple effect at the top. The sash windows on the floor above overlooked a triangular balcony with a pretty balustrade. It was white, like all the other houses on the street, and so was the wall that afforded partial privacy. The name of the house, traced above the door, was Blenheim.

The bell sounded a light note. The door opened and a slip of a girl stepped into view.

She had the body of a twelve-year-old, so thin that her collar bones stood out harshly from the neckline of her tunic. Fine chestnut hair was gathered into a ponytail high on the crown of her head. She looked frail, but she had eyes that were full of life.

"May I help you?" she inquired. I couldn't be sure of the accent.

I introduced myself. "I've spoken to Thomas Butler's secretary. I know that he is away, but I understand that he will stop here tomorrow evening between journeys. Is that right?"

"Why do you ask?" I hadn't expected this kind of self-assurance from someone who looked so fragile.

I offered her my business card, and the envelope with the contract. "Mr. Butler has hired me to do a job, but I need his signature first. There's a letter in here"—I tapped the envelope—"that should explain everything. Could you see that Thomas Butler deals with this before he leaves London? Please?"

"Certainly." The slight hand that took the folder looked odd somehow, and with a jolt, I realized that the two top joints of her forefinger were missing. She didn't flinch from my gaze. But after glancing at my card, her composure slipped. "You're a private investigator? A detective?"

"Yes. But I'm not with the police."

She hesitated, then surprised me with a question. "Would you mind telling me how you go about tracing a missing person? You *do* do that sort of thing?"

"I do, from time to time. It's most a matter of being systematic. Of starting, say, with family members and friends and workmates. Of asking questions, finding out everything you can." I stopped. "Why? Do you need help to find someone?"

"No, no, I just wondered," she said, flustered for the first time. She took a steadying breath. "But there is something you could help with. To recover something. Something that's been stolen from me."

"What sort of thing?"

"My wages," she said, pointing her mutilated finger emphatically at her thin, little chest to underline the *my.* "My money. That I earned, that my last employer didn't give me . . ."

"Hang on now," I said, glancing at my watch—I had plenty of work waiting—"this sounds like a long story. And if we are talking here about a problem with your employer, it may well be that you need a solicitor rather than a private investigator."

"You won't help me, then." She looked deflated, crestfallen. I felt like a big meanie.

"Tell you what. When I come back to get those papers, let's have a longer talk. You can tell me exactly what the problem is. Maybe I'll be able to think of some way to help." I had a quick look at my diary. "Wednesday. Will you be here at around ten in the morning?"

"I'll be here," she assured me with a radiant smile.

3

At Aardvark Investigations, the investigators had enough to do. There was Thomas Butler's theatrical thief and Mrs. Jamieson's truant husband. There was a security job in Glasgow that had been on hold for weeks. And there was all the routine work that had piled up while Stevie was in the States acquiring a tan and a self-satisfied smile.

It is a principle of business, as of meteorology, that it never rains but it pours. Or perhaps I should say, when referring to paying customers, that the sun never shines but there's a heat wave. Speaking from experience, it seems to me, you *can* have too much of a good thing.

"A Cambridge client," Sonny said, pointing at the telephone extension. "Could be yours."

Marcia Shields had been burgled. I assumed the mantle of the disinterested consultant. "Some of your taxes,"

I advised, "go to support a police service who'll have a pretty good crack at catching burglars." Funny how quickly struggling entrepreneurs can become blasé. Only a couple of years ago I was worried about the overdraft, and now I was contemplating turning work away. "So why come to us?"

The Cambridge woman wasn't put off by my telephone manner. "The straightforward answer," she answered straightforwardly, "is that I'm not sure that I want these burglars apprehended. At least not by the police." Shades of Butler. Two in-house theft cases in a single week?

I stalled for time, asked her where she got our name. Marcia reported that a neighbor—a man whose business had benefited from my attentions—had recommended Laura Principal as a female PI who was tough and smart and honest too. I made a note to put him on our Christmas-card list.

I had a day in hand before Butler's contract could be recovered—and let's face it, flattery will sometimes get you somewhere. Feeling tough, smart, and honest too, I headed down the M11 toward Cambridge. The car engine, which had stalled a couple of times as I pulled away from traffic lights in London, seemed more amenable on the open highway. I put a blues instrumental on the CD player, turned up the volume, and sang my way to Cambridge. Before you could say, "Woke up dis morning . . ." I had reached the commuter belt adjoining Cambridge Station. I negotiated my way along the cycle route to Lyndewode Road and nosed the car into Marcia Shields's narrow driveway, behind a Saab that was certainly newer and most likely in better nick than mine.

"Yours?" I asked the client with a nod at the Saab and a flash of fellow feeling.

"Don't remind me." She explained that she was counting the cost of a radical reconstruction of her car's electrical system—so far successful—and felt less than affectionate toward the Saab.

Marcia Shields was a free-lance designer in her early forties. She was pretty in a contrived sort of way, with long hair that blended several shades of blond, most of them the products of human ingenuity; you'd never accuse Marcia of letting herself go.

The story Marcia Shields related was short and far from sweet. The previous weekend she had crossed the Channel to visit an old friend who lived in Paris. She had dropped the Saab at the garage, taken a cab to Stansted Airport, and meandered for a carefree couple of days along the boulevards with her pal. In her absence, she had unexpected guests. When she returned to Cambridge on Sunday evening, the front door of hor houco wac ajar and a dozen paintings had gone walkabout.

There was no play of self-pity in Marcia's account of the burglary, not even when she confirmed that the paintings, which had belonged originally to her grandfather, were valuable and uninsured. Others might cry over spilt milk, but Ms. Shields was made of sterner stuff.

Except when it came to her sixteen-year-old daughter. Layla had stayed with a friend while Marcia was in Paris, and Layla had nothing to do with the burglary. About this Marcia was vehement. Her loyalty did not, however, extend to Layla's friends. Marcia's description of Layla's boyfriend, in particular, was acid enough to burn holes in the carpet. Either maternal protectiveness had warped her perception, or Vic was a nasty piece of work.

I summed up. "So you fear that some of Layla's friends may have taken advantage of your absence? That's why you haven't gone to the police?"

"In a nutshell," Marcia agreed. And things in the household had been miserable ever since. It's hard enough dealing with a teenage daughter with less-than-likable companions, Marcia pointed out, but relations become even trickier when you suspect her friends of daylight robbery.

I inspected the damage. Marcia had left the house much as she found it on her return from Paris, under the misapprehension that the scene of the crime would yield its secrets to one such as me. The high-ceilinged sitting room overlooking the garden was lovely—or would have been had not someone done their level best to destroy it. The glass fronts of the china cabinet had been smashed. Drawers in the yew side table had been prized open, chipping the veneer. Slivers of glass scrunched underfoot. Books were strewn on the floor, and a porcelain vase lay on its side on the hearth, a cruel crack slicing through the glaze. None of the obvious damage was as telling, however, as the discolorations on the buttermilk walls that testified to the absence of the paintings. The only other missing items were seventy pounds in cash, removed from a briefcase, and a bracelet of freshwater pearls. Other jewelry—some of it much more expensive—had been left untouched.

Marcia was adamant that the doors had been secured when she left, and that the windows were still fastened on her return. I checked for myself, but could pick up no signs of a break-in. The thieves appeared to have come and gone in conventional fashion, through an open door.

I tracked the keys for front door and back. Marcia had

a set, as did Layla. A cleaning woman—who, like the paintings, had been in the family for years—kept the third set.

"Any others?"

Marcia shrugged. "I'm divorced and my ex-husband makes himself scarce. Who else would have a key?"

I had learned my lesson with Butler. No stinting on the paperwork this time round. Marcia read the contract carefully, signed and dated it, gave me the address of the cleaning woman (who could, she avowed, be entrusted with the crown jewels), and finally constructed a list of neighbors' names. You don't cart off a dozen substantial oils without someone in Lyndewode Road catching a glimpse.

Eventually Marcia left the house for a meeting, leaving me alone to examine the sitting room on hands and knees. I used my palms to sweep the wool carpet at the base of the wall where the paintings had hung. This treasure hunt turned up two small objects: an earring in the shape of a silver sunburst, and a minute gold pin, blunt tipped, with grooves around the edge of the head. Nothing, not even dust balls, under the sofa; I can't say for sure that the cleaning woman would keep the crown jewels safe, but by this evidence, she would certainly keep them clean.

I was still crawling about with my bum in the air when I was startled to hear a shuffle in the hallway. "You're the private investigator," a voice declared from the doorway. It sounded like an accusation.

"Laura Principal," I confirmed, standing and smoothing my tights. "And you must be Layla." Layla's style, like her mother's, was decorative, but in a less bourgeois mode. She wore a crocheted top, a long skirt of Indian cotton, black Doc Martens, and jewels in unexpected parts of her face. Except for her complexion and her build, testimony to rude good health, she might have been taken for a New Age waif.

She twined a strand of hair the color of shadows around her finger and looked sullenly away. I tried again. "I guess if those were family paintings, they were yours too. Did you like them?"

"Yes," Layla said, shyly now, but as if she were pleased to be asked. "There is one I especially liked, of a fair-haired woman with a cameo at her throat and a man standing behind her. They remind me—"

She stopped, abashed. Went back to twiddling.

"A man and a woman," I repeated. "Your mother and father?"

For the first time, Layla looked directly at me. "How did you know that?"

I laughed at her astonishment and delivered an exaggerated wink. "Private investigator. Remember?"

She laughed then, and when she relaxed, she had all of her mother's good looks and none of her mother's detachment. She readily answered the rest of my questions.

About the objects I had found: the silver sunburst was hers, but she didn't know what the blunt gold pin was, let alone whom it might belong to. I decided to hang on to it for a while and told her so.

About the events of the weekend. Layla didn't like going over this—she sighed the sigh of the persecuted teenager called to account—but she told me nonetheless. How she had stayed with a chum from sixth form college, name of Barbara Thoday. How they had watched videos, gone shopping, gone to The Junction to hear a South African group. How they hadn't—most emphatically—popped back to Lyndewode Road. When asked directly whether she knew anything about the burglary, Layla's face flared with denial. The indignation, at least, was genuine.

About her friends. Here there was no hesitation. She mounted a vigorous defense of Vic and Petersee (no, not Peter C, she corrected when I had written it down), and Tenko. Her mother thought they were slobs, she said, didn't approve of their scruffy clothes, was scornful of Petersee's dog. Most of all, Layla insisted, Marcia objected to the fact that Vic didn't have a job.

"She was a hippie herself in the sixties!" Layla wailed. "She's always going on about how she spent a month on the Spanish Steps and stuff like that. She ought to understand."

"Understand . . . ?"

"That Vic doesn't want to live like everyone else, all work work work and conform conform conform. He wants to be free."

Don't we all. Tell it to the unemployed. "Maybe to some people, Layla, Vic might sound arrogant. Or," I added, testing the waters, "stupid?"

Layla bypassed the argument and defended the boy. "Vic is really smart," she retorted loyally. "He's got a degree. From Cambridge," she added in tones of triumph. "But that doesn't make him better than anyone else, he says. A degree comes from just learning to say what they want you to say."

She was quite confident on this ground, her cheeks pink with energy. I could sympathize with Marcia's unease. It doesn't do a lot for your daughter's motivation to have her boyfriend—who already has a degree, thank you very much—heaping scorn on education.

On the way out, at my request, Layla lifted a raffia bag off the floor and produced from its depths two keys.

"The front door," she informed me, extending a Yale with one hand. "And the back," she finished, brandishing another.

"So as far as you know, no one other than you, your mum, and the cleaning woman can get into this house with a key?" I checked. Just for the record.

"Well, there's mum's friends the Mertons," Layla mused. "But why would they want to come in?"

Last year, Layla explained, when she was away on a school trip, her mother had locked herself out of the house and the next day had deposited a spare key with Kay and Terry Merton, just in case it should happen again.

"Your mother didn't mention this key when I spoke to her. Why do you think that would be?"

"Dunno," Layla said shrugging. "She's probably forgotten all about it."

Something resembling defiance crept back into Layla's look when I said I would like to talk to her friends. What could be the harm? I urged. Maybe, if I could prove they weren't involved in the burglary, her mother might be persuaded to give them another chance. When Layla looked hopeful, like a child whose runaway kitten has been spotted on the roof, I had to deflect a stab of guilt.

I pocketed Layla's promise to arrange a meeting with her friends and headed off to the bank.

The cash dispenser on Mill Road provided me with money. It seemed wasteful not to use it, so I nosed around the Chinese supermarket, purchased a packet of dried mushrooms, and felt better for the browse.

Then, just as I was about to drive off, a wild horse on Gwydir Street persuaded me once again out of the car.

This stallion was an antique creature made of wood

with eyes on a level with mine. It bore little relation to the my-little-ponies that simper their way around fairgrounds today. And even less to those mild-mannered rocking horses that are designed to fit at great expense into pine-furnished playrooms. No fantasies here of a benign animal world.

No, this was a savage, a proper, carousel horse: nostrils flaring, eyes white with panic, tendons in its neck standing out in harsh relief. At one time, it had been painted in garish colors, but now the red halter and gilt bridle had flaked away.

The horse dominated the front window of a shop whose sign designated HARDING AND CALLOW as dealers in objets d'art. I couldn't resist stepping inside to check the price tag, to trace my fingers along the runes of its mane.

On the while-you're-there principle, I also checked out the pictures. There were a few on the walls, mainly etchings of uncertain provenance. Nothing to write home about. And nothing certainly that had come from the home of Marcia Shields. "Interesting, aren't they?" a sleek-looking woman asked. I couldn't imagine her spending a lot of time in dusty attics and auction rooms.

"What I'm really looking for," I answered, "is a painting like one my grandmother had. A woman with a cameo brooch, and a man standing behind her. Anything like that . . . ?"

I could see the look of appraisal in her eyes. She knew that this wasn't a casual inquiry. "Sorry," she said, and managed to look as if she meant it.

I didn't leave empty-handed. With great satisfaction, I bought a mellow boxwood surround for my photograph of Claire. "Don't bother to wrap it," I advised. "I'll use it straightaway." The sleek young woman put away her tissue paper and placed the purchase in my hand.

But when I reached the car—frustration and panic. I opened up my briefcase and found nothing there but stationery, an A–Z, and sheaves of paperwork. I fanned the envelopes and the pages of the writing pad just in case, but no black-and-white image of a twelve-year-old with eyes bright as berries flicked into view. I even scrambled awkwardly into the backseat and scoured the floor, just in case. I found an ice cream wrapper and an Ordnance Survey map, but I didn't find the photograph of Claire.

The loss of a credit card or an umbrella—of any everyday object—can be unsettling. But the loss of this particular photograph, with the telephone number penciled on the back, rocked me in a more profound way. On the journey back to London, I detailed the obstacles that now stood between me and Claire: no home address in Canada, no name or address for her London friends, no clear date of arrival, and a million passengers rolling through Heathrow Airport every week. By the time I reached Camden Town, I had worked up a shimmer of panic. My chances of locating Claire, I calculated, were less than my chances of winning the jackpot on the National Lottery. And I hadn't even bought a ticket.

I parked in my usual spot behind the Satay Palace and dashed up the three flights of stairs to the office. This constitutes my regular test of fitness—cheaper than a checkup at a private clinic, more revealing than a visit to the GP—but I did it today merely to burn off excess adrenaline. Stevie was ushering a client out the door as I came in. I shook hands with him and waited impatiently until Stevie turned her attention back to me.

"That photo, Stevie. The one you were looking at the other day? The picture of Claire? I thought you put it back in the briefcase."

Stevie looked at me mildly, unimpressed by my sense of urgency. "I did. Anything wrong?"

You might say that. "It's not there now."

"Let me see." I handed her the briefcase. Stevie laid it on her desk, clicked it open, and pulled out the rearmost manila envelope from the stack. "You don't think I'd put your precious photo away without some protection, do you?" she asked dryly.

"Oh, Stevie, thank you." She deserved a grateful smile, and I deserved a telling off for giving in so quickly to anxiety. I slit the envelope open with a penknife. There was no photo inside. There was a contract form, blank. And a letter, addressed to Thomas Butler, with my signature at the bottom.

Stevie peered over my shoulder. "Wrong envelope," she commented, catching on immediately. "So you've left Claire's photograph with this Butler chap, eh? I wonder what he thinks of that."

"He'll think," I said with a surge of embarrassment, "that he has hired himself a hell of a fool."

4

A light wind drifted down Palace Gardens Terrace. Pink cherry blossoms scattered like confetti over the pavement and pointed the way to the Butler house. I touched the doorbell. This time the gentle ping brought no response. No skinny girl with a mutilated finger rushed to answer the door.

It struck me that there was something lifeless about Blenheim today. It had the same prettiness as the day before yesterday, and the mountain ash in the shelter of the white stone wall still displayed the unguarded greenery of spring. But there was a faint aura of decay that I hadn't noticed on my previous visit.

I rang more insistently, uncomfortable at the prospect of another wasted journey. At the count of fifty, I heard a quiet tread. The door opened. Thomas Butler looked at me vacantly, without a trace of recognition.

"Laura Principal," I nudged.

"Ms. Principal." The smile that washed across his features was formal. There was none of the easy rapport of our encounter at his club. "What is it you want?" He didn't invite me in.

"I'm sorry to trouble you, Mr. Butler, but you had to leave your club suddenly on Monday, and we didn't get around to signing a contract. I've brought one with me now. If you could just take a look at it . . . ?"

He shuffled his feet uneasily, retreated an inch or two away. "Actually, Ms. Principal, this isn't a good time. Ring my secretary and perhaps we could meet tomorrow, in my office."

I interrupted, "Your secretary has the disadvantage of not knowing your movements. According to her, you should be in New York by now."

"Change of schedule," Butler stated in a clipped tone. Interesting to note the edge of annoyance in Mr. Genial's eyes. "I don't really see, Ms. Principal, why I should have to explain to *you*." He began to withdraw.

By now, there must have been a glint of annoyance in my eyes, too. I can butter up clients with the best of them, but I mean business, and I like to know that clients do too. Butler's behavior was beginning to smack of a runaround.

"Mr. Butler, give me a chance to explain." Politely, but the pressure of my palm on the edge of the door conveyed that I intended to be heard. "You rushed out of your club on Monday, leaving no opportunity to discuss terms. I need your signature on a contract before I can start work. I learned you would be out of town all week except for a brief visit to your home on Tuesday evening. That's why I deposited an envelope, to await your return, with the girl who answered the door. Now, if you would be kind enough—"

"What young woman?" Butler interrupted. His puzzlement could have been genuine.

"She was hardly more than a girl. Sixteen, seventeen years old. She came to the door on Monday. She promised she'd be here today."

Butler looked at me strangely. I carried on, exasperation coloring my tone. "This girl was exceptionally thin with a chestnut-colored ponytail. She had a trace of a foreign accent. She may have been Malaysian, or perhaps from the Philippines. I thought she might be a domestic helper?"

"Ms. Principal, you're talking gibberish. This house was empty until I came home last night." His voice was becoming louder, less controlled. "There is no envelope here and no Filipino teenager. Nothing to detain you a moment longer. If you send a contract to my office, I'll look at it later. In the meanwhile, good day."

This was becoming undignified. I released the edge of the door, but made one last attempt to get through to him. "What about that black-and-white photo?" I shot back. "The one I left here by mistake. What have you done with that?"

"Photograph? I don't know what you're talking about." And he slammed the door closed. But not before I saw his pudgy face go the color of soft ice cream.

Being a persistent sort, I of course rang Butler's secretary and wangled an appointment. But when I showed up, instead of being directed into Butler's office, I was presented with a letter. In it, Butler expressed his confidence that the problem of the theatrical thefts had now been resolved; my services were no longer required. He was sorry if he had put me to any trouble, and for my effort, a small check was attached.

These judgments are, of course, relative. But *small* is not the word I would select to describe a sum of money that would cover—depending on your priorities—a term's fees at Harrow or a Nicole Farhi wardrobe. For a check that size, the term I would use is *something to hide.*

Butler's receptionist assured me that Thomas Butler had now definitely departed for New York. She kept a beady eye on me while I read the letter. Maybe she feared that I would make a scene. I moved to reassure her, by admiring the celebrity photos on the walls—Michael Crawford, Robert De Niro, David Suchet, Maggie Smith—smiling broadly all the while. I mentioned that I would like to take some friends to see *Inside Sherwood Forest.* Did she have details of advance booking arrangements?

"Why certainly," she said with a look of relief. "Just a moment." She walked over to the filing cabinet and extracted a paper. She even offered to photocopy the details for me. And while she had her back turned using the photocopier, I leaned toward her desk, ran my eye down the typed itinerary, and noted the name of Butler's New York hotel.

If Butler had been hoping to persuade me to drop off his trail, he couldn't have found a less effective way of doing so. I didn't like the fact that he had given me the runaround. I didn't like the fact that he had lied. I have no objection to being paid, and even less to being paid a lot; but I don't like being paid off.

And I couldn't live with the unanswered questions. "I'll be here," had said the girl who answered the door at Blenheim. Who was she and where had she gone?

What was her interest in missing persons? Why did Butler deny all knowledge of her? And last but not least, why did the blood drain from Butler's face at the mention of Claire's photograph?

Unanswered. But not for long, I resolved.

Later that day I sent a fax to Butler's private number. It was phrased in my best business language, but the gist of it was simple: *Keep your check. You have a photograph that belongs to me and I intend to have it back. I won't get off your back until I do.*

I sent the same fax to the hotel that was, apparently, Butler's New York base. This hotel, or so I've heard, is an exceedingly circumspect establishment. It's not the sort of place where Macaulay Culkin hangs out alone over Christmas. It *is* the sort of place where a wealthy man could with impunity entertain a girl young enough to be his daughter, as long as the girl in question is well-spoken and discreet.

But not in this case. Just to be sure, I rang the desk and said that I had a confidential message for the young woman who had accompanied Mr. Butler. The concierge avouched in chilly tones that Mr. Butler was, as usual, traveling alone.

Well, at least as far as this slip of a girl was concerned, I could narrow my attentions to this side of the Atlantic. I dredged up a fundamental tenet of investigation and acted on it: that in the search for a missing person—as in many other things—there is no place quite like home.

I popped back to Blenheim three times that day, but of my slip of a girl there was no sign.

The bell echoed eerily in an apparently empty house. A light snapped on once, behind the curtains of the first-floor bay window, creating the illusion of movement. A time switch, I reckoned, not a flesh-and-blood hand. Even more than before, the house felt lifeless.

"Forget it," Sonny said, or words to that effect. "It's not worth the trouble."

Not worth the trouble! "Sonny, how many times do I have to tell you, there's something weird going on in Palace Gardens Terrace. This girl—who looks like something out of an Oxfam ad—she asks me for help. We arrange to talk at Blenheim on Wednesday. But when Wednesday comes, she has disappeared."

Sonny refused to be impressed. "So? Maybe this Malaysian girl—"

"Filipino teenager. That's what Butler said."

"Wasn't it 'no Filipino teenager'?" Sonny asked pointedly. "Perhaps she was simply a visitor, and now she has gone home."

Not good enough. " 'I'll be here,' she said, Sonny. As plain as day. Why would she say that if she was about to board a flight to Manila? And what would Butler stand to gain by pretending that she never existed? Butler's up to something. And what about Claire's photograph? Butler had obviously seen it; he looked completely poleaxed when I mentioned it. Why? Why not return the photo to me and be done with it? Why did he lie? None of it makes sense."

"You're right. It's as fishy as the North Sea," Sonny conceded with a shrug. "But it's not a paying case."

I managed to stay in rational mode—just. I didn't dwell on the fact that someone had asked me for help and I had shouldered her aside. I didn't go on about how Butler's curt dismissal rankled—which it did, in a big way. I didn't linger over the fact that Butler had given me a right royal runaround.

I went straight for the kill.

"I wouldn't have gotten involved with Butler in the first place, Sonny, except that *you* persuaded me to come to London. If it hadn't been for pressure from you, I would have stayed in Wildfell and counted the baby seals on Blakeney Sands. Butler and his little Filipina would be your concern, not mine. So"—I was fired up now and the words were flowing—"if you want to object to my search for the little Filipina, you can simply consider me on holiday."

So there.

On a perfect April morning, cool and sunny, I parked at the Notting Hill Gate end of Palace Gardens Terrace and began a serious assault on Butler's neighbors.

The houses on either side of Blenheim yielded nothing and no one, their occupants off, presumably, on the duties of the day.

At the next house I bumped into an impatient woman with a sports bag in hand. She was on her way to jazz ballet and shook me off with one brusque statement. No, she knew no one in Blenheim—ridiculous name for a terraced house—and she didn't care to know. Not, I concluded, the neighborly sort.

It wasn't until I crossed the street that I struck lucky. On the other side of the road from Blenheim and off to the left stood an austere house, the front garden buried under slabs of concrete. Six steep steps had to be mounted to reach the door. The woman who answered the bell was a Filipina in her thirties. She wore a black dress neatly fitted over her stout figure, and an expression of lively curiosity. From the way she sized me up and down, she must have noticed me knocking on other doors in the street.

"The new housemaid, yes," she volunteered after my introduction.

"You know her?" I had steeled myself for disappointment and couldn't conceal my excitement.

"Not precisely." She looked hard at me. "Identification?"

I passed her my business card. She skimmed it, glanced at me again, and made up her mind. "You're not from the immigration people. Are you?" It was more of a statement than a question.

"No connection at all."

She offered me coffee. I introduced myself and offered my hand.

"My name is Carmen," she announced. When she smiled, the skin around her eyes formed tiny pleats.

I followed Carmen out of the wind and into a dark-toned corridor. Directly in front of me was a flight of stairs, the banisters crudely altered to accommodate a chair lift. I could make out a metal platform in the gloom at the top.

When we were settled in the kitchen, I told Carmen of my doorstep encounters at Blenheim.

"So Mr. Butler says he doesn't know her?" she asked, shaking her head. "Well, I've heard some odd things from that family, but this takes the biscuit." Carmen slicked her hair tight against her skull. "She is thin, yes? With her hair pulled back like this?" I nodded. "It must be the same girl. Very early Monday morning, when I stepped out to fetch the milk, this girl was going up the front steps—slowly as if she were ill—and Mrs. Butler seemed to be supporting her."

"Thomas Butler's wife?"

Carmen nodded. "Penelope, she's called. I've always

liked the sound of the name." She chanted *Penelope* under her breath for a moment, pleased by the rhythm.

Well, I thought, that will teach me to interrupt.

I prompted Carmen to bring her back on target. On Monday, apparently, she saw nothing more. The following day, looking out the window, Carmen spotted the thin girl scrubbing the steps at Blenheim. She was wearing, not a tacky overall as on first sighting, but jersey leggings and a tunic top. She seemed to be in distinctly better fettle. It was then that Carmen recognized the girl as a compatriot. She resolved to introduce herself, but by the time she stepped outside, the girl had gone.

"Did you go and look her up?"

Carmen pursed her lips. "You've obviously never worked as a domestic."

"I did a summer stint as a waitress at the Pizza Express. While I was an undergraduate," I said, chancing my arm. "Does that count?"

"What I mean," said Carmen, ignoring my last comment, "is that many domestics are not allowed to have visitors. If I had asked to see the new household worker, she might have been sacked."

"But you've been very hospitable to me."

"I said *many* domestics," Carmen shot back firmly. "I didn't say *all*."

"Sorry," I said, palms up in a gesture of submission. "Go on." But there was nowhere to go. Carmen had never seen the thin girl after that.

I asked her whether she could tell me anything about the Butlers. "More than I ought to." She giggled, obviously keen on the chance for revelation. The information Carmen provided on Thomas and Penelope Butler was of the quality that Sonny and I call horse's mouth. As in straight from.

Carmen's employer was an elderly invalid who depended upon Carmen and her British-born husband to keep the house, maintain the garden, and cook the meals. She had lived in Palace Gardens Terrace for five years, and during that time she had seen a great deal of Mrs. Butler. "Not socially," Carmen was quick to point out. "No, I'm the *little woman* who does Penelope's little chores." I glanced at her in surprise, the sarcasm unexpected. Her expression was all innocence. There was a lesson here on the need to cultivate the respect of the domestic help—one that the Butlers clearly hadn't learned. This little woman knew things about the Butlers that they would rather not have in the public domain.

Knew, for a start, that Thomas Butler adored his wife. Would do anything for her. *Worshiped,* was the word Carmen used. And like most worship, it only went one way. Penelope appeared in public with him, looked the part of the loving wife—"She's a beauty, you know," Carmen added—but in private, she didn't give him the time of day.

Knew (or rather surmised, in answer to my question) that Mrs. Butler cared for only two things. One of these was the garden established in Kent by her late mother. Penelope spent more of her time there than in London and made liberal use of Carmen's services—arranging repairs, taking deliveries, turning out the spare room, and so forth—to keep Blenheim ticking over in her absence. She paid sometimes, a little. More often it was just a would-you-mind-awfully neighborly request. Unreciprocated, of course.

"And the second thing?" I asked.

Her daughter, Beatrice. Pretty, sweet-tempered, and the apple, apparently, of Penelope's eye. "Of course,"

Carmen said pointedly, "Mrs. Butler would like a child who looks good. It reflects well on her."

Knew, also, something of the reason why Penelope stayed with Thomas when she clearly didn't care for him. Penelope sometimes spoke to Carmen openly about her husband, and with a coldness that shook Carmen.

"She confides in you?" I asked.

"Telling me," said Carmen dryly, "is not like telling anyone who matters."

On one such occasion, Penelope had revealed that she had resolved years earlier to leave Thomas. But then he had his huge international hit. Penelope wanted to be part of that success, and Thomas of course begged her to stay. They did some kind of a deal.

What kind of deal? Carmen didn't know precisely. It had to do, she assumed, with Penelope spending most of her time in the country. And she assumed, also, that it had something to do with why Thomas Butler was one of the saddest men she had ever met. Lonely, she said. Maybe guilty too.

I asked one last question, before I left the kitchen, just to round things off. "When you said that the Butlers did some odd things, Carmen, were you referring simply to the way they conduct their marriage? Or is there something else?"

The something else—for something else it was—was most intriguing. "Last summer," Carmen explained, "when Penelope was in Kent, a young man came to stay at Blenheim. I caught a glimpse of him two or three times. But later when I mentioned it to Mrs. Butler, she said coldly that I must have been seeing things. And that evening, the Butlers had a furious row. The windows were open, I could hear their shouts from across the street."

The little Filipina was, apparently, not the first visitor whose presence the Butlers had tried to cover up.

Carmen received my thanks for her help with a glint. I was glad for her sake that she could still take pleasure in revenge; the worst effect of petty insults, delivered day after day, is that some people come to accept them as their due. Not Carmen. She even provided me with Penelope Butler's address in Kent.

"You're certain this won't get you in trouble?" I checked.

Carmen drew herself up. "You came looking for Mrs. Butler. Why should I not refer you on? She's not the queen," she added with dignity.

No, indeed.

5

Fired by success, I continued to tap my knuckles on the sturdy doors of Palace Gardens Terrace.

I rousted out one more domestic, an arthritic old woman whose knees had (I hoped) seen better days. She wasn't a Carmen and I couldn't make myself understood. My didactic gestures in the direction of Blenheim prompted a shrug that verged on the comic. If her sly smile was anything to go by, she was putting me on.

Beyond that, I spoke to a plumber who was applying draining rods to a blocked sewer and who assumed, when he heard the bell, that it would be his mate; a graduate student, a chatty young man, who rented a room in one of the shabbier houses; and an American woman, oozing East Coast charm, whose terrier harried my ankles as we spoke.

None of them shed light on the Butler household.

Odd, I thought. Such a cozy-looking neighborhood, and yet, apart from Carmen, the residents might as well have lived in separate tower blocks for all they knew of one another's life.

I called it a morning. I wandered to the end of the street and crossed the barrier that protected Palace Gardens Terrace from the main flow of traffic around Notting Hill Gate. The Mall was smoky, but it offered freshly squeezed orange juice. First I retreated to the loo and slipped on a new pair of tights from the supply in my briefcase. Never did care for terriers. Then I took my orange juice to a quiet table near the window and sat down to write up my notes.

They didn't amount to much. I began with observations and questions about the Butlers and their household arrangements, moved on to details about the girl who was missing, and concluded with a calendar of sorts. Monday: the little Filipina entered Blenheim in the company of Mrs. B; I met Butler at his Mayfair club; I delivered (what I thought was) a contract to Blenheim and saw the girl for myself. Tuesday: Carmen noticed a girl scrubbing the steps. Wednesday: I visited Blenheim and found no one there but a taciturn Thomas Butler. The thin girl had disappeared, it seemed, sometime between Carmen's sighting of her on Tuesday and my encounter with Butler on Wednesday morning. Yesterday.

I strolled back to the car, mulling over these fragments, oblivious to the world around. When someone tapped my shoulder from behind, it affected me like an electrical impulse.

"Sorry to startle you," Carmen said. "He wants to see you." She moved off at a trot toward her house. I followed behind.

"Who wants to see me?" Had Thomas Butler returned?

"Mr. Scorsese. You know, the old man I work for." She stopped me on the landing and dropped her voice to a whisper. "He claims to know what happened to the little Filipina."

She started up the stairs. I needed a moment to orient myself. I beckoned her back. "I thought he was disabled?"

"He is. Hasn't walked for years. But there's nothing wrong with his mind."

"What's he like?"

Her smile, affectionate and a touch condescending, said volumes about their relationship. "He's a nice old fellow really. Eccentric, a bit of a racist, but there's no real harm in him. Now, can we go?"

"Lead the way," I conceded, following her up the stairs.

The old man lived in a square, high-ceilinged room at the front of the house. On one side of the room was a narrow bed, a wardrobe, and a writing desk that had been specially built, by the looks of it, to accommodate a wheelchair. The wall opposite was dominated by an overbearing cabinet in dark oak and a matching set of shelves.

A figure was seated in a wheelchair. He had his back to the bay window, partially blocking the light.

"Mr. Scorsese?" I asked before Carmen could introduce us.

"Sit down, sit down," he exclaimed impatiently. Clearly not one for formalities.

I spotted a chintz-covered wing chair and dragged it near enough to the old man that I could make out his features against the light. He was scrawny. His cheeks were sunken, his neck pathetically thin in a shirt collar several sizes too large. I wondered whether it had once fitted. In his temple a vein throbbed remorselessly.

"So you're a detective," Scorsese growled. The tone of voice implied *Prove it.* I reached for my handbag, but he stayed me with a gesture. "I've already got your card, if that's what you're looking for. Had to threaten her with the sack"—he scowled over my shoulder—"before she'd give it up."

I turned to look at Carmen. "I think I'll make tea," she announced, treating me to a wink that made her wrinkles dance again.

"Coffee, woman," the old man bellowed after her. She didn't turn back. He glared after her retreating back for a moment, then turned his fierce gaze on me. Suddenly I had the oddest sensation that I had seen him before; more than that, that I had spent quite a lot of time watching him. I had seen him—what?—standing in the distance, squinting into the sun?

I shook my head. Time to take control. "Mr. Scorsese," I said firmly.

"Martin," he shot back.

Surprised again. "Martin?" I asked incredulously.

"Martin," he repeated. His aggressive manner had left the room with Carmen. In its place he had assumed an air of vigorous good humor. "Martin Scorsese."

Could he be serious? I didn't want to ask.

"Okay, Martin," I agreed. I tested the waters. "Carmen tells me that you saw a young woman at the house of Thomas and Penelope Butler earlier this week."

"At Blenheim, you mean. Saw her three times," he asserted with pride. "Monday, just a glimpse, when she answered the door. Tuesday morning, I saw her out the front of the house, sweeping the walk. And the last time, Tuesday evening."

I was excited, but decided to move cautiously. "What can you tell me about her? And about those three occasions?"

Scorsese gave a description of the girl that coincided down to the last detail with my memories and those of Carmen. He added one thing only: that she had long, slim feet. "Big feet for her size," he insisted. "Skinny girls with big feet shouldn't wear leggings, it makes 'em look out of proportion."

I passed over the recommendation without comment. My residual doubts about the authenticity of his story— he could be repeating something he had heard from Carmen—evaporated when he added pointedly, "And you should be careful about pine green yourself."

"Beg your pardon?"

"Pine green," Scorsese emphasized. "That jacket you had on when you went to Blenheim on Monday wasn't a good color for you. A pale green, hmmm, maybe a duck's egg, would be better with a complexion like yours."

What did the old guy do, run a franchise for Color Me Beautiful on the side?

"Thanks," I said. Why sneeze at free advice? "I'll check it out in the daylight. But perhaps we could get back to the girl? The first time you saw her was when I called at the house, right? The second, she was sweeping the walk. What about the third time? What was she doing then?"

Scorsese drew himself up to full sitting height. "Picture the scene," he instructed, using his hands to create a frame. "Tuesday evening, sometime before nine o'clock, the Butlers had a visitor. I didn't see him arrive. I must have been watching television."

I hadn't seen a television in the room, but I didn't want to interrupt his flow to say so. I had learned my lesson with Carmen.

He continued, again using his hands to illustrate. "Sinister-looking, he was. Big and muscle-bound, like Schwarzenegger. Or Robert De Niro, in *Cape Fear.* You know, with the tattoos."

"This man had tattoos?"

"No, no," he snapped. "De Niro was the one with the tattoos. Anyway, this man came out of the Butler house, and—here's the part that will interest you," he insisted. "He had a girl close in front of him. He had a tight grip on her arm. And the girl, she had a shawl over her head."

"She was wearing a shawl?"

"Hah," he said, eyes gleaming, "I thought that would get you going." He gloated for a few seconds, then the momentum carried him on. "It was a blue wool shawl, no pattern. Over her head. Not"—he shot me a glance to make sure I was hanging on his every word. I was— "not on the back of her head, the way a shawl is usually worn. But pulled *forward,* so far that the front edge hung down near the tip of her nose. She couldn't hardly see where she was going."

I ignored the bad grammar and went for the soft underbelly. "Below the tip of her nose, huh?" He nodded. "Covering all of her hair, then? And her eyes?" Nodded again. "So how do you know it was her?"

He was ready for that one. Had probably been looking forward to it since the minute I came into the room, combative little shit. I had walked right into it.

"The shawl didn't cover her feet," he announced, quivering with triumph.

I got the point. "Long, thin feet?"

"The very same. You want me to go on?"

Scorsese related how the young girl was propelled out of Butler's house, down the walk, and toward the corner where a van was parked. There was a scuffle, a bit of a struggle. Then the man looked around furtively, opened the back door of the van, and pushed the girl inside. He had been gripping a carrier bag and threw it in after her. He swung the door to and locked it.

At this point, Scorsese closed the narrative. He folded his hands in his lap and gave me a what-do-you-think-of-that? grin.

I had no intention of reviewing his story before we'd reached the end. "So? What happened then?" Still that smug smile. "Come on, Martin, tell me what happened."

"No idea," he responded blithely.

What?

"No idea," he said again before I could find my tongue. The air of indifference deepened. "It was nine o'clock. *Raging Bull* started at nine. I had to hurry away from the window. I almost missed the titles," he complained, shaking his head as over a near-disaster.

"Are you serious? You saw a man force a girl into the back of a van, and you wheeled away to watch *Raging Bull?* Didn't you tell anyone? Didn't you ring the police?"

"I'm telling *you.*" Scorsese looked serene. I could have wrung his skinny neck. "No way I want to get involved with the police," he muttered. "Hey," he exclaimed, brightening again, "do you realize what's missing?"

"That girl from Blenheim," I shot back, furious.

"No, our coffee. Carmen! Carmen!"

With impeccable timing, Carmen crossed the landing and entered the room, pushing a wheeled trolley. She placed this near Scorsese's right arm. When he saw the teapot with its crocheted cozy, he fumed. Carmen ignored him.

"This isn't coffee," he growled.

She offered me a muffin before turning back to Scorsese. "One cup per day," she said mildly. His hostility didn't shake her one bit. Perhaps it was this that made him so sharp with her. Perhaps her kind acceptance of him enhanced his sense of ineffectuality. The old man couldn't move himself as freely as he would like, he couldn't move events, and he couldn't even move his housekeeper to anger.

This exchange interested me, enough so that I could set aside Scorsese's infuriating indifference to the fate of the missing girl.

"You're very observant," I noted, breaking the silence that had set in when we had received our tea. Carmen didn't leave the room, but sat down on the edge of the narrow bed, behind me, and quietly sipped a cup of tea herself. I suspected that she was accustomed to sharing his teatime.

Scorsese looked directly at me, some of his spirit returning. "Mavis always said so," he agreed with emphasis. "That's my wife. She died in 1986. She said I was the only man she knew who always noticed what women wore. I can describe the wool coat she was wearing when we met down to the last satin frog."

"Quite a talent."

"It is one thing to look," he added sagely, "but it's another thing to see. If anyone comes down Palace Gardens Terrace when I am at the window, I make a point of noticing everything about them. Weeks later, I could tell you how they looked, what they wore. Everything."

"Test out that skill now," I suggested, "on the man who put the girl in the van on Tuesday evening."

Scorsese screwed up his eyes. When he opened them again, he was ready. "Not easy. Because of the dark, and the way the girl was in front of him most of the time. He was five feet eleven, maybe six foot, and, like I said before, big. Big shoulders. His black hair was receding on top and he had thick sideburns." Scorsese snorted, none too delicately. "Looked ridiculous, like the hair had slid off his forehead down onto the sides of his face."

I refused to dwell on that image. "His coloring?"

"Oh, sure. He was black."

"Black?" A tantalizingly unspecific word, *black.* "Afro-Caribbean?"

"No." Scorsese shrugged scornfully. He jerked his thumb in Carmen's direction. "Black. Like her."

Carmen gave me an I-told-you-so look and carried on leafing through a copy of the *Radio Times.*

"And his clothes?"

"Heavy shoes with thick soles, the kind that are waxed, you know?" Sure. "And a dark roll-neck top. And a trench coat."

"You mean a raincoat or a proper trench? With all the tabs and so forth?"

"Sure, a proper trench. In that awful color, that brown mixed with gray. What's it called?"

"Taupe." Carmen supplied. Her first statement since sitting down.

"Yeah, taupe," Scorsese confirmed.

"Anything else?" I asked, not really expecting more.

"That's it," Scorsese concluded chirpily. "And don't

ask me about the van," he warned, holding up a hand. I had been just about to do so. "Because I don't like cars, never have. Can't tell one from another. The only thing I noticed about this van—I was watching the people—was that it was indigo, you know, dark blue. And it had some gold lettering on the side. Made it look kind of jumped-up, like one of those butchers' vans that call themselves 'Purveyors of Meat to the Queen.' That sort of look."

Hopefully again, I asked about the lettering. Logos or stickers? Special aerials? But Scorsese wasn't listening. He had glanced at his watch and wheeled close enough to the bookcase to snatch a remote control device. He held it outstretched in front of him, snapping his thumb vigorously up and down. The unwieldy cabinet on the wall opposite him opened, its top flattening against the wall. And from the cabinet rose, like Botticelli's *Venus,* a television screen of astonishing proportions. Three foot high and four feet wide.

Light waves danced across the screen for a moment, then a color picture snapped into place with what I thought was probably the opening sequence of *48 Hours.* Scorsese stared at it, his powers of concentration now devoted utterly to the film.

Carmen tapped me on the shoulder and said in a quiet voice, "You might as well go now. He won't say anything more."

I looked back at Martin's profile, his eyes fixed on the screen. Clint Eastwood: eyes screwed up, staring into the sun. That was whom he reminded me of. Make Clint Eastwood twenty years older and six inches shorter, and the match would be complete.

It felt uncomfortable to leave without even a farewell. "He wouldn't have heard you," Carmen soothed as I followed her down the stairs. "He is so good at noticing things precisely because he only does one thing at a time. Films are his passion. Since he has been confined to that wheelchair, he's lived for them. His favorites are the slice-of-life, sleazy-side-of-town kind of film. Makes him feel he's been somewhere, done something, something that works by different rules than those that order our lives here in Palace Gardens Terrace."

"He must enjoy the films of his namesake, then. Like *Mean Streets* and *Taxi Driver.*"

Carmen laughed. "Of course," she said, amused that I hadn't twigged before. "That's how he got his name."

"Sorry?"

"You didn't think that was his real name, did you? He changed it two years ago, after watching *Taxi Driver* for the umpteenth time. By deed poll. I had to get him all the forms. 'Mavis wouldn't approve,' he said, 'but since Mavis up and died, I guess I can call myself what I like. Just don't expect me to start eating pizza,' he warned. 'I'm too old for that.' "

"What about this young girl?" Carmen asked as we stood on the doorstep. "Do you think we should go to the police?"

"Not a lot of point, I'm afraid. We could say someone has gone missing from Blenheim; the Butlers would say not. We don't know her name. We've hardly spoken to her, we can't prove she ever existed, we have no relationship to her, and we have no tangible leads by which she might be traced."

Carmen understood, only too well: "The police won't act on a report like that."

That was putting it mildly.

And yet, I couldn't stop thinking about the young Fili-

pina who looked as fragile as a child and who was gone.
Girls don't just disappear into thin air. Do they?

One more thing to do before calling it a day. Thanks
to Martin Scorsese, my slip of a girl now had a more
detailed description—right down to her long, slim feet—
and an exit. *Tuesday evening,* I wrote. *Last sighting.*
Taken away from Palace Gardens Terrace by a balding
man with sideburns. In an indigo van.
I hadn't decided how much reliance to place upon
Martin Scorsese's account. He was an acute observer, no
doubt about that. He had noticed me arriving on Monday and recalled, even if he didn't approve, the color of
my clothes. But how much of his story was memory,
and how much was imagination working on overtime?
The relish with which he told the tale would fit either
hypothesis equally well.
One little phone call couldn't hurt.
"The Old Manse?" Penelope Butler had a childish
voice. Her sentences tipped up at the end, turning every
statement into a question, as some Americans do; but
judging by her accent, she was English through and
through.
I explained who I was and what I needed: I needed,
I said, to trace the girl who had been staying—and probably working—at Blenheim earlier this week. Did Penelope have her current address?
Three seconds is a long time in the context of a phone
call. You can hear the silence pressing down the line.
"I— Perhaps you've made a mistake about the address?" When Penelope spoke, the words came out rac-
ing, as if she wanted to get them over with quickly.
"There is no girl in our house in Kensington."
I felt like the schoolyard bully, pressing for answers

from such a quavering voice, but this initial response just wouldn't do. "Mrs. Butler," I tried again, resolving not to mention the witnesses for the time being. "Mrs. Butler, there is no mistake. The girl was at your house on Monday and on Tuesday for sure, and now she is gone. She may have come to harm. If you don't know where she is, at least let me know her name, so I can begin to trace her."

"I've told you, I don't know this young person." The voice was firm now. Either she had had time to compose herself or my mention of the girl coming to harm had somehow hardened her. "I'm sorry"—she didn't sound it—"but I cannot be of any help. Good evening."

She waited the space of a moment that politeness requires, then replaced the receiver.

So. They were all at it. If I was going to find the girl—as of course I was—it would have to be without the help of Ma and Pa Butler.

6

On Friday morning I realized with a start that I had promised to begin pursuit of Marcia Shields's paintings that very week. "Smart, tough, and honest" was what the client believed of me; if I wanted to deserve this reputation, I had better forget the missing Filipina for a few hours and fulfill commitments in Cambridge.

After a light breakfast, I dressed in a linen trousers suit, shielded my eyes against the glare of the April sun, and cut across to the M11. I put my driving self on automatic pilot, so to speak, and used the hour and some on the road to organize my thoughts about the Cambridge case. In the days when I was an academic, reflection and planning waited always on a quiet room and a tidy desk—but since my study was rarely as quiet as I might have wished, and my desk hardly ever tidy, reflection had been often, even in that most contemplative of callings, in short supply.

Things are different now. The business of private investigation is full of long lonely hours—waiting for illicit deliveries, monitoring the movements of an errant spouse, tracking clients from place to place—and most of the time, you either do your planning on the hoof or you don't plan at all.

Before I knew it, I had an agenda for action, and I was driving past Quayside in Cambridge, where a row of punts was neatly tethered waiting for the tourist trade. I braked suddenly to allow a cyclist her wobble as I passed over Magdalen Bridge. A right turn at the lights, a left turn up the hill, an easy curve, and there I was. Home.

Home—a two-bedroom Victorian terrace—is the only legacy from my ill-fated marriage to Adam. In the early days of our relationship, Adam and I sanded these floors, bracing together against the storm of dust. We should have known it wouldn't work: the house turned out to be the only joint project in the entire marriage. Although we were both historians, our specialist areas and our approaches were wildly different; so were our views of students, of other historians, and of life. Adam had his heart—no, rather his mind—set unswervingly on a fast-track career. He was ready to sacrifice everything else in pursuit of a chair, and it slowly dawned that he was prepared to sacrifice me as well. It was not that he wanted an uneducated wife. What he wanted was a historian who would devote herself to his career— manage the house, proofread the articles, and assess archival sources too. I tried for a while to find a way to bridge the gulf that separated us. But Adam's only strategy, faced with difference, was to bring it to heel, and I wasn't prepared to be house-trained.

When I first tried my hand at private investigation, Adam was appalled. It was, he asserted without irony, an unsuitable job for a woman. Nor was Sonny easily convinced. Sonny Mendlowitz and I met at a jazz club on Chesterton Lane. When they told me what the good-looking man who made the clarinet sound like dark chocolate did for a living, I assumed that they were pulling my leg. Seedy little men, that's how private eyes were fixed in my imagination—part cynics and part debt collectors, who wore slouch hats and smoked too much and swept up the debris of other people's lives. None of that fitted Sonny.

We took to meeting from time to time—a drink at the Eagle, a dinner in college, a walk by the river—and I came to understand that Sonny's work was more lively than delving away in dusty archives, and better rewarded too. When the perfect case came up—involving a business where someone had been selling secrets to competitors—I turned on the charm and my powers of persuasion and urged Sonny to let me have a go. He wasn't what you would call confident about my capacities. "This isn't the university library, Laura," he'd said, finishing his pint. "These guys can get rough." But he accepted my argument that, with the right clothes, I could blend into the office much more readily than he. "Just this once," he said.

"Just this once," I agreed, the picture of compliance, and bought him another pint.

But when I identified the bad guy in no time flat, when I whizzed into that office and out again leaving only a satisfied client behind, it was the first in a sequence of successes that led eventually to our partnership. Not bad, Sonny said, for a historian.

So I courted—and won—a new career. And while I did so, Adam courted Isabel. It was a relief to all of us when he said good-bye to me and I said good-bye to academia. As if it were haunted, my Cambridge home echoes with these transitions in my life; that is one of the reasons that I resist the sometimes siren call to sell it.

Enough reminiscence for one morning. I wandered through the rooms, checking that everything was all right. Then, seeing that it was, I pocketed my post, locked up again, and launched myself upon the good citizens of Cambridge.

My plan of action was as simple as pie. First, check Layla's alibi; a visit to Barbara Thoday, the friend with whom Layla said she'd spent the weekend, should do the trick. Second, speak to as many as I could manage of Marcia's neighbors, one of whom might have noticed a dozen oil paintings being frog-marched out of Marcia's house. Third, check whether the other people who had keys to Marcia's house—the cleaning woman, and, if Layla was correct, Kay and Terry Merton—were still in possession. There is little point in pondering the problem of entry if the answer lies with a missing key.

Barbara Thoday was an A-level student at Long Road Sixth Form College, and with the connivance of the college secretary, I lay in wait for her in the corridor after sociology class. Streams of students pressed past while Barbara assured me that Layla was with her all weekend. She accounted for their time together in tedious detail, from the playing styles of members of the South African band, to the booty from a shared shopping expedition. It constituted a substantial alibi. In fact, Barbara's story was of such elaborate particularity that I suspected—for the first time—that she and Layla were selling me a pack of lies.

My dealings with Marcia's neighbors were more straightforward. Their responses to questions traced a map of local concerns. I encountered clashing views of the cycleway that threaded along Lyndewode Road; divisions about the development plan for Parkside Pool; accounts of other burglaries. I was accosted by trippers, fresh off the train, who had become mazed in their search for what the guidebooks call the Historic City Contor. And I personally profited from the day, in unexpected ways. I received geranium cuttings from a woman who was planting out her tubs, concert details from a notice on a window, and a blessing from a nun in Glisson Road.

What more could a girl ask from a day's doorstepping? Only information relating to the loss of Marcia Shields's paintings. And, as luck would have it, I got that too.

On the Saturday of the weekend that the paintings went walkabout, the manager of a nearby bed and breakfast, strolling out to have lunch with his cousin, had noticed a white van parked in the narrow driveway alongside the house that belonged to Marcia Shields. He had noticed it, he said, because it resembled a British Telecom van. He had logged a request with British Telecom to repair a fault on his phone, and the thought that Marcia might have got in first had left him aggrieved.

BT checked their work schedules. They hadn't been to Lyndewood Road on Saturday. So it was someone else who had pulled into Marcia's driveway while she was in Paris. And that someone, unless I was much mistaken, had entered her house and carted the Shieldses' collection of paintings out the back door and into the van. No muss, no fuss, and a very tidy profit.

In the evening, I treated Helen to an early supper at Browns. The supper constituted a small thank-you for her effort with my flora and enabled me to confirm, in passing as it were, that she hadn't just by chance kept Claire's letter. Helen had tossed it out as I'd told her to do.

Then I went checking on the whereabouts of keys. Marcia's cleaning woman had hers tucked away in the bottom of her handbag. Our interview took less than five minutes and left me wishing there was someone like her in London to deal with the more recalcitrant regions of Sonny's flat.

Terry and Kay Merton lived fifty yards or so past the entrance to Homerton College on Hills Road. Their spare key was harder to locate than the cleaner's, and its guardians were more difficult to like. When I explained my business, Kay Merton recoiled. It was the kind of reaction that might be expected if I had turned up out of the blue offering to appraise the family silver.

Mrs. Merton was a conventional-looking woman who wore a Jaeger two-piece and a grimace of insecurity. Suspicion oozed out of every pore, which made me keen to hang around a little longer. My interest in her wasn't, apparently, reciprocated.

Was Mr. Merton home? I wondered whether I might fare better with him. Just as Kay's tight mouth framed the word *no,* a heavyset man emerged from a room to the right of the hallway. Mrs. Merton made a gesture of resignation and retreated toward the back of the house.

Terry Merton was indistinguishable in appearance from a thousand British businessmen. He had a placating manner with his wife, a peremptory one with me. I was willing to bet that the peremptory approach was closest to the real Terry. But maybe that's unfair. He seemed genuinely upset to hear that Marcia had been burgled and could offer no reason why she might have neglected to mention to me that the Mertons had a key. "You see," Terry Merton added, "we haven't seen Marcia much at all for the past year or so. It's rather an oversight that we still have her spare key. *If* we still have it."

He gestured me into the sitting room. I watched as he went to the mantelpiece and opened first one, and then another, silver box from a collection that was expensive rather than attractive. "Here it is," he said with relief in his voice. "I'm certain this belongs to Marcia. Perhaps you had better take it. Return it to her with our best wishes, please."

So I did. I was fairly certain that Kay Merton was listening in the hallway during my conversation with her husband, but there was no sign of her resentful face as I made my own way out.

The next day, I awoke in London to the sound of automatic gunfire. Sonny was doing his Saturday-morning tortoise imitation, body buried in bedclothes, head hidden beneath the pillow, and I managed to shower, dress, and blow-dry my hair without interrupting his performance.

Dominic and Daniel were curled up on the sofa, watching a video of the *3 Ninjas.* Two empty cereal bowls testified to an attempt at breakfast.

"Anyone for pancakes?" I called softly.

"One here!" Dominic returned, his eyes not leaving the television set. "With maple syrup, okay?"

Daniel slid off the sofa and made his way to my side. His dinosaur slippers whooshed faintly on the carpet. "Can I whisk?" he asked.

We worked our way companionably toward pancakes.

Daniel weighed, I poured. Daniel broke eggs and whisked. I fretted the melting butter. I flipped (badly) and he flipped (worse). The results were ragged but delicious. We joined Dominic for the last action sequence of the movie and cheered as the grandfather quite improbably defeated his younger and nastier opponent.

The cheer woke Sonny. He merged in time to challenge for the last forkful of pancake. I won, popped it into my mouth, and then admitted that there were two more buttery crepes with his name on them in the oven.

After we had eaten, Sonny settled down to skim through the news section of *The Guardian.*

"That girl you're looking for. She's from the Philippines?" he asked a few minutes later.

I confirmed.

He passed the paper over to me and tapped an article under domestic news. It described, in the driest of terms, how the Home Affairs Select Committee a House of Commons standing committee whose remit included immigration—was investigating the use of special regulations under which foreign domestics came to Britain. "Home Office concessions," these special regulations were called. And the largest proportion of people admitted under such "concessions" were, apparently, Filipinas.

"So?" I asked.

"Isn't it obvious?" And of course once he said it, it was. If a girl enters England under something as grand as a "Home Office concession," then there might yet be a way of tracing her.

I nipped out to our corner shop to check the rest of the newspapers, but none of them, as it turned out, had a fuller account of the committee's work.

When I returned, Sonny had roused himself from his

snail's-pace approach to the day and presented instead the very picture of a purposeful man. I watched quietly from the doorway as he pulled one end of a measuring tape to the floor, secured it under the skirting board and stretched up, his thumb skimming the surface of the tape. He marked the wall with a soft pencil, checked the height swiftly, then repeated the exercise farther along the wall. He was, as far as I could make out, preparing to mount shelves in the alcove adjoining the fireplace.

It is moments like this that reminded me that Sonny never had a proper home. His father, Alex—now a sad old man—was, during most of Sonny's childhood, a sad man of middle age, embittered by what he saw as failure and stunted emotionally by the early death of his wife.

Alex had been the deputy headmaster at a minor public school. He had tried to convince himself that this made him a person of some importance, but his lack of conviction revealed itself in anxiety about status. He was, not surprisingly, an unpopular master. And it is also not surprising that the other boys made life difficult for Sonny. With cruel intuition they knew that getting the son into trouble was the best way to embarrass their deputy head. If his father had been a demonstrative man, if he had been able to show the affection for Sonny that he almost certainly felt, it would have been easier. But for Alex, affection was swamped, always, by the apprehension that something Sonny might do might diminish the standing of his father in the eyes of the school.

Like Rumpelstiltskin, Sonny spun gold out of straw. He developed a charm and an assurance—not to mention a talent for cricket—that eventually won the other boys' respect. And he constructed an emotional world centered on a suburban villa miles away, where his grandmother offered warmth and acceptance, and the chance to figure out who he was when he wasn't his father's son.

When Sonny was at university, his grandmother died, quietly, in her sleep. Male undergraduates are allowed to be indisposed temporarily by the death of a grandparent. Sonny was flattened. The university failed to understand and he left at the end of his second year. He took his grandmother's small legacy, moved to London, and set up in business for himself. In spite of his narrow upbringing—perhaps in reaction against it—Sonny was an intensely practical young man. After a few successful cases, and two years' hard slog, he found himself on the top of the list of recommendations of several firms of solicitors. The survival of Sonny Mendlowitz, Private Investigator, was assured. He had found a place in the world in which his responsibilities were to something other than the honor of his father.

But old insecurities—like old habits—die hard, and nest-building is an occasional form of reassurance that Sonny can't resist. I should have guessed, when he started sizing up the alcove the other day, that we had an attack of home improvement on the way.

The warmth from the fire released the pungent smell of four lengths of beechwood, propped against the wall. Sonny turned to pick one up and saw me. He smiled a smile of invitation, and I began to wonder whether the current flurry of activity had anything to do with me. Sonny has always hankered after a more structured kind of relationship, and I have been most adamant that commitment needn't mean living in each other's pocket. But lately Sonny had been making the running, and I sometimes saw my separate world slipping into shadows. I hoped that this wielding of masculine tools was something more subtle than an unacknowledged victory dance.

He set down the plank, picked up a bracket from a pile on the floor. "Hold this for me, will you, Laura? Just here"—tapping a spot on the wall—"while I put the screws in."

I lined the bracket up to the mark he indicated and waited there while Sonny trotted off to the cupboard. With every passing second, I was reminded of a home truth: that holding brackets, passing tools, steadying ladders, is not for me. I'd rather someone else did it (single-handedly) and boasted about it later; I have no objection whatsoever to giving credit where credit is due. Sonny returned, clutching the cordless electric drill that my mother had given him for Christmas. He accompanied the blasts of the drill with whistled snatches of Mozart. As soon as the bracket was firmly in place, I fled.

"Hey! We've got three more to do. Where are you off to this time?" he asked as I laced up my boots and took my jacket off the peg.

"Tell you later, Tarzan," I stalled, kissing the end of his nose.

On Earl's Court Road, the air was spiked with sunshine. It had enticed the locals out of their bed-sits and onto the streets. Traffic was steady for midday on a Saturday. Driving as slowly as I dared, I scanned the shops in the vicinity of the underground stations: a *bureau de change,* Snappy Snaps, a down-at-heel Baskin-Robbins, and yet another bureau de change. It doesn't take a detective to figure out that Earl's Court is a magnet for long-term visitors whose incomes don't qualify them for American Express.

Kenway Road was on the right. And the telephone

directory hadn't mislead me, for there, squeezed between a launderette and the Prince of Teck pub ("No,"
I told Stevie later, "I didn't make it up") was the Filipino Store. It looked like a cross between a greengrocer's
and one of those stalls that clutter the dingy streets near
the Vatican.

The Filipino Store was long and narrow and stocked
with an impressive range of foodstuffs. Tins and jars
with faded labels and calorific contents—coconut
spread, sweet sugar-palm fruit, banana blossom in
brine—studded one long wall. A butcher's case offered
crabs, sprats, and varieties of offal that few native Brits
would know how to prepare. In addition, there were
baskets of bread and floursticks and pork crackling,
there were sacks of meal, and there were stacks of staple
vegetables, from yams to baby aubergines. Above the
doorway at the back of the shop hung a small shrine, no
more than a foot square. A plastic Virgin with a sequin-
studded skirt of starched blue net crouched in a forest
of candles.

I put some excellent yams in my shopping basket,
added a bottle of garlic sauce, and took my place in a
queue. While I waited, I scrutinized the signs behind
the counter. *Komiks 50p. Videos: Please rewind the film!*
and, on a large display board, *Peso Express: Today's rate
39.72. The best remittance service in London.* I wondered how many elderly parents, how many sisters and
brothers, in Manila and Quezon City, relied upon this
service for the money that would pay school fees or the
mortgage on a piece of land. I thought unwillingly of
the Hallmark sign *Love means always being there.* For
migrant workers the world over, love means having to
go away.

After making my purchases, I explained to the Filipino man behind the counter that I was trying to trace a girl who had disappeared. He gestured toward the back of the shop. "You can put a notice there," he said, handing me a filing card. "Fifty p for a week." His unreflecting eyes refused any comment on my request.

Two weeks' worth wouldn't break the bank. I got out a pen and composed a brief message, describing the skinny kid who had vanished, and offering a reward for information. Beneath my name and telephone number I added, as an afterthought, "I have nothing to do with the police." It wouldn't do as a general statement, but in respect to my search for the little Filipina, it was more or less true.

Sonny and I had our sights set on a quiet evening, but Justine, my brother Hugo's wife, persuaded us to make up the numbers at a dinner party. My sister-in-law's devotion to cooking never fails to impress me. Scouring the markets for the perfect plums, chopping and blanching and sieving, disciplining wayward pastry, devising remedies for a meringue that fails to peak—as far as I can tell, these constitute her favorite agenda for a weekend. *Vive la différence.* The meal was, as always, glorious.

"Especially the pudding," added my brother with a contented smile. "Justine, why don't you skip the opening arguments in your next big case and simply present the judge at an early stage with an almond soufflé?"

"Hugo!" she remonstrated, but she didn't look displeased.

Sonny and I stayed behind, after the others had left, and had a late-night drink. Sib's privilege, this delicious exchange of pleasurable and provoking moments. The evening was officially declared a success. There were one or two treasurable bits of gossip, the conversation had had enough of an edge to be absorbing, and the company was agreeable—all but one, I demurred.

Sonny returned to the one I would have preferred to forget. "Your face was a picture, Laura, when Sarah was talking your ear off before dinner. What was all that about?"

"So you did notice," I said accusingly, but it was too late now. The one disadvantage of eating at Justine and Hugo's is the risk of finding their neighbor, Sarah, among the guests. I don't like her, can't like her, won't like her, and yet she always seeks me out. The loquacious Sarah, who had *rocketed* her way—her word, not mine—from nursing to a *very* senior position in the regional health authority, had cornered me and devoted ten long minutes to her early career in Saudi Arabia, reliving memories of a British chap named Cracknell who knew *everyone who was anyone* in the Middle East, and who used to regularly—she whispered with a girlish giggle—deliver a bevy of British nurses to high-class parties in Riyadh. If my memories were this sleazy, I would censor them. But then, perhaps, I'm getting old. I had glanced wistfully at Sonny, but he was deep in conversation and didn't look in the least prepared to mount a rescue operation.

"You don't want to know," I replied belatedly.

"Hey," Hugo exclaimed, recalling an exchange he had had earlier with Sonny, "is it true, Laura, that you've heard at last from Claire Atkinson?"

"Ships that pass in the night," I said as lightly as I could.

And then I shared the bad news. How Claire would be staying for a short time with friends in Islington—name and address unknown. How my only point of contact with her was a telephone number, and that had been lost: how Claire's photograph with the number on the back had vanished into a house on Palace Gardens Terrace, never to reappear, and Helen Cochrane had—on my instructions—tossed the original letter away.

"It's not that bad," I concluded. "She'll probably ring me anyway when she arrives. I know Claire."

"Knew," Hugo corrected. There was a pause.

And that's the moment Sonny chose to pop the question: "What about Provence?" To a circle of blank looks. "Provence. In August. Didn't you hear what Sarah had to say?"

Shakes of the head and looks of puzzlement all around.

"Sarah and her ex-husband own a massive stone farmhouse in southern France," Sonny explained. Nods of understanding at last. "It stands empty most of the time because their new spouses have other ideas. But they can't agree to sell. So . . ."

Justine clapped her hands in appreciation. "So why don't we all go!"

"Precisely," Sonny concluded. "Rumor has it, there's a stream at the bottom of the garden and the nearby restaurant welcomes children. Florence would love it," he exclaimed, invoking Justine and Hugo's offspring. "Dominic and Daniel would love it. Damn it, I would love it!"

I examined each of the three faces in front of me—my family, cherished and cherishing—with care. Sonny was wearing his boyish face, enthusiasm peeling off years. Hugo looked intrigued. I could see his pragmatic mind ticking away, a checklist of questions and possibilities passing behind his smile. Justine had a dreamy look.

Either the farmhouse inspired romantic thoughts or—more likely—she was simply exhausted from cooking.

Why not? I thought to myself, astonished at how easy it would be. But the old caution hadn't abandoned me altogether.

"Let's think it over," was what I said aloud at the door as we made our good-byes.

At Sonny's flat, I was still hanging up my coat, when he pounced.

"Sshh!" I whispered. "The sitter!" Sonny saluted me, took a deep breath, and went to do his paternal duty. But as soon as Sue had been chatted with and paid and could decently be made to exit, we fell back into each other's arms.

"What do you mean," I demanded—offering a mock resistance—"what do you mean by introducing the idea of *les vacances* in front of my brother and his wife before you had even breathed a word to me?"

"Ooh, my darling," Sonny crooned with exaggerated sympathy and a caricatured French accent, "did I put you in an awkward position?" As he asked this, he bent me over backward at an impossible angle.

"Nothing I can't straighten out," I said, laughing, twisting into an upright stance. "But what makes you think that a family vacation is the best thing for us anyway? What about your private time with your boys? What about *my* time with Helen and Stevie at Wildfell? What about our—"

"—separate but parallel existences." Sonny took my hand and led me toward the sitting room, where the embers still glowed. I lounged on the hearth rug and slowly relaxed.

"I'm not saying we should spend every minute together in the future, or live in each other's pockets,"

Sonny soothed, undoing the buttons on my silk blouse. He kissed me gently. "Nor"—this came out throatily— "nor am I suggesting that you should abandon holidays in Norfolk with your girlfriends." Sonny's kisses lingered longer and my concerns about Provence receded.

"Just come with me this once," he urged. I was becoming more sympathetic to the project by the moment. "See what fun we can have. Together."

And we did.

8

I dialed the switchboard at the House of Commons first thing Monday morning, and—as if thoughts were wishes—I was ushered two hours later into a wood-paneled interview room at Westminister. The Home Affairs Select Committee—responsible among other things for monitoring immigration policy—was investigating the status of foreigners who did private household work; Reena Kaur was a senior member of the committee staff.

"Thank you, Mrs. Kaur, for agreeing to see me so quickly."

"Not at all." She was in her midthirties. In London, not the most stylish of capitals, to say someone is as intelligent as she is well-groomed might imply a put-down. In the case of Reena Kaur, it was unmistakably a compliment. "Monday morning we have very few visitors." With one stroke she waved aside my thanks and made it clear that it was circumstance, rather than influence, that had got me here.

I went straight to the point: Could she explain what was so special about the status of private household workers? Why the select committee would want to investigate?

She certainly could. At her tone, I braced myself for a lecture.

Under British immigration rules, apparently, work permits are not issued to private household workers from outside the European Union. However, many wealthy foreign families visit Britain regularly—some even maintain homes in London—and it doesn't suit them to be without their servants. Some come from countries—such as certain Gulf states—whose labor forces depend heavily upon the recruitment of migrant workers from their poorer neighbors.

"Did you know," Reena asked—but of course I didn't—"that every year some thirty thousand Asian women go to Saudi Arabia to work as housemaids?"

According to Mrs. Kaur, the Home Office, eager to ease the movement of wealthy people into this country, issues concessionary visas so that they can bring their live-in servants with them. Hundreds of domestics enter Britain every year and live and work under these regulations.

"But I fail to see the difference between—"

Reena Kaur forestalled my question. "No. It's not the same as entering on a work permit. When Filipinas come—or Moroccans or Sri Lankans or Bangladeshis—they are given leave to enter as members of the household. They are not classed as workers."

"Semantics?"

Mrs. Kaur's reply was a flat and unnegotiable negative.

"Not at all. These are different legal statuses. And the difference has life-and-death significance." She reached in her desk drawer and took out a package of cigarettes. She lit one and drew deeply. It was then that I noticed for the first time how tired she looked, under the flawless makeup. She faced me again, a trail of smoke snaking over her shoulder.

"You must understand this, Ms. Principal. Women and girls who are not classed as workers have no employment rights. No right to change households. No right to leave a tyrannical employer for a fair one. If employers pay the woman less than agreed—or if, as sometimes happens, they do not pay her at all; if they compel her to work all hours of the day and night; if they prevent her from contacting her family—she is, in effect, at their mercy."

"Do you mean to tell me," I asked, finally getting the point, "that employers can mistreat domestics and get away with it? But surely, if a woman has been beaten, say, or if she has not been paid her wages"—*like my Filipina*—"then she can go to the police?"

"Yes, I do mean to tell you that." Mrs. Kaur replied coldly. "Your point is precisely the one the government spokesman likes to make. 'If any woman has a complaint against her employer,' he says, 'she should not hesitate to seek the help of the British police.'" Her impression of the minister—given their differences in gender, age, ethnicity, and intelligence (let's face it, she's a bright woman)—was astounding.

Reena Kaur picked up my card and checked my name. She also, I noticed, took a steadying breath. "But he is wrong, Ms. Principal. If she complains to the police, she will be sacked by her employer and evicted in one fell swoop. She will be homeless, in a strange country, and she will have no entitlement to health care, to legal aid, to welfare. Not even the right to work for a living. Hardly a victory for justice."

"But that's absurd. It's catch-twenty-two. Why, it's a form of servitude!"

"Right on all three counts. Besides which, if a domestic worker leaves her employer—even to escape abuse—she becomes classed as an overstayer, liable to immediate deportation." Reena Kaur leaned forward and fixed me with an intense look. "As one member of the committee put it—bluntly, perhaps, but accurately—British immigration rules provide structural support for slavery."

She looked at her watch. "Now, Ms. Principal, before you leave, is there something specific that you wanted to ask?"

I described the girl I was looking for. Explained that she had been working, apparently, at a house in Kensington; that she was there one day and gone the next.

Reena Kaur shook her head. "So far, I've taken statements from over one hundred women and girls, but I can't recall any who had a mutilated finger. You don't have a name for her?"

Unfortunately not.

She stood up, then paused. "I can do one thing for you. The Commission for Filipino Migrant Workers run a crisis center for girls who get into difficulties. Many runaways eventually find their way there. The place is run by Father John, an excellent fellow. I can ask him to let you know directly if this girl comes to them. Shall I do that?"

"I'd be very grateful. And if there is anything I can do in return . . . ?"

"The center is a charity. Always short of resources," she observed with a smile.

While I was writing out a check, I returned to the work of the committee, with one last question that was bothering me. I had read in the papers about a young Jamaican woman whose employers—doctors in Surrey, as I recall—had been fined heavily for mistreatment. If she could bring them to court, why couldn't others?

Reena brushed a fleck of ash off her skirt. "The exception that proves the rule. You know the center I mentioned a moment ago? In the first six months of last year, two hundred and forty-seven domestics left abusive employers and sought the center's help. Two hundred and forty-seven. Only two or three cases reached court. What does that suggest to you about the odds of a domestic servant getting legal redress for abuse?"

"I'd say that a smoker has more chance of getting a centenary telegram from the queen."

Reena Kaur tapped another cigarette out of the package and placed it between her lips. She reached for the cigarette lighter. "You can bet on it," she said.

"Desiree, you're not thinking of coming in here with that dog, are you?"

Desiree is Dee to her chums in the theater, but I like the lushness of the original name. I had asked her to put in a couple of days that week, but I hadn't expected her to come dragging a grumpy bullterrier at the end of a blue retractable lead. The poor beast's claws screeched on the floor, like chalk scraped over a blackboard. Come to think of it, perhaps *poor beast* was the wrong term.

"Looks awfully like a pit bull to me," Sonny warned.

"Don't be absurd!" declared Dee, jumping to the defense of the mutt she had in tow. "He's a British bullterrier. Nothing like a pit bull. Look at that neck. Don't you know *anything* about dogs?"

"I don't know much about dogs," Sonny replied, sensing an opening—

"—but I know what I like," I finished for him. "And it's a dog in the office—*not*. Pit bull or no."

Dee subsided. She turned around, retracted the lead a few more inches, and headed back toward the door, mumbling over her shoulder, "I'll leave her on the landing, then." The mutt managed to secure a grip on the carpet and came to a halt. Dee appeared in the room again.

"Will one of you help me?" she pleaded.

I looked at Sonny. Sonny demurred with a be-my-guest flourish. I approached the dog warily from behind, placed the tip of my boot under the base of its short, stiff tail, and pushed. The terrier turned its head toward me. The black patch that covered its eye made it look like a pirate. Ho-ho-ho, I thought dryly. Slowly I lifted my boot. The terrier shook itself vigorously at last and trotted to the door.

When Dee reentered, she looked crestfallen. "It's proving harder than I thought," she complained. I presented her with a cup of coffee. "Milk please," was all I got by way of a thank-you.

Sonny couldn't contain his curiosity. "Why a dog? And especially, why one of those mean-looking brutes? Anyone who saw the dog first would expect to find a swastika tattooed on your forearm." Since Dee was plump and playful looking, expectations would clearly not be met.

"It's all part of the part," she explained. Once you register that Dee is an actress, some of her more cryptic statements begin to make sense. "Ivy Malone is a burglar

and a psychopath, you know, and Justin—our director—
reckoned that the dog would make her the female coun-
terpart of Bill Sykes. But we couldn't afford a pedigree
bullterrier, so I had to borrow this one from a friend of
a friend. And—well, you can see," she wailed, "she
doesn't seem to like me."

"She?" I asked, perhaps a little coldly.

"Fifi." Dee had the decency to look embarrassed. "It's
a girl. Or maybe a woman? I don't know when dogs
grow up."

"So why's she here?"

"Justin says I should take her everywhere. We should
look completely natural together. Fifi should be my Sia-
mese twin, like we were joined at the hip."

This simile didn't do much to convince me of Justin's
artistic judgment. I wasn't especially looking forward to
attending (though I knew I would) Dee's performance.

We shut the door to dull the sound of Fifi's whines,
and I explained to Dee how I wanted her to ring around
the domestic agencies in West London, making inquiries
about my missing Filipina.

"You'll like this job, Dee. You'll be warm and cozy,
here in the office. And," I added with a stern look
toward the door, "you'll be dog-free."

"Bitch." Stevie commented, joining the conversation
for the first time.

"I beg your pardon!" Dee's cheeks were flaming.

"She's a female. She's not called a dog, she's called a
bitch." Stevie sipped her coffee contentedly.

Bullterrier aside, this was shaping up to be my kind
of day. I had started the morning by sliding into an
opening in Reena Kaur's diary. Now, I took a phone
call from someone who had come across my notice in

the Filipino Store. She wouldn't leave a name, but she agreed to a meeting back at the shop at the end of the day.

The Filipino Store was quieter than it had been on my previous visit. The only person there was the man to whom I had spoken before. He was wearing a NEW YORK YANKEES T-shirt and leaning alongside the cash register reading komiks.

I suppose I must have been hoping that this would be the end of my search. That the caller would turn out to be a skinny kid with her chestnut hair in a ponytail; that my missing Filipina would be missing no more. But the young woman who entered the store a few minutes later wasn't the same person at all. Her name was Sofia Perez. She was in her late twenties. She had a bottom that was big and shapely, and she walked with an unself-conscious wiggle—a true fifties swivel—that would have done Marilyn Monroe proud.

Sofia was simply dressed in black capri pants, Chinese slippers, and a long red cardigan buttoned down the front. From a distance, she looked—there's no other word for it—cute. Closer up, she had a face that was round and warm, dark, springy hair, front teeth that overlapped, and a smile that hovered on the verge of laughter.

But when I described the girl who had come and gone so rapidly from Palace Gardens Terrace, Sofia Perez wasn't laughing.

"It's my cousin Marilou," she whispered. "She has been out of touch for weeks." She was just this side of tears.

"Is there somewhere we can go to talk?" I asked, offering her a tissue.

She pointed out the window to a Filipino restaurant

on the other side of Kenway Road. "Fine," I said. "I'll buy you an early supper." The man in the YANKEES T-shirt watched covertly from under lowered eyelids as we left.

Sofia seemed intent, at first, on confining herself to soup. She wasn't accustomed to dining out. To overcome her embarrassment, I ordered for both of us—pan-fried roast pork and vegetables and rice and a sweet dish, all served together in the Filipino style—and we tucked in together. The food was tasty, but not half as absorbing as the story Sofia had to tell.

Sofia Perez's little cousin—seventeen years old—was christened Maria Luisa Flores, but like so many Filipinas, she preferred to be known by her nickname—Marilou. Their families were close, and as children, Marilou and Sofia had spent a lot of time together. Marilou's mother was a teacher of English. Her father had been a construction worker, but two years before, he had developed a chronic disorder and was dismissed from his job. The family borrowed money against their plot of land to pay the medical bills. It was always intended that their clever daughter should finish high school and train as a teacher. But Marilou wouldn't be dissuaded: at sixteen years of age, intent on paying off the family debts, she applied to a recruiting agent to work in the Gulf.

The agent found her work in Qatar, Sofia recounted, for a large fee of course, which had to be borrowed too. And eventually Sofia received a letter saying that Marilou would be coming with her employers on an extended visit to England.

Sofia, who had worked for a Kuwaiti family since her late teens, and who spent part of every year with them in London, was delighted. Spending time with her cousin would be almost as warming as a visit home.

But something had gone wrong. No one—here or in the Philippines—had heard from Marilou since she'd left Qatar.

"Do you have an address for her here in London?" I asked.

"Yes. The Qatari family have a residence in Holland Park. But I couldn't go there," Sofia said, alarmed at the idea. "Not unless I was invited."

"Maybe *you* can't," I said firmly. "But I can. But first, tell me a little more about Marilou. Was she pleased about coming to London? Seeing you?"

"Thrilled. Not only because of me, but because of what she called her secret passion."

"Aha," I muttered. *Cherchez l'homme.*

But I was mistaken. Marilou's heart beat faster for Jane Austen. She had always been a bookworm, Sofia explained, poring over the books that her mother brought home from the English tutorial school. To her, England was the country of *Sense and Sensibility.*

Umm. She must have had quite a shock. I was working to get a grip on this determined little exile. "What kind of employee would she be?" I asked. "Hardworking? Pliable?"

"Pliable?" Sofia laughed. "Marilou was always the stubbornest child in our barrio. And what a temper!"

And that's when she told me about Marilou's forefinger. One year her grandfather carved for her a small wooden doll. Her brother hid the doll, to tease her. Marilou was furious. She shouted at her brother, she begged, and at last she threatened.

"Threatened?"

"The only threat she could make against a brother older and taller than herself. We were playing outside. She looked around wildly—I shall never forget the look

94

on her face—and then she snatched up my father's machete. 'Here,' she shouted at her brother. 'Here, if you
don't give Bobo back, I'll cut off my finger.' She positioned her hand over the edge of the wall and looked at
him defiantly. Julio moved towards her. He grabbed for
the machete just as Marilou—eyes squinched shut—
smashed it down. We watched in horror as blood spilled
over the wall. The end of her finger still hung by a sliver
of skin, but the community doctor wasn't able to save
it."

Sofia laughed uncertainly, shaking off the memory.
"Marilou was like a queen when she left the surgery.
We were all in awe of her."

"So, if an employer tried to push your cousin around,
she wouldn't take it meekly."

"Not Marilou," Sofia said proudly. "She is a sweet
and generous girl, and a bit naive perhaps. Inexperi-
enced. But when it comes to standing up for herself,
Marilou Flores is a tough little cookie."

9

Marilou Flores's Qatari employers had a house just off Holland Park Avenue. Sofia chose to accompany me—I had stirred up thoughts of family, and she was eager to talk—to the end of their street. She wouldn't go a step farther. I left her pacing on the corner, attracting admiring glances of which she was clearly oblivious from passersby, and went to interview the people who had brought Marilou into the country as a member of their household.

The double-fronted house on Abbottsbury Road spelled, to a British observer, serious money. Money to purchase a house of those proportions in this street, and money to maintain that impeccable facade.

To a young servant from abroad, it might look different. The wrought-iron bars that protected the ground-floor windows from intruders would also make it difficult for insiders to leave. Had Marilou peeped out from behind those heavy curtains? Had she watched the street, hoping to see a girl from her own country, someone to talk to? Had she had other servants to share the work of maintaining all those rooms, or had she shouldered that responsibility alone? Was she expected to look after the children, to fetch for the adults, to cook, to tend the sick? Had she allowed herself to imagine having someone—a mother, a sister—to tend to her and put her needs first? Or at age seventeen (an age when British children are considered too young to vote, too young even to watch certain kinds of films) had Marilou already learned to suppress the yearning to be cared for?

When we found her—*if* we found her—we could ask her.

The door was opened swiftly at my summons by a Pakistani woman, slight and stooped, who wouldn't make eye contact. When I explained why I had come, she shook her head and stared at her sandals. "Gone," she said in a voice barely above a whisper. "Marilou is gone."

"Was she a friend of yours? Do you know where she is?" I pleaded.

The servant shook her head. "Marilou was very young. She didn't understand about life in England." She shook her head again, chasing away some memory that lodged there. "I couldn't help her," she said sadly.

"Why did Marilou need help?"

Before she could answer, there was a call, loud and insistent, from the top of the staircase. I edged forward, trying to see. The maid moved hurriedly away and was met by a cascade of rapid-fire speech.

Unless I was really misreading the signs, the mistress of the house (the *madam,* Sofia had said) had clearly

just emerged from bed. Her hair was dirty and disarranged. She glared at me. "Well? What is it you want?"

At the mention of Marilou Flores, she became enraged. "Hopeless," she declared, as if I had asked for a
reference. "Lazy, incompetent, good for nothing at all."

The long and short of it was that, according to the
lady of the house, Marilou was gone. Decamped without
a trace. Just—the madam demonstrated with an aggressive snap of her fingers—like *that*.

"We were packing to go skiing, and she ran away. In
the middle of the night! And she stole from me. She
took the money for the milk."

"Was it a great deal of money?"

That glare again. "More than she deserved. She is a
little thief!"

The Pakistani servant had retired out of sight down
the corridor, though probably not out of earshot. The
madam seemed keen to vent her spleen, so I provided
the excuse.

A few mild questions—how long was she with you?
How did she spend her time?—were all it took to elicit
a pretty clear (though not very pretty) picture of Marilou's life before she ran away to the Butlers: working
unlimited hours, forbidden to leave the house except on
errands, forbidden even to go to church.

"I had no choice," the madam declared with the moral
certainty of someone used to organizing everything for
her own convenience. "In Qatar, she behaved herself.
But in England, she was too forward. She wanted to
go out, to visit a cathedral in Hampshire. She wanted
to *sightsee*."

"To Winchester? Where Jane Austen was buried?"

"What does it matter which cathedral it was?" the

madam snapped. "She would have run away. We had to keep her in."

"So you kept a seventeen-year-old girl a prisoner in your home."

The lady of the house was shorter than me, but rage made her formidable. She stabbed her small finger at me, her gold rings glinting like knuckle-dusters. "Marilou was my servant!" she shouted. "She had no right to *sightsee!*"

When Marilou had run away in the middle of the night, they had washed their hands of her. In her desperate rush to leave, the girl had abandoned most of her possessions. The slugabed madam, eager to be shut of her, had promptly ordered them burned.

"She's brave, your little cousin," I said to Sofia. I had related to her the gist of my conversation with the employer from Qatar and was trying to offer a crumb of comfort. "Not every teenage girl would have the guts to escape, in a strange land, where she knew virtually no one, and under threat of a beating. It's not far to Palace Gardens Terrace from here. She may have gone there straightaway. Perhaps she was taking shelter in their garden when Mrs. Butler found her—and presumably invited her in."

I also wondered again why Marilou had asked me about tracing missing persons. At the time, I had assumed there was someone she wanted to find. But now, it occurred to me, Marilou might have feared that the family from Qatar would trace her and force her back. Perhaps that was why she hadn't contacted Sofia, even after her escape.

"But why did she run away a second time?" Sofia

asked. "Why did she disappear from the house in Palace Gardens Terrace too?"

Then came the difficult part, telling Sofa what I had so far kept to myself: that her cousin may have been abducted, taken away from Palace Gardens Terrace by force. I tried to soften it a bit, to suggest that the witness, Martin Scorsese, may have been mistaken or may have misunderstood—but that kind of soft-pedaling is seldom convincing. I didn't believe it, and neither did she.

"You know what you have to do now," I said gently. "As her next of kin."

Sofia's troubled eyes were uncomprehending.

"You have to report Marilou's disappearance to the police. Enlist their help to find her."

"But—"

I set Sofia's protest firmly aside. "It's too late now to protect her from immigration officials. Marilou has been missing from the Butler house for days. She is only seventeen, and no one—not even her family back home—knows where she is. We have to hope the police can find her, before she comes to harm."

"This will take a while," I warned Sofia as we entered the station. Truer words were never spoken. As we entered, the sergeant was occupied with arranging the release of a stray bicycle to its owner, an owner whose response was anything but grateful. You might think that the poor old sergeant had made off with the bike himself. The paperwork took ages—policeman's revenge?—and Sofia and I were left twiddling our thumbs.

Eventually we were seen. I explained that Sofia had come to report a missing person. The sergeant rang through for someone to assist and showed us into a small interview room. We waited there for the duty inspector to arrive, and with her, we filled in a missing person's report. The only place where I contributed was in relation to the girl's time in Palace Gardens Terrace. I told them about my meeting with Marilou and about Thomas and Penelope Butler. I referred them to Carmen and to Martin Scorsese and told them how a girl was led away with her head shrouded by a shawl.

"That sounds like abduction to me," I said blandly. The duty inspector made no reply.

I wasn't surprised that the tension eventually got to Sofia. By the time we left the interview room, it had really hit her: this wasn't another childhood adventure. Marilou had disappeared and it was a matter for the police.

I sat her down on a bench near the front door and went to fetch a drink of water. When I returned, Sofia was crying and the loneliness of her situation swept over me. I sat down next to her to see what comfort I could offer.

A voice rang out, sharp and almost certainly intended for me. "Just what have you done to make this young woman cry?"

It was Nicole Pelletier. Before I was reincarnated as a private investigator, in the days when I earned a living teaching history, Nicole had been a student of mine. And one of the unsung perks of being an academic— especially in a small town like Cambridge—is that, over the years, many a noteworthy niche in your community comes to be filled by former students. Wherever you go, they are there, living testaments to continuity and to change. My students run the loans department of my local bank and buy men's underwear for Marks and Spencers; they draft the Cambridge planning regulations;

at Nadia's Bakery, they cut (for me, anyway) extra thick slices of pecan pie.

And sometimes, like Inspector Pelletier, they work their way up through the ranks of the CID.

I allowed myself a few seconds to reorient. Time, that is, to size up Nicole, who was towering over us, and to try to figure out what she was doing here, in Kensington Police Station, rather than in Cambridge.

"Secondment?" I guessed.

"Special assignment. One year, senior posting." The trace of smugness in her tone was intended to make me understand—if I didn't already, and I didn't—that this move confirmed her reputation as a highflier.

"Congratulations, Nicole." I inspected her with the eye of a former tutor and approved. Nicole is a capable woman and a handsome one. As an undergraduate, she was casual to the point of sloppy about dress, but her talent for netball produced a physical confidence rare among her age group. She looked robust and comfortable in her body still. And in addition, since the last time I had seen her, her clothing had moved upmarket, as if she had attended a course on power-dressing and then adapted the rules to exclude narrow skirts or high heels.

If Nichole's clothes had changed, her hair hadn't. It was still that blue-black color rarely seen on Europeans; as ever, it refused to be restrained. She had tried to secure it with a band, but the hair had other ideas and burst the bounds of convention.

"And what are you doing here?" she asked. Not smug this time, but territorial.

I was tired of being towered over. I patted Sofia on the arm and rose from the bench, standing full height so that I looked slightly down on the policewoman. "We're here because of Sofia's cousin. Marilou Flores, seventeen years old. She has gone missing. And there's reason to fear that she may have been abducted."

To Nicole's credit, she softened instantly with a sympathy that could only be genuine. She told Sofia how sorry she was, noted the name and report number. She nodded to me, a nod that was easy to read: we go back a long way. "I'll nose around," she told me. "See what's cooking."

I was glad to hear it. Not because of the way she said it (Nicole was never known for an elegant turn of phrase), but because a statement of interest from DI Pelletier meant that this missing person's case wouldn't merely drift to the bottom of the pile.

10

She-who-must-be-obeyed (my diary) instructed me on Tuesday to make a progress report to Marcia Shields about the theft of her paintings and the complicity or innocence of her daughter's friends. In spite of my preoccupation with Marilou Flores, I had to attend to my Cambridge case.

Three telephone calls smoothed the way.

The first was from Marcia's daughter, Layla—she of the shadow-colored hair and the boyfriend that her mother despised. Just as I was thinking of putting the pressure on for a meeting, Layla rang and invited me to have a cup of tea with her friends—Petersee, Tenko, and Vic—in the Roma Cafe in Cambridge.

The second call was to Marcia herself: I confirmed an appointment for that afternoon and, in passing, checked that the electrical system of her Saab was better for its recent repair.

The third call was to Marcia's garage. None of my visits to Saab garages in London lately had been a conspicuous success, and I was convinced that my car deserved better. So I persuaded Marcia's workshop to squeeze me in for an estimate—only an estimate—if I could present myself in Cherry Hinton, on the outskirts of Cambridge, by ten o'clock that morning.

So the doings for Tuesday just sort of fell into place, and the place was Cambridge. The manager of the Saab garage had a gangly quality disconcerting in a man whose fortieth birthday was surely a matter of memory rathor than of dread. IIe wore a suit that might have been nicked from the wardrobe of a much bigger man. The jacket bagged in the shoulders and straggled in the hem. But in spite of sartorial shortcomings, he was attentive to his customers—or to me at least—and that, in the end, won me over. I told him how the Saab's acceleration had become unreliable. He listened as if he really cared. I accoptcd the offer of an immediate diagnostic check and forgave him his ill-fitting suit.

My feelings about the rest of the staff were less positive. I entrusted my keys to a bold young mechanic with his name embroidered on the pocket of his boilersuit. "Harding" made far more eye contact than is called for in a transaction of this kind. "Leave it to me," he said with a wink. I was less than reassured.

The Roma Cafe, where Layla had arranged to meet, proved to be an unobtrusive little place near the Grafton Centre. Glass-fronted cases offered assemble-on-the-spot sandwiches and salads, on one side, and ice cream and pastries on the other. The cappuccino machine kept company with the pastry, and a thin-faced waitress raced between the two.

The red lino floor accommodated four small tables.

Two were empty, if you discounted—as you should—
the fake rosebuds. A round man sat at the third reading
the *Financial Times,* his briefcase clenched between his
feet. The remaining table was occupied by a young fellow with a golden tone to his skin that didn't match the
English weather. He wore a checked woolen jacket and
bleach-washed jeans. Around his neck was a purse on a
thong. He looked at me as I entered, a long plait of blond
hair flipping over his shoulder as he turned.

No sign of Layla. I decided for the moment not to
approach Petersee—the golden boy was too young to be
Vic—and took a seat instead at the empty table that had
the best view of the door. The waitress was beside me
before I had hung my jacket on the back of the chair.

"Hmm." She cleared her throat nervously. The gesture
was right at home, somehow, with her narrow features.
"Are you looking for Layla Shields?"

No point in disguising it. "I hope she hasn't been de-
layed?" What I really meant was that I hoped Layla
wasn't mucking me around. There may have been a period of my life when I found that kind of thing amusing,
but it belongs to an era when my diary was less full.

"Oh, no," the waitress replied. Obviously a girl with
her customers' interests at heart. "She'll be here any
minute now. That's Petersee over there. If you want to
meet him . . . ?" Her voice trailed off uncertainly.

I flashed her one of my special smiles. Sonny once
labeled that smile "maternal." I prefer to think of it as
reassuring. "How about asking Petersee to join me?
And . . . " I placed a hand on her arm to detain her. "I'll
have prawn and avocado with dill mayonnaise on white.
Perhaps Petersee wants something too, on me."

After the message had been delivered, Petersee rose
from his chair with a great deal of bumping and

scraping. He leaned over. It was only then that I noticed the dog under his table.

"I hope you don't mind," he said. "The dog, I mean." The animal looked wistfully up at me, its top incisors slightly overlapping the lower lip. "I'll tie him up outside if you would rather. But he gets upset."

"What's his name?" I asked, feeling like a fraud. I don't usually care to know dogs' names. Especially when they look at me as if I might be their only hope of happiness. What had I done, I wondered, to deserve three dogs in one week?

"Trevor," he replied. Trevor's tail began to wag at the sound of his name, and he focused his longing on Petersee again.

The dog provided an opening. I had no difficulty persuading Petersee to answer my questions. He seemed as transparent as cellophane—an optimistic kid, hanging out and retaking examinations in the face of A-level results too modest to gain entry to the university course he wanted. I wondered how his parents, who had coughed up the fees for Bradfield's School, felt about that.

Petersee, it turned out, fancied the New Age life on the open road. He spoke enthusiastically of tepees in Wales, where friends braved the winter cold with only their drugs to keep them warm. He waxed eloquent on the sense of community generated by the hardship of homelessness. Only a guy with a secure roof over his head could really believe that, I thought. And sure enough, the would-be traveler lived in Newnham with Mum and Dad.

From the corner of my eye, I saw the door of the café open and two people come in. They looked our way. The man put his arm around Layla's shoulders in a possessive movement and kissed her. The gesture—I had no doubt it was a gesture, produced either for my benefit or for Petersee's—was crude and unconvincing. A macho pose rather than an expression of affection. Petersee lowered his eyes and tucked into his sandwich.

Layla pulled away, embarrassed. She was a half an inch taller than her boyfriend, and her open expression was the antithesis of Vic's guarded look. His hooded eyes were his most arresting feature. They flashed at me for a second or two, dark and hostile, and then the lids twitched down as if pulled by invisible threads. He lifted his chin so he could see across the room in spite of half-closed eyes.

Layla led the way toward me, smiling nervously. Mr. Cool trailed behind, unconcerned, his top-of-the-range Doc Martens scuffing on the floor. She introduced me to Vic.

"So, the lady dick," was what he drawled by way of greeting. No effort to conceal his contempt. "And sandwiches too." He swept his eyes over the table, taking it all in, calculating. "I'm pleased to see you made yourself at home. Wouldn't want you to feel uncomfortable. Now would we?" He gave a cynical laugh, looked sideways at Petersee and Layla. Neither met his eye.

"Layla," I said, nodding. "Would you like anything to eat?"

"No, no really, I'm fine," she said, flustered. "Well, a cup of tea, maybe."

I looked at Vic, resisting the impulse to narrow my eyes and drawl back. Some affectations are catching. "You look hungry," I said pointedly. "How about an Eccles cake?"

He sat down with a clatter and was probably pleased when the round man picked up his briefcase and exited the café in mild alarm. I decided to ignore Vic, at least long enough to get the better of my irritation before it got the better of me. I recognized his type, and the shock of recognition was anything but pleasant.

I ordered the tea and finished my sandwich, slowly.

"So," Vic snarled, tired of not being the center of attention, "Layla's old lady has decided to stick the blame on us. And you're here to do the dirty work, are you?"

I wiped my hands on a serviette. "Only if you call it dirty work to talk to people with a view to disproving the possibility of guilt. I don't," I added mildly.

"And why should I want to talk to you?"

"Simple. If you had nothing to do with the theft of Marcia Shields's paintings, maybe I can establish that. It must be unpleasant to have a cloud of suspicion hanging over your friendship with Layla."

Vic's scowl was the first reaction of his for which I felt any sympathy. It indicated that he did indeed care about Layla's opinion of him—not that he wanted her to know it.

"I'll give you three questions, lady dick. Ask me three questions. But make them good, because when I've answered them, I'm off."

"A nice coincidence of desire," I muttered to myself. He wasn't alone in wanting to keep contact with the current company to a minimum.

"What?" he demanded, the hoods of his eyes retracting suddenly. He was furious at the slightest hint that someone might be making fun of him. No sauce for the gander here.

"Fair enough," I translated. "Question one: Tell me what's made you the person you are today."

Silence as Vic tried to figure out where this was heading. "What's that got to do with the paintings?"

"I'm the one who's doing the asking. *You* can have three questions, if you like, when I've had the answers to mine."

"Hard times," he drawled. I knew he wouldn't be able to resist. His kind can never turn down a chance for self-dramatization. "I've known hard times all my life. My father is a butcher, doesn't know culture from a pig's liver. Never earned more than one hundred and fifty pounds a week in his life. No fancy boarding school for me," he said with a jeer at his friends. Layla squirmed, as he meant her to do. "No paintings on the wall for me, no family treasures—not unless you count the figure of the cart horse that my father won at the fair. It sits on top of the television, on a doily. Very tasteful," he sneered.

I nodded at the blue-and-white scarf draped with artful carelessness around his neck. "Peterhouse College, Cambridge, I believe." It wasn't a question. I merely wanted to establish that the hard-times-at-t'-mill theme would only play so far.

Vic almost stuttered in his anger, his eyes virtually closed and his chin pointed aggressively in my direction. "Have you ever tried it, lady dick? You just try being an undergraduate in Cambridge when everyone else despises you for your accent, your clothes, your lack of money. When you can't afford to go out for a drink, let alone to a May ball. When people in dining hall think you're quaint because you went to a comprehensive school. So . . ." Vic paused for breath, took himself in hand. "If you want to know what makes me tick, it's that I'm a survivor. And that I've rejected all that crap about working hard to be a boring little mortgage-payer, just like the rest of them. I'm a bad boy," he drawled, "because I see things as they are."

So now we knew. The butcher's son had absorbed the aristocratic stance—all that contempt for ordinary people and everyday aspiration. He had deployed it aginst his parents and, in the end, against himself. Self-hatred is a nasty thing.

"Question two." Move on before he sank into self-pity. "Where were you on the weekend that Layla's mother's paintings walked? And," I emphasized, "only a full itinerary will do."

Vic dredged up a cold smile. It didn't improve his looks. He claimed he had been playing with a rock group on Friday evening, sleeping and hanging out with friends on Saturday and Sunday, and with a chick all Saturday night.

"A full itinerary? You want to know *precisely* what we were doing?" he asked cynically, referring of course to the chick.

"I'm not interested in the details of your love life, if love it is. I'll settle for simple information. Like where you were on Saturday night, and the name of the person you were with."

As if I didn't know already—Layla's blush was there for everyone to read. She looked nervously at me as Vic confirmed that Layla had snuck away from the Thoday house on Saturday, with Barbara's connivance, and joined him at his place. I let it pass. But I had the impression that Vic got perverse pleasure from her discomfiture.

"You've only got one more question, lady." He looked triumphant now.

I watched as Petersee surreptitiously slipped Trevor the ends of his egg mayonnaise sandwich. Trevor didn't look wild about the egg, but he was grateful for the attention. Maybe I have underestimated dogs. I passed Petersee the last morsel of my lunch and felt a certain satisfaction when Trevor gobbled it up.

At last I addressed myself to Vic. "Question three, then. Where—precisely—did you get the money for those boots?"

He didn't like it, I could see that. All the better. I gave him an opportunity to compose himself. "Since you don't approve of working, I assume your benefit check covers the necessities and little else. If I can believe what you've already told me, your father hasn't much to spare towards hundred-pound boots for his unemployed son. So you can understand," I said with a self-deprecating shrug, "why someone like me might be curious."

Of course he was ready now, as I knew he'd be. "Savings," Vic offered. "I saved for these boots over weeks and weeks."

"How very prudent." Then I turned to Petersee.

Petersee ran through his activities on the weekend the paintings were stolen: from Friday evening in this very café, through homework and videos and sleeping on Saturday, to Sunday lunch at his gran's and Sunday evening at the cinema with Tenko. Uneventful, and easily checked.

"And Tenko?" I asked, turning back to Layla. "Couldn't she make it today?"

Layla looked startled. "Didn't you know?" She beckoned to the waitress. The narrow-featured girl brought the coffee jug for refill when she came. "I'm so sorry, I assumed you'd met. Laura, this is Tenko."

I gave myself the mental equivalent of a slap on the wrist. "Tenko," I responded, catching her eye. "Can you join us?"

"Order something first, and then it will be okay."

So I ordered two large mushroom pizzas, and coffees all around, and as soon as Tenko had relayed the order to the back, she pulled a chair over from the adjoining table—the one vacated by the round man—and squeezed in between Layla and Petersee. Some of the anxiety rolled off her shoulders when she sat down. Maybe she was just tired.

She warned us that her break was short, so I took a different tack. I asked her what she thought of the paintings in Layla's house.

"I wouldn't want them on my walls." Tenko had a clear, precise little voice. "They were kind of somber. I was surprised they were worth so much money."

"How did you know their value?"

"Mrs. Shields told us," she said forthrightly. "Didn't she, Layla?"

Layla nodded. Nervously.

"Yes," Tenko continued, "Layla and I were looking at a painting of a man and woman, and I traced the woman's face with my finger, but Mrs. Shields came in the room and asked me not to touch them. She told me that the pictures were very old and quite good, though they weren't done by a famous painter, like Picasso or anyone. And that she imagined they'd fetch perhaps a thousand apiece at auction. So to be careful."

"Were the others," I asked, indicating Petersee and Vic with a nod of my head, "surprised when you told them?"

"Vic wasn't, were you Vic?" Vic refused to meet her eyes. "He had already guessed that they were valuable. He knows quite a lot about art, you see."

"I see," I said solemnly, not glancing in Vic's direction. "And what do you know, or imagine, Tenko, about the disappearance of those paintings?"

She had no ideas, apart from general indignation. She didn't even seem to realize that she and her friends were under suspicion. She ran through her weekend, quickly, and as far as the naked ear could detect, without guile. A large part of it was spent working, in this very café. Her story confirmed Petersee's on two counts. It was only as she got up to attend to a buzz from the vicinity of the pizza oven that she lobbed her grenade over the parapet. I wouldn't quite call it a bombshell, but it certainly did explode.

"Are you coming around to mine this evening, Tenko?" Layla asked.

Tenko looked at her thoughtfully, glanced in my direction, and replied, "I better not."

"Why? What's wrong?" asked Layla, clearly surprised.

Tenko glanced at me again, then, with a sigh, decided to unburden herself. "I really wouldn't know what to say to your mum. You see, I know—I guess I'm the only one here who knows—that Mrs. Shields never went to Paris."

Even Vic sat up and took notice. His malicious smile overshadowed the dividing up of the pizzas. Tenko explained. She had kept this knowledge to herself for too long and was relieved to share speculation as to its meaning with others.

The Saturday of the weekend of the burglary, Tenko had gone to London for an interview. As she emerged into the daylight at Kings Cross, she saw a Mercedes-Benz pull up near the curb. A woman jumped out and signaled the newsagent for a copy of *Time Out*. Tenko recognized Marcia Shields immediately. And when Tenko approached Marcia, she had the impression that Marcia's glance fell on her and flicked away. It was then that she had concluded that Layla's mother's trip to

Paris was an invention. She was staying in London and had chosen to hide this fact from even her own daughter.

I turned to Layla. "Did it ever cross your mind that your mother might have a lover, perhaps?"

"Once or twice," she said, nodding, a hint of the penny dropping in her voice, "my mother reacted oddly to telephone calls, speaking in a stilted way when I came into the room. I shrugged it off at the time. But now I wonder . . ."

"Does she have a boyfriend that you know of?"

"She sometimes goes out with a man called Christopher, but Chris is gay. They are certainly not—you know—lovers. And there would be no reason for them to hide it if they were."

I paid the bill, and left a hefty tip. "I'm going to have a word with your mum now, Layla. Do you want to share my cab?"

Layla looked as if she might like to be spared the walk home. But she glanced at Vic, whose sullen face was tantamount to a threat. "Not this time. But thanks."

Marcia was doing a spot of gardening when I showed up. A buddleia had broken free of the brick wall, and she was trying to get it back under restraint. She led me into the garden, but she wasn't particularly welcoming, and her high color suggested that my arrival made her nervous. She needed to know what I knew.

"A simple matter," I answered her. "I understand now why you didn't go to the police. They might have been suspicious about your own part in the burglary when they found out that you had spent the weekend, not in Paris, but in London, after all."

Marcia paled. "I was in Paris ..." she whispered, without conviction.

"No. You were in London. And late on Saturday morning, you bought a magazine at Kings Cross Station. Who was driving the Mercedes?"

"I can't tell you," Marcia said, all the bouncy self-confidence of our last meeting gone. "He's married, you see."

"How long have you been involved with him?"

"Almost six years now. Don't think I like this stealth and sneaking around," she said, giving in. "I hate it. But he says that his wife must never be allowed to know, that she would pull her money out and his business would collapse. He made me promise. If anything got out, he would never forgive me."

"Marcia," I said more gently, "how much of the rest of your story is true?"

"All of it," she insisted, her contact-tinted eyes awash. "Everything, I left the house when I said, took the car to be repaired, went from there in a taxi. The only difference is that I went to the train station rather than the airport. We had intended, you see, to go to Paris. That was our plan—a spring break. But something came up. He had to be in London for a meeting on Saturday afternoon, so we altered our plans."

"You never went back to your house before Sunday evening?"

"No. I came home on Sunday evening just as I said and found the paintings gone."

I didn't press Marcia for the name of her lover. Instead, I held out the house key that I had retrieved from Terry Merton. "With Terry Merton's compliments. But not those of his wife. Can you suggest any reason why Kay Merton might recoil at the mention of your name?

Other than the obvious one—that she already knows you are having an affair with her husband?''

Poor Marcia. Her face told me all there was to know. Terry had been stringing her along, pretending that his wife didn't know and mustn't know. All that stealth was merely a ploy so that Terry Merton—like many another philanderer—could retain his long-term lover without disrupting his domestic life.

She listened while I summarized my inquiries so far into the stolen paintings, though her heart wasn't in it. And she agreed that once Layla's friends were in the clear, I could talk to the police.

I left her still wrestling with the buddleia. "Stupid thing," she declared with feeling as it refused to fall into line. "Why won't you give it up?"

I fitted in a few other chores while I was in Cambridge, and by the time I got back to the garage to pick up my car, the heel bar on one side and the computer-components shop on the other were decisively shut. The forecourt door was partway down. Underneath it, only a concrete floor was visible, oil and grease reflecting the gleam from a fluorescent light. Inside, someone was whistling, and there was an occasional crash and bang, but no hum of machinery. The workshop was virtually closed.

With commendable tact, no one in the office mentioned that I was late. The manager confirmed my suspicion that the fuel-injection system was wonky—my word, not his—and warned that it would soon need to be replaced. When delivering the estimate of cost, he kept his eyes fixed to the worksheet. Delicacy, I decided. He probably couldn't bear to see me flinch.

He called the receptionist, who entered from a back

room wearing a coat and an aura of hairspray. She flipped open the workshop diary and waited impatiently, her fingernail tapping on the open ledger, while I ran through my own appointments. At one point, the tapping ceased, and I glanced up to see her cast an enticing smile in the direction of my bold mechanic from earlier in the day. Even I had to admit that without the overalls, he looked exceptionally smart, leather jacket and wool trousers straight out of the window of the posh shop on Benet Street. The manager averted his eyes. Was he keen on the girl himself? I wondered. Or did he simply, in his ill-fitting suit, feel upstaged?

I weighed up the disadvantage of being without a car against the risk of waiting to repair it. I did my calculations aloud, to the annoyance of the receptionist. "Friday week," I concluded, arranging to drop the car off on my way to Stansted. "I've got a job to do in Glasgow," I explained. The mechanic looked at his wrist—which was odd, since he wasn't wearing a watch—nodded at the manager, and did a passable impression as he exited of a well-heeled young man-about-town. The receptionist scribbled my details in her ledger, snatched up her handbag by its gilt chain, and dashed off after him. The cloying smell of hairspray stayed behind.

11

"**G**ood morning, Mary Sunshine. Another gorgeous day in London. Up and at 'em." The voice was Sonny's. The alarm call was unwelcome. "Wakey, wakey."

"Go away. I'm taking the morning off."

He tried to snatch the duvet away, but I held on for dear life. "Go," I repeated pleadingly. "I'm sleeping."

But of course, by then, I wasn't.

Sonny retreated, leaving me at last to peace and quiet. And ten minutes later, I was up, making coffee. But even the prospect of a lazy morning was denied me, because my thoughts soon turned to the slip of a girl. Who now had a name.

Marilou Flores, I breathed to myself: Where are you?

Nicole wasn't in her office when I rang, but the duty sergeant tracked her down. "Any news?" I asked. "About that missing Filipina?"

"We've done the rounds," Nicole volunteered. "Thomas Butler, Martin Scorsese—can you believe that guy?—the former employer, Home Office records."

"And?"

"So far, zilch. She came into the country on December eleventh. The family from Qatar gave her a hell of a time. She ran away—more power to her elbow. According to Scorsese, she moved into the Butler's home in Palace Gardens Terrace and was abducted from there; according to the Butlers, she was never there in the first place. It's what you'd call a standoff. And"—Nichole got in quickly, before I could object—"we have no other leads. No suggestions as to places where she might be. No names of friends or contacts, other than the cousin. Nothing to go on. I don't see what else we can do."

"The indigo van?" I asked, knowing it was hopeless.

"Between you and me—my governor would never have authorized it—I had a peek. The register doesn't run to indigo. In London alone, there are almost a thousand vans that are blue or navy. One of those thousand owners may well be a man with thick sideburns who's balding on top, but there's no way we are going to send out officers to check. We'll just have to wait until the girl surfaces again of her own accord. Sorry, Laura."

I downed my coffee and moved to bury anxiety in action.

In what I hoped would be a once-and-only gesture, I rang Sarah, my brother's motormouth neighbor. Reminded her of the man, the British fellow, who on her account knew *everyone who was anyone* in the Middle East. Derek Cracknell, was that his name? Did she have any idea where he might be found?

Sarah certainly did have an idea. Or two. She almost fell over herself in her eagerness to discover my business with Cracknell. "He's sure to remember me," she insisted. "I could come with you, introduce you. I could assist you."

"With my inquiries?" I asked wryly.

Thanks, but no thanks.

Cracknell's office was in a run-down building in North Kensington. His two rooms were at the front of the second floor, within coughing distance of the fumes of the Westway. The location and the furniture suggested that whatever their actual line of business, Cracknell Associates were hanging on by the skin of their teeth. Cracknell's assistant took my business card and disappeared into the next room. After a moment, I snuggled down into the chair, and—closing my eyes—drifted away.

And opened them again, suddenly. Someone, a man of substantial proportions, stood directly in front of me. He was an inch too close for comfort. What a difference an inch makes. I quelled the impulse to run and straightened in my chair.

"Derek Cracknell?"

"At your service." Cracknell was built like a rugby player with a deep chest and muscled thighs. Maybe a former rugby player. He had the surface softness that suggested his game was followed by a few pints too many.

"Would you mind stepping back? You're making me nervous." I flashed him a smile that was meant to take the sting out of my words.

Cracknell stepped a pace away and lobbed me a return smile. "Delighted to meet you, Ms. Principal. My very first female private investigator. I must say"—and here he looked me up and down in what he meant to be an appreciative gaze—"you're not at all what I expected. I imagined someone hard-faced, masculine, badly dressed. Not a young woman who looks as if she just pranced off the catwalk."

This was, as the Pythons used to say, getting silly. Naomi Campbell I am not. And I objected the word *pranced.* I stood up and faced him squarely. That seemed to quiet him down.

I mentioned Sarah's name (he didn't remember her) and flattered him outrageously. As I told it, the Cracknell reputation put him right up there with Lawrence of Arabia.

"Apparently, you know everyone who's anyone," I concluded.

"I get around." A touch smugly. "Why don't we step into my office, where we won't be interrupted?"

The outer reception room was drab but tidy. Cracknell's office was merely drab. The extent of the clutter suggested a man with too many things on his mind. There were certainly too many things on his desk.

He showed me to a seat too close to his and swung his chair to face me. His after-shave had a note of blackberry, the kind of smell that makes you long for summer. I try to resist snap judgments, but so far this after-shave was the only thing about Cracknell that I liked.

I explained why I had come. "To ask you for help in tracing a missing Filipina. Her name is Marilou Flores."

Cracknell's eyes slid away from mine, as if he didn't want me to see what lay behind them. He backed his chair an inch or two away.

"This Marilou," I continued, watching his face, "entered England in December as a housemaid for some people from Qatar. Then she ran away."

"Ran away where?" He was anxious to know. Or to know if I knew?

"That's just it, I've no idea," I replied, keeping the Butler card close to my chest. "She was sighted a couple of times after leaving her employers, but now she's disappeared, it seems, for good. I can't help but wonder if she has found work somewhere else, perhaps with another family from the Gulf. She has to live somehow."

"And you think I can help?" Cracknell assumed an ingratiating expression, but his voice had about as much warmth in it as an iron bar. My opinion of Sarah sank even lower. What kind of a woman would find Derek Cracknell worthy of a giggle?

"I don't expect you've come across her"—Cracknell shook his head vehemently—"but I thought that, since you know everybody who's anybody, you might be willing to ask around."

There was a snap of resolution in his eyes and he suddenly looked downright eager. "No problem. I'll take care of it. I'll make inquiries and get back to you in say—a week or two?" He made some notes on a clean piece of paper and added it to the rest of the clutter on his desk. "You can just leave the whole thing to me."

"Kind of you," I murmured. If he had been a bit less keen, I might have been a bit less suspicious.

The internal phone buzzed. Cracknell excused himself and stepped into the outer office, but I couldn't make out the conversation that took place. On the other hand, I wasn't really listening. My attention had been snapped up by the brown plastic out-tray that nudged my left arm. With a glance over my shoulder to ensure that Cracknell was looking the other way, I riffled through the items in the tray.

An engraved invitation to a reception at the Kuwaiti embassy caught my eye. I admired the embassy seal and considered the yellow sticker with *NO* scrawled across.

I glanced at the door again, glimpsed Cracknell safely in conversation with another man, and slipped the invitation into the pocket of my jacket. Could be, I figured, a shortcut to getting further information about Cracknell himself. If they knew him well enough to invite him, then they might know him well enough to tell me a thing or two.

He returned, sat down close to me once again. I considered his pale skin, with darker pigment freckling through a pink sheen.

"You didn't get that tan here in London. Holiday in the Middle East?" I asked in a conversational tone.

"Business. I visit the Gulf every eight weeks or so. And sure," he picked up where we had left off, "I'll ask around for you. Better yet"—he looked at me appraisingly—"why don't you come out with me this evening and you can do some asking for yourself? I could introduce you to some of the right people." Cracknell's smile didn't obscure the strategic element in his faded blue eyes.

This was the man, I recalled, who used to regularly in Sarah's time deliver a bevy of British nurses to high-class parties in Riyadh. He still thinks he is supplying, I reflected cynically, but not nurses this time.

"Wish I could, Derek," I said, smiling broadly, "but I'm terribly tied up."

I moved toward the door. The invitation in my jacket pocket gave me confidence. "One more thing," I added, watching him closely. "How well do you know Thomas Butler?"

Cracknell earned a 5.9 for facial control on that one. The smile didn't slip, the eyes didn't narrow. But he didn't score so well on body language. His shoulders stiffened with the effort of concealing his alarm.

He denied it, of course. Claimed not even to have heard of Butler. But if Cracknell were on the stage, his "Who?" would have won snorts of disbelief from the stalls.

Being a well-brought-up girl, I merely smiled.

"It's only eleven P.M.!" squealed a girl who had just arrived. One look at the long queue for the midnight film was enough to make her meaning clear.

An hour represents a long wait on a chilly April evening, but if the truth be told, the wait was half the fun. Laughing, jostling, sharing Rollos or cigarettes or jokes, the young women and men—few of them out of their teens, some of them hoping that the manager didn't intend to enforce too strictly the rule of *18 and over*— were as good-humored a cinema audience as you could wish for. They marshaled themselves in twos or threes along the alley, leaving room for newcomers to trudge by in single file. With every new arrival who exclaimed at the length of the queue, those already waiting congratulated themselves afresh for engineering an early arrival.

A youthful extrovert entertained those around him with a caricature of Jason, the implacable killer whose exploits were being screened for their amusement that evening. Two girls buffered in duffle coats against the chill giggled merrily at his antics and shifted position to join in the fun. One offered Jason a swig from her bottle of Coca-Cola.

A wave of unease rippled down the queue. A gang of men reached the top of the line and took rough issue with the banter there. Their threats introduced a note of menace. It echoed off the wall of the cinema and rebounded down the line. Girls and boys shifted nervously, stifled their laughter, averted their eyes.

The newcomers were older and tougher and out for a fight. They shouldered their way down the alley, fists at the ready, their shaved heads and bomber jackets carrying the taint of the neofascist right. Giggles faded into fear as they approached.

The Jason impostor prudently abandoned the limelight and pressed back into the queue. He pushed his new companions behind him, but at that point the alley was narrowed by a plywood partition that screened the rubbish near the service door. The girls managed to retreat only a few inches.

The first tough refused to slow. He raised his hands and gave Jason a vicious shove. Jason plunged back against the duffle coats, and soft drink sloshed everywhere. The girls in turn tumbled onto the partition. The partition tipped, and the bags of rubbish that it was designed to conceal came into view.

The girl whose arm was drenched in cola screamed first. In a kind of reflex action, soon shrieks echoed up and down the line. People stumbled toward the high street, propelled by the smell of danger and a compulsion to escape. They collided with others who pressed toward the partition, determined to see for themselves.

The few who managed to get close enough to see almost wished they hadn't. The plywood screen had collapsed backward. Its top edge leaned at a crazy angle against the service door of the cinema. The bottom edge rested upon floods of human detritus, bits of hot dog and popcorn and slops of various kinds that had spilled out of the bags.

And some of the detritus was human in another sense. Adolescents who laughed at cinematic massacres, who groaned in amusement at dismemberment on the screen, struggled against the truly horrifying recognition that the pale objects protruding from the bags of rubbish were nothing other than the legs of a young girl. And that they were crusted with a hard brown glaze that wasn't cola.

They should have let the body be. The officers who interviewed them about their discovery found that they had watched enough police procedurals to know that. But the seventeen-year-old in the pink duffle coat had suddenly gone wild. She was what used to be known, without irony, as a good girl—friendly and honest, a companion to her mum, a treasure to her dad. The discovery of a girl buried under garbage had turned her simple world upside down.

In her scrabble among the rubbish, in her ghastly attempt to bring into view the rest of the body, she was doing just what she always did—trying to be helpful. Her chum had tugged at the duffle coat, attempted to stop her, but had been shaken off. Only when the body was fully revealed did the frenzied activity cease. She had stayed where she was, kneeling in the alley, she and the dead girl surrounded by a parapet of rubbish. Her breathing steadied, though tears continued to course down her face. She became very still.

She studied the dead girl, people reported, as if she were committing the details to memory. She began with the fine chestnut-colored hair. Some of it was gripped at the back with an elastic, but the rest had worked free and had swept across the face, hiding the features. A breeze gusted through the alley and lifted a strand of hair for a few seconds before abandoning it again. With a delicate touch, the girl in the duffle coat brushed the forehead clear and wondered that a face could be so cold. She caressed the ugly bruise on the temple. She considered the veins in the eyelids, the high cheekbones, the lack of makeup. She had known without knowing that the extraordinary pallor of the complexion was something achieved not by artifice but by death.

It didn't end there. She looked at the slender throat, the jutting collarbones, the tiny breasts, for the girl was naked. She saw the concave rim around the belly, so different from her own soft stomach. She saw the thin thighs and the blood-splashed legs and the beautiful toes. Nothing escaped her notice. Years later, when her husband had left her and she was struggling to bring up three children on her own, she would wake up in the night in a cold sweat, every detail of the body imaged in hard-edged clarity in her mind.

The first policeman on the scene found her like that, still staring. When he spoke to her, his voice seemed thin and unreal to her, like conversation issuing from the telly in an adjoining room. She was unable to respond.

But when he gently touched her shoulder, she rose and turned in one smooth movement and looked up into his eyes.

"She's no older than me," she whispered.

For a very long time, it was all she could say.

12

The following morning I was roused again from a deep sleep. Not a wake-up call from Sonny this time, but the *tring-tring* of the telephone and a voice with the grainy sound of officialdom.

"This is Kensington Police Station, Earl's Court Road. Will you hold, please? Inspector Pelletier wants a word."

"Who's that, Laura?" Sonny asked, surfacing. It was 6 A.M.

I couldn't bring myself to speak. Nicole wasn't ringing me before dawn, I knew, to invite me to her college reunion.

I inched myself up to a sitting position in bed, found Sonny's hand under the covers, held it against my cheek. When Nicole came on the line, I was ready.

"You've found her," I said.

"We've found the body of a teenaged girl, with part of a finger missing. The scenes-of-crime people have just finished with the body, and they've taken her off to the mortuary now."

"Where?"

"St. Mary's, Paddington."

"No. Where did you find her?"

Nicole explained about the alley next to the cinema in Notting Hill. About the poor young girl who had found the body. And about the poor young girl who was found.

No motorcycle crash for Marilou Flores, no overdose of ecstasy, no tumble off a bridge. These are the tragic, the unnecessary, deaths of the young. But Marilou's death had about it the whiff of evil.

The pathologist who had visited the alley couldn't be certain of the cause of death until he had had a look at the brain, but he had done X rays as soon as the body arrived at the mortuary. Marilou's skull was fractured, decisively. And her frail little body was extensively bruised and abraded, suggesting that she had been beaten pretty severely in the hours before she died.

Since there were no other relatives, Nicole asked me to accompany Sofia when she identified the body. She offered to send a car for me, but I preferred to make my own way there.

In the mortuary chapel, efforts had been made to create a safe atmosphere. The walls were backwashed with a soft light and the air carried a flowery scent.

The mortician was a motherly woman who seemed to know what she was doing. She didn't make the mistake of treating this as a social occasion. Her introductions— of the investigating officer, DCI Willis, and of the sergeant who was serving as coroner's officer—were minimalist. When introductions were complete, she stationed herself on the far side of a trolley where the body, overlaid with a plastic sheet, lay waiting.

"Are you ready?" Nicole asked gently. Willis remained in the background, watching.

Sofia gripped my hand, her knuckles pressing painfully on mine. "Laura?" she pleaded, her eyes focused on Nicole.

"Of course," Nicole affirmed, and I returned Sofia's squeeze.

We positioned ourselves near the head of the trolley. I wondered whether the mortician would warn Sofia about what to expect. She did. Even so, the face of the girl on the trolley was almost too much to bear.

Her body was hidden beneath the plastic sheet, so many of the most obvious of her injuries were concealed. Only her head and neck were visible. The fine chestnut hair had been tidied, smoothed back from her forehead and secured at the side. But there was no disguising the ghastly bruise that discolored her temple or the telltale stillness of her features.

"Do you recognize this young woman?" the pathologist asked.

"This is my cousin," Sofia confirmed.

She leaned forward before any of us could restrain her. "Marilou!" she whispered urgently.

It didn't work: there was no quickening of the complexion. The lips didn't start at the sound of her name, the eyes didn't open. Sofia waited a few seconds longer, then collapsed, sobbing, in my arms. For all Sofia's anxiety about the disappearance, she had always taken it for granted that her cousin would be found alive.

I rocked her for a moment, the warmth a comfort to

us both. But over Sofia's shoulder, my eyes never left the pale little face that had once been Marilou's. "I'll be here," she had said with a radiant smile and a confidence that was absolute. "Here" had been the Butlers' home in Kensington. So how did Marilou Flores come to be in an alleyway, at the bottom of a pile of garbage? Dead.

The news weighed me down. I couldn't summon the energy to run up the stairs to the office, and as soon as I was inside, I plumped myself down on the corner of Sonny's desk.

"They've done the autopsy," I said. "Subdural hemorrhage. Slow seepage of blood into the space between the layers of tissue covering the brain. Almost certainly resulting from a blow to the head."

"Laura," Sonny said quietly.

"The skull was fractured when it made contact with a hard object. Small, one or two centimeters in diameter, like a bolt, maybe. Or a metal lightswitch. Perhaps she fell onto it when she was attacked."

"Laura—"

"The seepage of blood would have been slow. For a few hours, or a day or two, she might have seemed all right. Apart from a headache. And then, maybe, she would have become drowsy. Or confused, like someone who had suffered a stroke. She might have been numb down one side of her body. She might have starting seeing double. And then at the end, she would have slipped into a coma and died."

"Did Nicole say anything about forensic evidence?"

"She said," I answered, still not meeting his eyes, "that Marilou had traces of skin under the fingernails of one hand but not the other. Meaning, apparently, that one of her arms was in restraint. Her wrist had been shackled in some kind of a metal cuff."

"Laura." Sonny stood up, came around the desk, and put his arms around me. He cast about for a positive note. "If there are skin traces," he suggested gently, "then it will be possible to identify her assailant."

"If only." Anger gave me a grip on myself. "But we have to catch the bastard first."

We left the office in the care of an answering machine and headed off to Highgate Wood. It was Sonny's suggestion, but I didn't take much persuading. The seashore—preferably wild and windy and empty of people—is number one for me when it comes to restoring the soul. But when ocean is in short supply, I can take a lot of comfort from a tree.

I relayed the rest of the information from the autopsy—courtesy, of course, of Inspector Pelletier—as we made our way toward Highgate Wood. That there were no signs of sexual interference: no semen, according to the pathologist, and no genital trauma. That Marilou had been badly beaten before her death: her legs were severely scraped and had bled extensively, as if she had been dragged over a rough surface, and bruises were scattered over her arms and torso. She had been killed somewhere else, at least twenty-four hours before her body was found, carried to the cinema, and deposited beneath the rubbish.

The wood when we got there was almost deserted. The trees stood at a decent distance from one another, their branches bare and still, tense with the waiting for spring. The sky was overcast, so that the wood looked a grayish brown—taupe, perhaps—and Sonny's red scarf stood out warm and garish against the monochrome background. Only the ground was textured with a mulch of leaf matter and twigs and mud that squished as we strode along. We held hands.

Sonny waited until we were deep in the heart of the wood, where, in better times, the dryads play, before he dwelt out loud on the meaning of the findings from the autopsy.

"No sexual interference," he noted, slowing his pace slightly to accommodate conversation, "but the body was unclothed. What do you make of that?"

"Could be that the killer removed the clothes to delay identification." My brain beginning to work again. I went over what we knew about Marilou's movements before her death.

"On Monday morning, Marilou was spotted wearing an old overall. Later that day she answered the door in smart-looking leggings and tunic. She might have brought them with her. But maybe—just maybe—a new outfit had been purchased for her that very day. By the person who helped her into the house, Penelope Butler."

"So," I added, "perhaps I'll hint to Nicole that a few of her officers make the rounds of the clothing shops near Palace Gardens Terrace with descriptions of the murdered girl and Penelope Butler in hand."

"Finding fresh evidence to link the Butlers with Marilou would put the cat among the pigeons. You're the one who has met Butler. Do you think that the conscience of the West End could really be a murderer?"

"Or his wife?" I speculated, striving for fairness. "Marilou was tiny, remember? Either of the Butlers could have done it. Physically, I mean."

And it went without saying that their continued denial of the girl's presence at Blenheim looked very curious indeed.

"But there's also the big man with the sideburns," I added, "the one Martin Scorsese saw push Marilou into the back of a van. He's a candidate for a grilling. But you can't grill what you haven't got, and we haven't got a single tangible lead on him."

"Leave him to the police, Laura. Let them track down this sideburned fellow." Sonny said this in a pointed way. As if he reckoned I was over the despondency that came with the autopsy results, so he was taking off the kid gloves.

"I'm counting on it." And that was the truth. But what I didn't say was that I had other fish to fry. Derek Cracknell, for one, deserved a little batter. When his name had first cropped up, I simply filed it away, on the understanding that a man who knows everyone is always worth an entry in my database. But once I had met Cracknell, my interest became more personal, so to speak. It wasn't merely that many of his business dealings never saw the sun. It was more the look in his eye— that shelving of bonhomie—that occurred the instant I breathed the name of Marilou Flores.

"A few more days," I insisted. "Just to tie up the loose ends."

Sonny agreed, as long as I kept the Cambridge case on the boil. "You've got to learn to compromise, Laura," he said. Not for the first time.

And then he reminded me, gently, that there were other deadlines. The people who owned the farmhouse in Provence were waiting for a decision.

Ever since Sonny had unfurled the banner of a family holiday in France, I'd come under pressure. From my sister-in-law, Justine, who experiences my hesitation about settling down to a coupled existence as a kind of reproach. From my brother, Hugo, who met my ambivalence with the suggestion that it was time, anyway, that Sonny and I consolidated our households. "That cottage is a financial drain," he had tossed in on his way past.

I didn't need to be paranoid to come to the conclusion that a month in Provence *en famille* was a code for a bigger set of commitments.

Sonny continued to press. "Come on, sweetie," he cajoled as we paused in a clearing to get our bearings. In front of us was an enormous tree whose lowest boughs drooped toward the ground, extending a clear invitation to passersby. Sonny swung himself up onto a long, strong limb and sat astride. After a second's hesitation, I took his outstretched hand and hefted myself up behind him. The warm, smooth bough swayed slowly up and down under our weight.

"There's a stream below the farmhouse," he coaxed. "Think of the sunny days. Better still, think of the long, warm evenings with lovely wine and lashings of Provençal food."

And bicycle rides down country lanes, and sampling the wares in the local market, and nights with Sonny in a big cool bedroom. Who wouldn't be tempted?

"But, Sonny, it won't be like a holiday *together*. We won't have any time on our own. Just say we did go to Provence. Would you be willing to follow that up in September with a week or so at Wildfell? Just the two of us?"

He made his usual apologies, but we both knew that they were excuses: at heart, Norfolk is just not his sort of place. "And," he concluded, trying to look regretful, "there's a limit to how much time we can both take off from the office."

That was precisely the problem. If we were to spend August in Provence, that would be *it,* more or less, for the year. And there was no guarantee that *it* would be enough. The very thought of passing through the drowsy days of summer without a couple of weeks at Wildfell filled me with a sense of loss.

Sonny and I clambered down from the limb and meandered farther until we came upon a clump of fading bluebells. Not a patch, I told Sonny, on the carpet of bluebells that had spread all the way from the top of Leigh Woods to the Clifton Gorge in Bristol when I'd picnicked there with Hugo as a child.

And maybe that's my problem, I realized, with a twinge. Too much thinking of the past. Times have changed now. Ginny is beginning to outgrow me; Helen is absorbed in her new job; and Stevie seems not to need anyone.

Or on the other hand, I reflected, brushing the edge of melancholy now, maybe my problem is that I want to have my cake and eat it too. Asking for too much: to preserve my partnership with Sonny and my alternative home at Wildfell too. Perhaps I do need to learn to compromise.

Or maybe, I concluded, it's simpler than that. Maybe it's just that an autopsy report on a girl you'd come to care about is a hell of a way to start the day.

Sonny sensed how near I was to sadness. He put his arm around my shoulders. I snuggled into the shelter of his body, and it helped, but I could still feel a chill.

13

My visit to the Embassy of the State of Kuwait was based on a simple desire: to know more about Derek Cracknell. And a simple logic: Cracknell, it had been said, knew everyone who is anyone in the Middle East. It followed, therefore, that everyone who is anyone would know Cracknell.

And where better to have a chat with everyones who are anyone than at an embassy reception?

I had no trouble at all gaining admission. I piled my hair high and put on a little black number—low enough in the back to look dressy but high enough in front that short men would meet with georgette rather than cleavage. When I alighted from the taxi at Queen's Gate, the VIP entrance was open wide and a uniformed guard ushered me smoothly inside. He glanced at my invitation and didn't challenge the claim that I was meeting Derek Cracknell at the party.

It was a glittering affair. Literally. The massive table at the end of the reception room had as its centerpiece a swan. And what a swan: some three feet in height, it had been carved from a single block of ice, and it flashed with light from the chandeliers. Candlesticks glimmered, polished floors shone, the gems worn by glossy-haired women sparkled. I hoped that, in the midst of this splendor, my little black number would be taken as a sign, not of poverty, but of the kind of understatement that marks the truly rich.

Just as I had selected my first knot of partygoers to tackle, I was swooped upon by an embassy official. "I don't believe I've had the honor?" he inquired with a practiced smile and enviable teeth.

"Claire Atkinson," I returned, taking the first name that came into my head. "A friend of Derek Cracknell."

"Derek!" he exclaimed, and looked at me more closely. "How do you do, Miss Atkinson." He glanced across the room, scanning the table where the swan nested. "Where is Derek? Getting you a drink?"

"He said he would get me a drink," I said, smiling, "but you know Derek."

"I do," he returned solemnly. "He's probably in some corner, cooking up a deal. Allow me," he added gallantly. "A glass of punch?"

If I have to. "You're very kind."

I wandered away in the opposite direction. The official caught up with me again. This time he was accompanied by a stout Englishman with a mustache that might have been considered dashing in the 1970s. Or maybe the 1870s. His leer made me glad of my georgette. The official introduced him as Stan Porton, a friend of Derek's. It was no surprise when Stan opened with the where-has-Derek-been-hiding-you? line.

"Did you know Derek when he lived in the Gulf?" I asked, using a Goldie Hawn character—any Goldie Hawn character—as my role model. The fact that I was almost as tall as this man dampened the effect.

"Derek and I go *way* back, love. We were in the Army together." For five minutes, which felt like fifty, Stan regaled me with the Middle Eastern adventures of Cracknell and Porton and pals. Most of these centered on illicit goods of one kind or another—smuggling in alcohol or women or pornography, smuggling out anything that would fetch a high enough price in Europe to make it worth the risk. Stan didn't quite put it like that. Boyish high jinks was more his tone. But it was clear that a position in British Army supplies opened doors that might otherwise have remained closed.

"So exactly what kind of goods does Cracknell Associates deal in now?" I pressed, remembering to smile.

"You name it, our Derek does it," Porton boasted. "Can't resist an opportunity. He's like little Jack Horner, finger in every pie." The lack of specificity was, I reckoned, deliberate.

"Connell! Kennedy! Over here!" Porton hailed. Two men moved immediately in our direction. One of them plucked a glass from a waiter's silver tray as he passed and drained it in a single gulp, before wrapping his arms as far as they would go around the sturdy Porton and slapping him chummily on the back. Stan introduced me. The backslapper, who barely acknowledged me, was clearly more comfortable with the boys. The other one—Kennedy—asked where Derek had got to. "I'm beginning to wonder that myself," I said with a suggestion of mild indignation. And sure enough, they seemed to find this vastly amusing.

I soon discovered that these three plus Cracknell were

regulars at a poker school that met on Wednesday evenings in the cultural office. An all-British gathering? I asked.

"Hell, no. The Kuwaitis—especially Ahmad Al-Sane—are terrific players. Besides which," Porton added with a wink at Kennedy and Connell, "if we played only among ourselves, the stakes wouldn't be worth winning." They waxed enthusiastic about the relationships built up through these tournaments. To hear them talk, you would think that it was poker, rather than oil, that had cemented the British-Kuwaiti alliance in the 1991 war.

I made one last effort to break into their gossip. "I've seen Derek with a fellow whose name I can't remember. He's a muscular chap, about six feet tall, balding on top. With long black sideburns. Is he a poker player too?"

Porton and Connell shrugged uncertainly. "Sounds like Norberto," Connell said. Porton nodded in agreement. "No, Derek wouldn't bring him here. Too unpolished for this crew. He keeps him backstage."

"Is he black?"

Connell made no attempt to hide his derision. "With a name like Norberto?" he scoffed. "He's Italian."

"And you don't know his last name?" I appealed to the others.

"Can't say I ever heard it, honey," Porton replied good-naturedly. "Hey, if you're looking for a bit of rough trade . . ." and he and his friends fell about laughing and returned to recollections of cliff-hanging moments at the card table. The boys scarcely noticed when I drifted away.

Two cliques, three hors d'oeuvres, and four abortive conversations later, I struck lucky again. In the loo. The woman who was standing by the mirror adjusting her lipstick as I emerged from a cubicle was small and glamorous and dark-haired. She looked at me as if I had blocked up the toilet.

"Do I know you?" I asked, curious to find out what I had done to merit such resentment.

"Let's just say," she said, setting down an ample evening purse, "that we have friends in common. Now that you're hanging out with Derek Cracknell." And when she said it, it didn't sound friendly at all.

"I'm Claire Atkinson," I said, extending my hand. "And I'm not as close to Derek as you might think."

"No one's close to Derek except maybe his poker pals," she said, looking at my hand as if she were thinking of spitting on it. "I should know. I was married to him."

"Mrs. Cracknell," I said in solemn acknowledgment.

"Elaine," she corrected, mollified. From the evening purse, she took out a cigarette case, a lighter, and a small flask of vodka. She rested her velvet-clad bum on the edge of the counter and took a long swig. I took one too. We stayed until the end of her cigarette, Elaine smoking, both of us drinking. And—though Elaine clearly hadn't been the kind of wife who immerses herself in her husband's business—she softened enough to sketch in the background on Cracknell Associates.

According to his ex-wife, Cracknell called himself a consultant. Elaine's voice conveyed clearly that that wasn't the word she would use. To sum up, Cracknell's speciality was the more unsavory end of the Anglo-Arab market: setting up deals, providing girls for parties, negotiating bribes, or acting as a go-between for exchanges that were just this side of legal. Handling the arrangements that the big guys want to rise above; running pretty close to the wind. I knew the sort of thing: a business where contacts are everything, a business dependent on backhanders and favors, on you scratch my back and I'll scratch yours.

"And how successful is he?" I asked, passing the flask back to Elaine.

Cracknell had extensive contacts in the Gulf, she explained, especially in Kuwait and Qatar. But he had had a long run of bad luck, she said with a satisfied smile. His finances were fragile. He often boasted about big deals, seldom pulled them off.

"So"—Elaine concluded her cigarette and brought her bean-spilling to an end—"I'd advise you to steer clear. But before you do, tell him from me to keep eating that cholesterol."

My perplexity must have shown on my face.

"All those years of watching his diet and protecting his health," Elaine explained, snapping her purse shut on the vodka flask. "I must have been mad."

I emerged from the ladies' and went straight back into the reception room. It didn't take long to find Stan Porton. He looked as if he had hardly shifted position since I'd left him an hour ago, though the groups may have eddied around him. His nose was red from drink, but his mustache was still erect.

"Ah," he said amiably, "Derek's girl."

Nothing ventured, nothing gained. "I met some people from Qatar the other day." I mentioned the family who had brought Marilou to London. "They have a house on Abbottsbury Road. Do you know them?"

"Know them? Everyone knows them. If you haven't got their blessing, you can't do business in Qatar. But," he said, chortling in advance at his own joke, "to know, know, know them isn't necessarily to love them."

Belatedly, Porton twigged to a possible connection. "So you met them, did you? Does that mean that Derek's back in their good books again? I thought they were still steaming after he failed to deliver on that other deal."

I was saved from constructing an answer—if *saved* is the right word—by the arrival of the official who had greeted me when I first came through the door. His practiced smile was strained now. "Hello again." He nodded at Porton and turned straight back to me. "Do you know," he said with a casualness that made me uneasy, "here's the strangest thing. According to the guest list, Derek Cracknell sent his regrets for tonight."

"Change of mind, I suppose," I said brightly. "Believe me, he's very much around. He went upstairs not five minutes ago, arm in arm with Mr. Connell."

The official was too polite to challenge me directly, but the furrows in his forehead deepened. "Perhaps I should go and find out what's happened to him. Shall I fetch you another glass of punch?"

The plaque on the end wall of the reception room commemorated the involvement of British forces in the 1991 war. I examined it while, from the corner of my eye, I watched the anxious official move away through the press of the crowd. When he reached the swan, he beckoned to an attendant, held a whispered conference, and pointed to the area of the room where he had left me.

I made swiftly for the cloakroom. My angora scarf was hanging where I had left it. I wrapped the scarf around my shoulders and stepped toward the door.

"Shall I call a taxi, madam?" asked the uniformed man on the front steps.

"No, thank you," I replied, setting off along Queen's

Gate in the direction of the Cromwell Road. "I can't afford to wait."

From the sublime—if that's the right term for an embassy reception—to the ridiculous: Sonny and I joined what seemed like a million other Londoners at Sainsburys the next morning. We loaded up with coffee and hummus and toilet rolls and fish fingers (for the boys), and Sonny threw in an especially nice bottle of wine. This was a consolation prize for me, I learned, since for the rest of the weekend, he was planning to be away.

The queue for the checkout was long enough to give us a chance to talk. While the woman in front of us flicked through *Family Circle,* and the man in front of her guarded his broccoli, I filled Sonny in on the embassy reception. I spared him no detail in my blow-by-blow description of Cracknell's friends and associates, from the disgruntled Elaine to the cardplayers.

"Poker and pornography," Sonny summed up. "Sounds like our Cracknell's a real man's man. I bet he doesn't spend his Saturday mornings in a Sainsburys queue."

The line was moving at last. "At least I've got a grip on his business now," I said, ignoring Sonny's attempt at humor.

"What you really need," Sonny said, switching into serious gear, "is something linking Cracknell to Butler."

"Don't I wish," I agreed fervently, edging the trolley forward. "Do you want to load the bags, or shall I?"

14

If you overlooked—as I meant to do—the outstanding work for my Cambridge client, I had three other urgent matters battering on my brain.

Above all, I needed to learn more about Marilou Flores's life in London before she arrived at the home of the Butlers: what did she do and where and with whom? Why, after sitting tight for several weeks with the family from Qatar, did she suddenly run away? Was there anything in this period of her life that would make her a target for a killer?

Also high on the list—in fact, long overdue—was a visit to Penelope Butler at her country place in Kent. Penelope and Thomas were not, Carmen said, the closest of couples; therefore, the fact that Thomas had clammed up needn't necessarily mean that Penelope would act like a mollusk too. But if I were to do more than simply harass her, I needed to find something that would persuade Penelope of the appeal of revelation—some shred of information to connect her to Marilou.

Finally (whatever Sonny thought about it) I needed to locate Derek Cracknell's rough-hewn assistant, his backstage boy. The Norberto who was mentioned by Cracknell's poker pals might not be the sideburned man who had abducted Marilou, but beggars can't be choosers, and Norberto was the only candidate so far.

I flipped a coin to decide where to begin. Kensington Gardens won. That's where nannies from Kensington or Knightsbridge air their little charges and where resident domestics spend their afternoons off. It was as good a place as any to search for someone who may have known Marilou Flores. I chose the Queen's Gate for my entrance and strode off on a damp Saturday afternoon in the direction of the bandstand.

My favorite walking pace is beyond brisk, so I had to rein myself in to a more leisurely stride. Slow enough to allow me to get a good look at my fellow pedestrians. Fast enough not to draw attention to myself.

The people in the park were few and tending toward the picturesque. An elderly man, bent ever so slightly at the waist, in a good quality anorak; he folded his hands behind his back and kept his eyes on the path as he walked. A policewoman riding a chestnut mare, with her long cloak spread around her like a tent. An old-fashioned nanny, with white dress, navy cloak, and a Boots carrier bag. And so it went.

It wasn't until I reached the Round Pond where the gray surface of the water rippled in the breeze that I found what—or rather, who—I was looking for.

A child leaned out over the water, stretching for the string of a miniature sailboat that had floated beyond reach. He seemed desperate to catch it and called what was surely a plea for help in a language I didn't recognize. The source of his desperation was less the escaping string, I suspected, and more the threat of the sib. A taller girl swept the water with her hand, aglow with eagerness to beat the boy to it.

"Careful!" From the nearby bench a woman rose and rushed toward them, her face concerned. Like me, she wore jeans, but in place of cotton pullover and suede loafers she sported a cheap sweatshirt and cheaper trainers. Working gear. If faces are anything to go by, she was from the Philippines.

She put a restraining hand on the shoulder of the young boy. The boat drifted farther away. I kicked off my loafers, rolled up my jeans, and tiptoed into the water. The twist of denim around my knee was wet by the time I placed the boat on the ground in front of the boy. The older sister snatched it up and turned to dash away, but her nanny stopped her. With an extravagant sulk, the girl abandoned the toy and uttered a series of words that could only be insults. Her brother echoed the phrases with glee. The nanny ignored them and returned the boat to the boy. She nudged him and pointed to me.

"Thank you," he whispered reluctantly.

"It was rather fun," I admitted, wondering why adults so readily relinquish the opportunity to wade.

The nanny had firm round cheeks and a bashful demeanor. Her eyes almost disappeared when she smiled, giving an impression—probably a false one—of merriment. I joined her on the bench while my feet dried.

"Your children?" I asked politely, though I was certain they weren't.

"No, no." She said this quickly, as if concerned that

someone might accuse her of misrepresentation. "These are the children of my employer."

"May I ask you a question?"

She nodded, willing but anxious.

"Have you ever seen this young woman?" I offered her a snapshot that Sofia had provided. "Her name was Maria Luisa Flores. She called herself Marilou. She lived nearby between December and April, may have come to Kensington Gardens during that time."

The nanny held the photo gingerly, as if a too assertive grip might damage it. She glanced at the photo, then sideways at me, unsure of what I wanted. I did what I could to prompt any memory she might have. Explained that Marilou had lost a lot of weight while she had been in England, was probably thinner than in this photo. "But there's one noticeable feature that won't have changed. She was missing part of her finger."

The nanny handed the photo back to me. "I'm sorry," she said, and she looked genuinely so, "but I don't know this girl. I've never seen her." She looked embarrassed again. "Did she work for you? Was she your maid?"

I swallowed with discomfort. So, here I was, thinking we were getting on like a house on fire, like equals, and she knew me right away for what I was. If not an employer—"No, no, nothing like that"—certainly one of the class of employers.

So I disclosed that Marilou had died and I was attempting to find out how she had spent her time prior to her death—to fill in, I explained, the missing pieces of the puzzle.

The nanny stood up and began assembling her things, stuffing articles of clothing into a canvas bag. She turned back to me. "So you're from the police," she stated coldly. She called to the children, who were playing on the grass close behind the bench, urged them to hurry.

"No, I'm not." I touched her arm. She wouldn't look at me, beckoning to the girl who lagged behind. "Please. I'm not from the police. Or from immigration. I'm a private investigator and the only thing I want to do is to make sense of the last few weeks of Marilou's life."

"Why?" She looked at me directly this time, but she didn't wait for an answer. A terrible sadness was in her face. "Thank you for retrieving the sailboat," she said politely. And then she was gone.

Sometimes, of course, it pays to be persistent. But when you are looking for information from a group of people for whom "investigation" rings alarm bells, persistence is likely to win you repeated rebuffs. What I needed now was an insider. After a few more encounters in Kensington Gardens that went nowhere. I retreated to a call box and sought the help of Sofia Perez.

"Tomorrow," Sofia agreed promptly. We made a date.

I also rang the number of Cracknell Associates in North Kensington. "Is Norberto there?"

There was a pause. "Norberto who?" Cracknell's assistant wasn't giving anything away.

"Afraid I don't know his last name. He works for Derek Cracknell."

"Not in this office," she said, and rang off.

The abortive visit to Kensington Gardens left me just time to swing past Cracknell's office building before closing time. Cracknell's premises may have been nondescript and fume-ridden, but I had noticed on my previous visit one positive feature that must have gone down well with the tenants: underground parking. My mother, Dorothy, who has decided views on most things—including footwear—claims that you can tell a woman by her shoes, and a man by his car. I hoped she was right. And if there was the slightest chance that Cracknell kept an indigo van in the space below his office—an indigo van with some gold lettering on the side—better to know about this sooner rather than later.

The entrance to Cracknell's car park angled in and down from the road that ran alongside his building. At the bottom I was halted by an automatic barrier, the kind that prefers security passes to coins. I offered it an account card for Heffers Booksellers, a phonecard, and my ticket to the University Library. None of them got chewed up by the persnickety barrier, but none of them gained me entrance. So I was forced to beat an ignominious retreat.

I parked on a nearby street and returned on foot. The car park wasn't large and, since it was a Saturday, was less than full. The cars ranged from an old banger that probably wouldn't make it up the driveway, to a scattering of fleet cars, last year's Fords and Vauxhalls. On a quick survey, there was no indigo van, lettered or otherwise.

Alerted by a scuff of steps from the office stairwell, I dashed between two cars in the row nearest the inside wall and waited. Few things are more conspicuous than a pedestrian in a parking area, and I had no intention of becoming the object of a call to the local nick.

A man entered the car park with a woman in tow. From my crouched position, the top of his head seemed to scrape the ceiling. I could see his shoulders—massive they were—and the tabs of his trench coat. I could see his sleek sideburns and the shiny dome of his skull where most other adults have hair. He strode quickly toward my hiding place.

The woman was black and delicately built, dressed in a pencil skirt and high heels that were selected with something other than speed in mind. She tottered along behind, anxious to match his pace, and failing. Her ankle twisted sideways—the stiletto's revenge—and she paused to massage the place where it hurt.

He looked back over his shoulder to see what was keeping her. Made no move to help. "Hurry the fuck up," he snarled. Maybe chivalry *is* dead.

He lowered himself into a vehicle farther down the row. For a tense moment, no sound issued from the car, and I wondered whether I had been spotted. But then the woman hobbled up to the passenger side and settled in, there was the bounce-bounce-bounce of Eurovision pop, and the car pulled away.

As I peered around the Citroën that sheltered me, I saw a maroon Jaguar passing the security barrier on its way out. Couldn't make out the registration plate. I raced toward the driveway and managed to catch a glimpse of him as he blended into the traffic. By the time I had hotfooted it to my own car, the Jaguar was gone.

Seated behind the wheel, cruising in the faint hope of glimpsing him again, I breathed deeply to calm myself and chanted my favorite mantra: "Little by little, little by little, little by little . . ." Eventually the steadying syllables restored my confidence. The man in the Jaguar was gone, yes: but if he turned out to be Derek Cracknell's backstage boy, then I was definitely edging closer.

It could, of course, have been sheer coincidence. This muscular fellow had hair that appeared, to borrow Martin Scorsese's words, to have slid off his forehead onto the sides of his face; he parked his car beneath Cracknell's office building; and he wasn't the sort you would want to marry your daughter. But he might still have been an innocent, if unpleasant, passerby. Or if he *was* Norberto, Cracknell's right-hand man, maybe Norberto was not the man who had abducted Marilou. Or—just to complete the thought—the driver of the maroon Jaguar might have been the right (that's to say, the wrong) man where Marilou was concerned, but could still be someone other than Cracknell's backstage boy. That's the chance you take.

But coincidence, sheer or not, wasn't convincing. I would have bet all the fees from my Cambridge case that those three fellows had a birthdate in common: that Norberto and Marilou's abductor and the unchivalrous thug in the maroon Jaguar were one and the same.

And slowly but surely, I intended to find out.

At that precise moment on Ladbroke Grove, an idiot in a rusty Cortina elected to do a U-turn out of his parking space. My thoughts and my car jerked to a halt. Behind me, a cabdriver leaned on his horn in protest, a pointless gesture that would speed up nothing but his pulse rate. The Cortina was almost horizontal now across the busy street, blocking traffic in both lanes; no amount of honking would hurry it on its way.

Behind me, I heard raucous shouts. I checked the wing mirror and saw the cabdriver's head projecting out of his window. In his fury he resembled an orangutan, except that there is wisdom in the eyes of an orang.

And saw, still farther back, behind the cab, a maroon Jaguar parked at the curb.

I looked properly then, just as a man with sideburns emerged from a newsagent. He glowered at the traffic jam and slammed the car door shut. Balding, six feet tall, and swarthy. Allowing for Martin Scorsese's indiscriminating use of the term *black,* this could be the bad guy all right, with a *Sun* in his hand. And guilty knowledge of Marilou in his head?

Which went to prove, perhaps, that bad manners have their place: I forgave the Cortina owner for driving as if he were the only boy on the road. I double-parked, ostensibly checking a contact lens in the mirror. The Jaguar overtook me.

Most of the way we had a smooth ride. He drove the way I hope Ginny will drive when she is old enough to get her license—every stop preceded by early braking, every turn signaled well in advance.

But toward the end of the journey, after we had wormed our way onto Portobello Road just south of the Electric Cinema, I was thwarted. The indicator blinked, the Jaguar angled right into a narrow one-way mews, and I realized just in time that this was not a route to follow. Not unless, that is, I wanted to end up bundled into the back of a car myself.

Little by little. I stopped to watch the taillights of the Jaguar bouncing slowly down the mews. Nothing to do but circle around to the right and try to pick him up when he exited at the other end.

Little by little by less. At the corner, a van driver in front of me stalled his engine just as the lights turned green, and in spite of persistent horn-blowing—not a cab this time, but a matron in a Mondeo—he didn't manage to recover before the green was gone. When finally I snailed past the narrow snicket that served as an exit from the mews, there was no Jaguar and no trench-coated driver in sight.

Naturally, I checked. I traipsed the length of the mews on foot. The narrow street was paved with granite and had an uneven surface only slightly less hard on the soles of the feet than cobblestones. Along one side stretched a tidy row of mewshouses. They were modest and demure. They boasted hanging baskets and climbing roses and burglar alarms, and an ad hoc collection of dormer windows created a captivating roofline. Very Mary Poppins.

The other side of the mews told a different story. There was not a single dwelling in sight. Halfway along was a cobbled apron, a courtyard some twelve feet square. It had clearly been used as a dumping ground by stall holders from the Portobello Road. Rubbish bins clustered there, alongside a chain-link fence. There were market stalls that had been turned out to pasture, and the paving stones were sleeked with rotting vegetable remains. It was nothing short of sordid. I wondered that the inhabitants of the mewshouses didn't feel a collective urge to improve, if not the looks, at least the hygiene of the area.

On the side of the apron nearest the snicket was a vacant lot surfaced with cracked concrete. A wooden fence formed a decisive boundary between it and the overgrown garden of the modern flats beyond. Equally decisive was the chain-link fence some twelve feet high that surrounded the lot on the two sides accessible to the mews. The heft of the padlock that secured the gate suggested its owner left little to chance. And yet the only treasures defended by this protective paraphernalia appeared to be an old Ford Anglia up on blocks, an ancient prefab the size of a horse's stall, and a stack of milk crates.

On the other side of the apron was a large brick warehouse that ran to the Portobello Road, dominating the first fifty yards of the mews. Its long wall faced the mewshouses, high and dark and forbidding. The only openings into this expanse of brick were two apertures on the long side, probably added decades after the building was completed, and a pair of wooden doors that opened onto the apron. All three entrances were firmly shut.

Clydesdale Mews—the name was etched on a small plaque—looked closed for the duration. I could hear traces of music or television from the direction of the mewshouses, but apart from that the place was quiet as Christmas. There was no Jaguar, no sideburned man, and no reason for me to hang around any longer.

There was also no answer to the questions that persisted: Did Norberto (if Norberto it was) suspect that I was following him? Did he swing down the mews on purpose in order to lose me? Or did he have some business there—in one of the mewshouses, in the warehouse, in the vacant lot? And if he had business, would he return?

Instead of answers, what I got were goose bumps. My light jacket was not proof against the chill of an April evening. I took deep breaths to control the shivers. I was rewarded with an infusion of lilac from the overgrown garden behind the council flats.

Sofia Perez was waiting on the doorstep of her employer's house, friendly face soaking up the April sun, when I pulled up in front on Sunday afternoon. "Am I late?"

"No. I was just sitting in the sun, thinking about Marilou. They won't release the body yet for burial."

"I'm know. I'm sorry."

Sunday was Sofia's free afternoon, and not hers alone; once lunch was cooked and on the table, she assured me, most resident domestics would be out and about. I had come equipped with a picnic, courtesy of a local deli. Sofia and I chose a spot in Kensington Gardens near the intersection of several major paths and settled in for the afternoon.

Sofia was energetic and systematic in her inquiries. "I must have something to tell Marilou's mother," she explained, and convinced herself that this was the way. She intercepted Filipinas who ventured through the park, urged them to come and speak to me. Most were willing but unable to help. All were delighted to share in the meal. It didn't take long to confirm Sofia's claim that to some of the women who lived with their employers, a drumstick of roast chicken and a piece of fresh fruit would constitute a feast.

But none of the women we spoke to could give information about Marilou. "Nothing," Sofia sighed as we trudged the remains of our picnic back toward the car. "Nothing at all. As if Marilou didn't exist."

Two women were on a bench near the gate, wearing the pink-checked uniforms of care assistants. Sofia begged me to wait a moment longer. We could come back another day, I suggested, but the pleading in her eyes won me over.

I remained apart, picnic basket at my feet, while Sofia struck lucky. Body language left no doubt that the women on the bench recognized the photograph of Marilou. When Sofia beckoned me over, I was already on my way.

I met Gloria, a tall woman with a silver cross hanging from a chain. She did all the talking. Her companion, whose name was Shally, stared mutely at the photograph of Marilou with an expression that looked like longing.

"We know this girl," Gloria stated firmly, leaning forward to tap the photo with a neat pink fingernail.

A month or so ago, she explained, they had seen Marilou in Kensington Gardens with two toddlers. She had approached them quickly and had asked for advice.

"She was desperate to speak to someone from her own country," Gloria added. "She had just received terrible news and she didn't know what to do."

I had already known that Marilou had been virtually imprisoned in the home of the family who had brought her from Qatar. And with a little imagination, I might have realized that through long weeks of drudgery, the only consolation for the teenager was the thought that her wages—going directly to her mother—would release the family from debt. But even that crumb of comfort was, apparently, snatched away. Marilou had whispered to Gloria that she had discovered, quite by chance, that none of her wages—not a single pound—had ever been dispatched to the Philippines. Marilou's pay was being "retained," the madam had said when challenged, as a guarantee of good behavior.

No wonder Marilou had asked me for help.

"I told her that she must get out of that house," said Gloria. "That she must run away. That no one should be allowed to keep a girl locked up, to work her like a beast of burden." She looked angry at the memory and touched the silver cross. "And I showed her this."

She took a folded snippet of newspaper from the pocket of her cardigan and handed it to me. Opened out and ironed on my thigh, it was a cutting from the *Independent*. "Select Committee to Look into 'Slavery'," the headline said.

"You showed her this?" I asked, a little perplexed. "Why?"

"We told her the committee was going to do something about employers who behaved badly. We told her to contact them and ask for help."

"Did she say she would?"

"The minute she was out of her employer's clutches." Gloria nodded vigorously. "Marilou said she had found a window she could squeeze through—she was very thin—in order to escape. Once she was free, she would seek the committee's advice." But then, apparently, Marilou's consultation with the two older Filipinas had come an abrupt halt. The girl had been alarmed to see her driver striding toward her across the grass. Clearly frightened, Marilou had broken off their conversation and bundled the children away.

Shally returned the photograph of Marilou to Sofia and spoke in my presence for the first time: "She was very pretty." Her eyes brimmed with tears.

Sofia whispered in my ear, "She has a daughter in the Philippines. Almost the same age."

I wanted to ask Shally how many years it had been since she had seen her daughter, but didn't. Perhaps I couldn't bear to know the answer.

15

The clipping that Gloria and Shally showed me in Kensington Gardens reminded me of a job left undone. Only a week ago, when I had visited the House of Commons—when I had received from Reena Kaur a lecture on the conditions of migrant workers—I had been interested in a young Filipina for whom I had a description but not a name. Her chestnut hair, her thin body, her amputated finger: these meant nothing to Mrs. Kaur.

Sofia provided the name. Then Kensington Police provided the corpse.

Perhaps it was the rapidity of these transformations—from an unknown child to cousin Marilou, from Marilou to a body—that had made me overlook a crucial inquiry. I hadn't gone back to the committee, hadn't asked Reena Kaur if her records made any reference, not this time to an anonymous girl with a mutilated hand, but to Marilou Flores.

I recorded my question, belatedly, on Reena Kaur's answering machine, before seeking out Penelope Butler in Canterbury.

The A2 is hardly the most relaxing of routes. I don't normally undertake it unless I have a clear assignation at the other end. For Penelope Butler, I made an exception. During our previous telephone conversation, she had been unforthcoming. She had been questioned by the police before Marilou's body was found—and had remained, according to Nicole, cool as the proverbial salad veg. Nothing had occurred in the meanwhile to persuade Mrs. Butler to roll out the welcome wagon. Since another phone call would probably bring outright refusal, I decided to opt instead for a doorstep approach and see how far I could go on my personal charm.

The Butlers' country house, The Old Manse, was as handsome as their home in Kensington and three times as large. Although I had seen enough Sylvan Cottages in inner-city culs-de-sac and Belle Vues above the gas works to make me aware that house names have little to do with external reality, it was immediately clear that this particular title could be taken literally.

The Old Manse adjoined, as it should, the churchyard. The premises were separated in front by a tall hedgerow, and at the back by a wall of weathered brick some five feet in height. The extravagant size of the house and its imposing front aspect spoke eloquently of the esteem in which the vicar of the parish had expected to be held.

And rare among Victorian manses, it was immaculately maintained. It had escaped the look of dilapidation that overtakes many such buildings in the absence of staff and money. The windows sparkled. The stonework around the windows was beyond reproach. Someone here had the resources and the will to keep bleakness at bay.

I pushed the black button near the door and heard in the distance the undisciplined clanging of a bell. No one came. After a decent interval, I sought the stone path that ran to my right around the side of the house. The engaging quality of this path—the way that the moss besieged, but didn't encroach upon, the casual perfection of old stones; the tiny bulbs that nudged up the grass between the pavers—all of this should have prepared me for the sight that met my eyes at the back of the house. But even so, the sheer loveliness of Penelope Butler's garden took me by surprise. I was enchanted.

I don't know much about gardening, but I know just enough to recognize that good gardening presents itself to the uninitiated as effortless and artless. You know, of course, that the gardener in question has at some time labored over a spade and mucked about in the mud. You realize that she has committed to memory the Latin names for perennials and tested different techniques for tackling greenfly. But then you see one of those gardeners in action, as she drifts along with a trug on one arm, touching her fingers to this rose, stubbing with her toe the soil in that bed, smiling at the compliments visitors heap upon her head. In those moments, "gardening" is made to seem a mystical endeavor, and the finished garden appears as the spontaneous outgrowth of the gardener's vision.

Penelope Butler's vision was wholly delightful. The walls described a rectangle no more than fifty meters long, but inside was a secret world.

Drawing upon buried knowledge gleaned from my mother, I could see, even in the baldness of April, how the paths would ramble in the summer in and out of sight, how stalks of purple lavender would throng between the stones, how the surface of the tiny pond would be punctuated by water lilies, and precisely where the bush roses—probably white, with creamy pink centers—would overhang the path. How at midday the buzzing of the bees would lull you almost to sleep, and how at four in the afternoon the interplay of light and shade in the coolness of the shrubbery would refresh. It reminded me of the way I imagined *The Secret Garden* as a child, before the vision of my mind's eye was extinguished by the blatant bunnies and pushy crocuses of Agnieszka Holland.

The garden was empty. Rather fortunate that, I thought, given how boldly I had stood and stared. I shook off my reverie and prepared to leave, but as I turned around, I saw, silhouetted inside the French doors that gave entrance to the south side of the house, the tall figure of a woman. She shifted position when I sighted her, opened the door, and walked toward me.

It was easy to see why Penelope Butler had a reputation as a beauty. Her face was long and on the thin side, with a wide mouth that rendered it striking. She was one of those women who become, as they age, more compelling to the eye. Her hair, a honey blond, had touches of gray. It was carelessly coiled on the back of her neck. She had a serenity of expression and movement, that comforting kind of beatific aura often idealized by adolescent girls—until, that is, they realize that the cultivation of such an aura doesn't fit easily with the pursuit of most projects in the real world.

I expected from Penelope, the English rose, a harsh and haughty dismissal.

"You *do* like it," was what she said. Braced for a reprimand. I didn't catch her meaning. "My garden," she urged. Her eyes were fixed on my face.

Finally I understood. Penelope Butler had been positioned in that window before I stumbled into her secret world. She had observed my admiration and knew it to be unfeigned. She was flattered.

"If I tell you precisely how much, it will sound gushing."

"You needn't tell me." Penelope smiled, her full lips not showing any teeth but showing pleasure nonetheless. "Your face when you came round the corner spoke volumes. I so enjoyed being witness to your pleasure."

"Do you feel the way mothers do when someone admires their baby?"

"Not entirely." Distinctly cool. She didn't explain and she didn't expand. "Look," she exclaimed, leading me deeper into the garden, "look at what the birds have done in this shrubbery."

And so we progressed through the garden, exchanging comments as we strolled on everything from soup—sorrel soup, to be precise, the ingredients for which are available in Penelope's garden—to nuts. Though come to think of it, exchanging comments is not quite the right description. It was more like an audience: I provided openings in the form of questions or suggestions, and Penelope Butler held forth.

After a while, I began to get the measure of Mrs. Butler. She didn't seem necessarily to be a cold woman: I asked if she had children, and she told me with obvious affection of her daughter, Beatrice. But there was, I reckoned, something fundamentally dishonest in her presentation of self. It may not even have been her fault, I surmised. It was Penelope's blessing and perhaps also her misfortune to be born with a face that beamed beneficence, and so to receive routinely the gratitude that's paid to kindness without ever having to offer anything more of herself than a smile. That beatific smile served as a cover for an exquisitely developed self-centeredness.

I tested this hypothesis out. "It's so lovely here. I'd give anything to be in a position to have a garden like this." I waited for the queries as to where I lived, whether I had ever gardened.

Instead, Penelope looked at me without looking, if you know what I mean. A look unanimated by any spark of interest. She smiled her lips-only smile. "Yes, it is lovely," she said, and turned away.

It was ages before I referred to Marilou. Penelope—though she must surely have recognized my name when I gave it, must have known why I had come—displayed not the slightest interest in my business.

"All of this must take a prodigious amount of effort," I remarked at last, tracing a circle of the garden with my arm. "And of course, The Old Manse. But on top of this, you keep up another residence in London as well. How do you manage to do it all?"

She shrugged. "I used to be very conscientious," she said with the first hint of self-revelation. "I tried for years to keep the house in Kensington the way my mother kept our childhood home. A remarkable hostess my mother was. The sitting room was always ready for visitors, every detail from music to hors d'oeuvres fully thought through. Always flowers freshly arranged in every room."

She paused, thinking no doubt of the good old days. Or was it of loneliness? What space would there be for a child in such a home?

"She sounds like a hard act to follow."

"But then it was rather easier in those days, wasn't it?" Penelope's smile was a punctuation mark, a full stop that brooked no argument.

"Easier?" I asked, turning the full stop into a comma. It hadn't occurred to me that wartime shortages and the pressures of domestic conformity might have made housekeeping easier than today. But what I hadn't taken into account was the particular class context in which Penelope's statement was framed.

"Of course, easier. Mother had two Irish girls—a cook and another—who did the heavy work and handled day-to-day routines. They were with us for years and years, quite like members of the family. Mother depended upon them for everything."

"And today?" I asked, wondering when she would realize where this was taking us.

"Ah, today." Penelope turned away. "Today, of course, it is as much as your life is worth to find a little woman to come in once a week to do the floors." Penelope paused to pick up a plastic container. "Now how did that get here?" she mused, shaking her head. "Don't you just hate ugly things?"

I couldn't say I did. *Hate*'s a strong word. I could hate bad guys, depending on what they had done. I could hate racial intolerance. I might even go so far as to say I hate suet. But ugly?

Rather than disagree, I plugged back into the preceding line of thought. "So no Irish girls. Is that why, perhaps, you looked for a girl from the Philippines to help out in Kensington?" There. I had to say it sometime.

"Not that again!" So Penelope did remember me. "You seem determined to invent a housekeeper for me. But the plain fact is that I have never had a Filipina housekeeper. As I told you on the telephone—as I told the police—you've got some other house mixed up with ours. Anyway, what I can't understand," Penelope added, regaining control, "what I can't understand is why there is such a fuss about this girl. Foreign house-maids go missing every day. They run away, find an employer who is a softer touch, and that is that. Why all the fuss over this one? Why do the police insist on seeing me again tomorrow?"

"Didn't they tell you?"

"What are you talking about?" Irritated again.

"Marilou Flores's body was found in the small hours of Thursday morning. She is dead. She carried the re-sponsibility for her family's welfare on her shoulders, but she was still only a child. And she has been murdered."

The color drained from Penelope's face, and looking down, I saw that even the tips of her fingers went a ghastly white. So. She hadn't known. "Murdered," she repeated. It was a statement not a question. "Mur-dered. How?"

"The pathologist says that she died of a subdural hem-orrhage, a slow bleeding in the brain. Her brain was eventually compressed by the pressure to the point where she died."

"A hemorrhage?" Penelope asked, alarmed. "What caused it? Did the pathologist say?" This didn't feel to me like morbid curiosity. There was a sense about her of genuine need-to-know.

"An injury to the head," I replied, watching Penelo-pe's eyes. "Marilou's skull had been fractured. Cracked against something small and hard, like a bolt."

Penelope shuddered and her lids flickered delicately. But the color began to return to her complexion, and I was sure there was something in her face of relief. She tried to change the subject back to gardens again, but I wasn't ready.

"One more question." Penelope looked at me warily. "This girl from the Philippines who was never at your house. Does she have any connection with the young man who stayed at Blenheim last summer with your husband while you were in Kent?"

Penelope tried to rise above it. She aimed for the cool self-possession, the beatific smile, but she couldn't quite pull it off. Her nostrils flared in indignation and the smile had less charisma than a cold buttered parsnip.

"Servants' gossip," she snapped reprovingly. "I'm surprised you don't know better."

And that, as they say, was that.

We made it up, more or less. Returned to civility. Penelope even asked me whether I needed a cup of tea before driving back to London. It was a well-bred question, with no urging in it: if Penelope made the tea, it would be in response, not to her wish, but to my need. I declined. Or rather I tested the waters further by demurral.

"I wouldn't want to put you to any trouble."

"As you wish."

I picked my way back along the stone path, leaving her crouched over an early clump of peony shoots. As I reached the front of The Old Manse, an estate car rolled to a halt in the drive with a scrunching of gravel. The driver, her window rolled halfway down so that it hid her mouth like a veil, called cheerily to me.

"Halloo! Is Penelope around?"

"In the garden."

The back doors of the Volvo slammed open, and from each side a young person tumbled out. The girls were twelve or thirteen years old. Their pleated skirts and V-neck jumpers made them appear younger.

"Bye-ee," trilled the invisible mouth, and the Volvo retreated up the drive.

The girls picked up schoolbags and jackets and, in one case, a riding hat and whip, from where they had fallen in their evacuation of the car. I singled out the girl with fair hair in a French plait. "Where do you keep your horse?" I asked.

She had a gentle face, in feature like her mother's, but already bearing the stamp of a more vigorous engagement with life. "In the field, just over there. The other side of the churchyard." She had a slight lisp.

"I've just been spending some time with your mother," I said by way of explanation for my presence. The look of puzzlement smoothed off Beatrice's face.

"Do you ride?" The way she posed the question gave me to understand that this was one of the few things about adults that could possibly be of interest.

"When I was your age, I spent every free hour in a meadow on the outskirts of Bristol with a girl named Claire and a horse called Ophelia. She was fifteen hands high—Ophelia that is . . ." And the three of us laughed.

Ophelia belonged officially to Claire, but Claire, generous in this as in everything else, had insisted that, unofficially, Ophelia should be mine as much as hers.

"What color was she?"

"Claire?"

"No, Ophelia!" Beatrice collapsed with laughter.

"Chestnut with one white sock. And she loved mints." As I spoke, I recaptured the sensation of Ophelia's lips, wet and scratchy, scrabbling up Polos from the palm of my hand.

It was as if an icebreaker had plunged up the St. Lawrence, slicing open a channel through which communication could flow. Beatrice and her friend Evie chatted as if they had known me all their lives. But our conversation was interrupted by the arrival of Penelope. She looked distinctly put out to find me still there.

"It's time for your tea, girls," she ordered. "You must let Ms. Principal make her way back to London."

"But, Mummy, we've eaten. Evie's mum bought us a lovely tea at Murcheson's on the way home."

The menu was reviewed. Penelope conceded that ham sandwiches, whole-meal scones, and fresh fruit (Beatrice put a canny emphasis upon the whole-meal) would meet midafternoon nutritional needs. She herded the two of them into the house to change into riding gear.

"Please, won't you come to the paddock with us and see Princess Di?" Beatrice begged. Her eagerness reminded me that one of the delights of having a horse is introducing her to others.

Beatrice persisted and her mother finally gave in. Tracking through fields with two amiable twelve-year-olds sounded more attractive than throwing myself back into traffic, so I skated around the glacial quality of Penelope's smile.

And by the time an hour was up, I was glad to have stayed for more reasons than one. Princess Di was a spirited horse, with a comic line in facial expressions. But it wasn't just that. When I was seated on her back, checking her reactions to the rein, something Beatrice said brought me up short. I had asked her if she had the opportunity to see her father very often, since he was based in London.

"Oh, sure," Beatrice replied carelessly, "he comes

down here most weekends. Except when he's abroad. Or when there's trouble with Timothy."

Timothy turned out to be the older brother. Son (though probably not heir) of Thomas and Penelope Butler. And not a favorite of Beatrice's. The terms she used for him went beyond the usual sibling ambivalence.

"I have a big brother too," I told her, stung by an absurd desire to defend the species. "Is Timothy *really* that awful?"

This tactless challenge—unexpectedly—worked. Beatrice snuggled her nose into the side of the Princess's head for a few seconds, and when she emerged again, she distinguished between her experience of Timothy and her mother's account.

"I don't really know. I can't honestly remember. I think he was quite sweet to me, when I was little. Some of the time, anyway. Once, I remember, Timothy made me a den out of blankets and sheets and chairs upside down, and we had a picnic in there, all hidden away. But Mummy—well, Mummy said he had made his usual mess, and she was very very cross with him for it." Beatrice's eyes, avoiding mine, tracked her friend Evie as she rode around the paddock. "Mummy says—"

She paused and began again. "Mummy says that Timothy made her ill. For months after he was born, she had to have a nurse, and she was never strong again after that. And Mummy says that—ever since I was little— Timothy hates me. That's what she says. All I know is that Timothy and Mummy were always quarreling. And then Mummy would be cross with Daddy too. That's why they had to send him away to Bradfield's."

"To boarding school? He didn't want to go?"

She nodded correct to both questions. "She did it for

me," Beatrice said plaintively. "That's what she said." Penelope Butler had delivered an ultimatum: either Timothy went to boarding school or the marriage was at an end.

"And have things been better since?"

"Well, maybe." Beatrice looked doubtful. "At least, Mummy is happier now. I like living here because I get to ride the Princess every day. But it would be nice"—she smiled shyly—"if Daddy didn't have to stay in London so much. Because of his work."

Interrogating a child is a delicate business, but the opening was too wide to pass by. "Does your father stay all alone, then, in the house in Kensington? I thought perhaps he had a housekeeper? A Filipino girl?"

Beatrice was emphatic. "No. I don't think so. I think, poor thing, he's always on his own."

"And Timothy? Where does he live?"

"He's at university in Reading. Studying chemistry or something boring like that," she declared with disdain, her lisp making *chemistry* sound like an exotic Andalusian disease.

"Does he ever come here to visit?"

She gave a negative shake of her head. "Promise me something," she said suddenly. I nodded. "Promise me you won't tell Mummy that I mentioned Timothy to you."

"Why not?"

"Mummy says we are never to mention him. She says it's better if we just forget about him. Then we can be a proper family again."

Unexpectedly, for her voice had been pensive, she chuckled. I looked and saw that Princess Di had turned her head toward me and was extending her lips in an outrageous gesture. "Ride or get off," the horse seemed to say.

I set off on a circuit of the field. Evie's horse loped along side by side with mine, the warmth from the animals bringing heat to our cheeks. For a moment, I could almost imagine I was back with Claire, in the vivid world of childhood.

16

I took the long way back to London. The very long way. I crossed the Thames by the Dartford Tunnel, negotiated the London Ring Road north, and exited onto the M11, heading for Cambridge. On the journey, I used old Canned Heat tracks to kick-start my brain.

So there was a son. A son whom Penelope didn't like—no, more than that, whom she rejected. Penelope claimed that, quite literally, Timothy had made her sick.

Penelope likes people whose appearances reflect well on her, Carmen had said. In answer to questions about children, Penelope had made no mention of Timothy. The favored child, the pretty Beatrice, had been told to pretend that her brother didn't exist.

The young man that Carmen had seen at Palace Gardens Terrace last summer—was that Timothy? Did Thomas maintain some contact, even though Penelope disapproved? Was this the deal that Carmen had referred to: that Timothy be expelled from home, shunted off to Bradfield's; that Penelope and Beatrice take up residence in Kent; that in return, Penelope would remain—in public at least—Thomas's wife, and that the image of what Penelope called *a proper family* would be preserved.

Timothy Butler had been shunted off to Bradfield's. I had a source for Bradfield's too: similar age, maybe even the same year. When a small percentage of children spend their adolescence in boarding schools, it is not surprising that one such boy will sometimes know another. Marcia Shields, my Cambridge client, had asked me to find out whether the theft of paintings from her home had involved any of the young people—Petersee, Tenko, or Vic—who were intimates of her daughter, Layla. Petersee, I recalled, had gone to boarding school. At Bradfield's.

The Roma Cafe near the Grafton Centre in Cambridge was much as it had been before, except that, in Tenko's place, there was a redhead who looked as if she might be into mud-wrestling on her days off. Not the type to argue with. "You'll have to order," she said, so—although I would have preferred the Curry Queen—I invested in cannelloni for me and a vegetarian pizza for Petersee.

Petersee had been reading a book by Douglas Coupland in the corner when I entered, his fingers tapping a solemn rhythm on the surface of the table. I gave the impression that I was expecting to see Layla. "But since I'm here," I continued, "I wouldn't mind a word with you."

"Me? Oh, my God," he muttered in a resigned voice, "here it comes." His long fingers on the tabletop didn't stop drumming, but the tempo doubled. Less Beethoven's Fifth, more William Tell.

"Here *what* comes?" When he didn't answer, I made a wild guess. "You know something, don't you? About the burglary?"

"That's what I was afraid you'd say," Petersee protested, his golden skin flushed with distress. "I don't know anything about the burglary, nothing at all. But I saw . . ." He stopped again.

"Petersee?" I tapped his arm gently, so that he turned and made eye contact. "The only way I'll clear you and your friends of involvement is by finding out who actually took those paintings. And for that I need information. Every little bit."

So he told me. How last week he had been poking around in an antique shop, looking for a beaded purse for Tenko's birthday. How, lifting a handbag from a hook, he had noticed, stuffed away behind, an oil painting of a woman and a man.

"And you recognized it from Layla's sitting room?"

In a nutshell, yes. Layla had once pointed out the painting that made her think of her mother and father, and—since the woman in the portrait did bear a resemblance to Layla's mother—it had stuck in Petersee's mind.

I noted the details, but couldn't resist asking, "Why were you afraid to tell me this?"

"You'll think this proves that we had something to do with it."

"Not at all," I returned, thinking what a nice kid he seemed to be. "I'm working on another possibility at the moment, Petersee, and if you are right about the painting in the antique shop, then it points the finger of guilt away from you and your friends."

"You sure?"

"*Never* sure." I laughed. "But pretty damn hopeful. And now that we've got that out of the way, can I ask you a couple of questions about something else?"

"Ask away." He looked relaxed again, the golden boy, the Glastonbury kid.

"It's about your school. You went to Bradfield's, didn't you? Do you mind telling me whom you spent time with there? Who your friends were?"

"Funny question, but no problem. There was a gang of us. The five musketeers, they used to call us. We were all in the first team for cricket, and we sort of hung around together generally." He named his friends.

My cannelloni arrived. It looked like the sort that had passed through too many hands on its way from the fridge to my table. Unnerved by the possibility that the redhead did have mud under her fingernails, I pushed it away and saved myself for a chicken *tikka*.

"This gang didn't include a fellow named Timothy Butler?"

If Petersee was lying, he was the Kenneth Branagh of the Roma Cafe. At the reference to Timothy Butler, his fingers recoiled ever so slightly, not enough to disrupt the syncopation, but just enough to convey distaste. "I knew him. He was in my year at school. But he was never what you'd call a friend."

I pressed further. What did he think of Tim? What sort of fellow was he?

"Look, all I can tell you is that Tim Butler wasn't really the kind of guy you'd want to know."

Touching, this concern. Apart from Sonny and my other closest friends, protective attitudes don't often come my way. "What kind of guy was he?"

"Well, he wasn't stupid or anything like that. He was

quite a good student, especially at sciences. Though after . . . after exams, I heard that he didn't make the grades that had been predicted."

"After . . . ? Not just exams?"

"No. There was some trouble." Petersee looked at my discarded cannelloni. "That pizza is taking a long time."

I caught the waitress's reluctant eye and signaled for the pizza. Petersee continued.

"He hit a girl from the village who worked in the kitchens at the school. They had words about something and apparently he just lost his temper. He hit her. Punched her, I mean."

"Did the school officials hear about this?"

Petersee nodded. "The girl went to matron in tears, and the matron took it to headmaster and headmaster hit the roof. Timothy got in trouble big."

"How did you get to know about it?"

"Oh, it was all over the school. We had lectures from the masters for days afterwards."

Curiosity got the better of me. "What did they say to you? 'Gentlemen don't hit ladies,' that sort of thing?"

Petersee nodded again, enjoying by recall some of the drama of the event. "That sort of thing, yes. And think of the damage to the school's reputation. And if we didn't want to have to cook our own dinner and wash our own socks, we had better look after the staff. And this was the housemaster," he added, reddening. " 'She wasn't his to abuse.' "

"Whose was she, then?" It's a bad habit of mine, blaming the messenger. "Sorry," I appended, grateful that Petersee hadn't risen to the bait.

So. Tim Butler had been a good student, until he had disgraced himself by ungentlemanly conduct. But he had still sat his examinations. "He wasn't expelled?"

"Sent down? No. His father came and pleaded for him. Said it was so near to exams and all, give him one last chance. Probably—that's what everyone suspected at the time—he offered a big donation to the school. He's got a lot of money, you know."

"So I've heard. Did Tim's mother come to the school too?"

Petersee shrugged. "Don't know," he said at last. "But there was a rumor—well, more like a cruel joke, I suppose you could say—that even his own mother couldn't stand him. He was almost the only boy, I do know that, who didn't go home for the holidays."

"Listen, Petersee, may I ask you one more question?"

He gave me the go-ahead.

"Before the incident. You weren't friends with Tim even then, were you? Why was that?"

"It's not easy to explain. He wasn't a bad bloke in some ways. He tried to be friendly, but—it's hard to say, really. He was kind of unhappy, and he had no confidence, and—well, he never got anything really right. I guess he was just dull."

"Dull?" I had expected something more dramatic.

"Yes, dull. Like if he happened to sit down next to you in the common room, you would think, 'Oh, no,' and move away. Or if he volunteered to do the fundraising for an event, you knew that they would run out of money. Or if he launched into a story, it would just fall flat."

"No charm?"

Petersee's glance fell on the just-arrived vegetarian pizza. "Not a sausage," he confirmed.

I was relieved to find that the antique shop where Petersee had spotted the painting was still open when I moseyed past. It was much as it had been on my last visit. The horse in the window still reared its displeasure at being held captive, the sign still designated Harding and Callow as dealers in objets d'art, and the youngish woman who answered the bell still looked far too sleek to be a frequenter of dusty auction rooms. I asked her—again—about a portrait of a man and woman, and she still claimed to know of no such picture. When people lie with such composure, you have little choice but to catch them in the act.

I poked around brazenly, moving just about every stick of furniture in the place, but turned up nothing. To compensate for all this shifting and shuffling, I bought an Edwardian letter-rack. It was small but rather pretty and would come in handy for Helen's birthday.

Before I left town, I also fitted in a chat—of a less than committal kind—with the Cambridge CID. Marcia Shields had said I could involve the police when I was absolutely certain that her daughter's friends were in the clear. I was halfway there.

On Tuesday morning, before I had time even to boil the office kettle, the telephone rang. Reena Kaur, the stylish woman who had set me straight on the workings of the immigration regulations, was returning my call. She had two things to report.

First, that on the very day I had left some papers with Marilou Flores at the Butlers' house in Palace Gardens Terrace, a girl of that name had rung the Home Affairs Select Committee and arranged to make a statement later in the week. She had been mistreated, she said, and she wanted justice. British justice. She had never showed up.

The first piece of information was—well, information.

Of the now-I-know variety. Whether Marilou's appointment with the committee had any bearing on her death remained to be seen.

But the second piece of information was riveting. Reena Kaur reported that Father John, the priest who ran the crisis center in Notting Hill, was interviewing a woman who had seen Marilou in the days between her abduction from Palace Gardens Terrace and her death.

I turned the kettle off, my need for caffeine drained away. I rang Sofia Perez and asked her to meet me at the center in Notting Hill. I bounded down the stairs, pulling on my jacket as I went, considered the traffic, and decided to do without the car that day. Finally I set off at a jog for Camden Underground Station.

It was an endurance-testing journey. I secured a seat on the crowded train, but almost wished I hadn't, as I spent the next twenty minutes in closer company than I would have wished with a stranger's intimate parts. Poems on the Underground came to my rescue. I scanned the verses above my head, and within two stops I had become absorbed in ditties from my school days. "The Bishop of Inchcape Rock," that moralistic old rhyme, came flooding back. I reached the center for migrant workers virtually on the punch line of the ballad, where the wicked bishop gets his comeuppance; and on that stirring note I was immediately buzzed in.

It was impossible to say what the main room of the center might look like on a normal day, because the layout had been skewed by preparations for an evening's disco. A boom box was plugged in and ready for action. Room dividers had been removed and furniture had been pushed back against the walls. There were too many pieces of furniture and too few walls; armchairs and desks and cardboard boxes had been stacked two or three deep. It reminded me of one of those furniture warehouses where you have to dig out from under more pretentious pieces the lampstand that will turn your bed-sit into a paragon of style.

One corner of the room was given over to food preparation. An enormous sack of carrots leaned against the leg of a table, and a woman with cowboy boots tackled the carrots gamely with a kitchen knife. No fripperies like food processors in a place like this.

I liked Father John at once. His eyes were shy, and his voice seemed to be permanently soft and cheerful, as if he were rehearsing jokes under his breath. He was holding the base of a ladder while a volunteer strung crepe-paper decorations from the corners of the room to the plastic fitting in the center of the ceiling. "One moment," he said, and saw the volunteer safely down before turning back to me.

I asked the volunteer to keep an eye out for Sofia. Then I followed Father John to a cubbyhole near the washroom, where a woman in her thirties—a widow, Father John had said—sat on a high, narrow bed, her legs dangling pathetically over the side. "This is Joy Escudero," the priest said. He spent a moment introducing me in Tagalog and, from his tone, assuring Joy that I was someone she needn't fear.

"Hello," I said softly. Joy had a nervous tic just below her left eye. Her smile, when it came, was the smile of someone who, like Anne Frank, persists against the odds in believing that people are really good at heart.

I inquired whether she was comfortable and whether I could get her a cup of tea. She shook her head, yes and no, in answer to my questions. But when I asked how she came to be here, she looked at Father John with eyes that begged for intercession.

"Joy would like me to act as her translator. She's too agitated to speak in English just now. Maybe later," he said.

I smiled encouragement. "Thank you, Joy, for letting me see you. Please, tell the Father what brought you to the center, and he will explain it to me."

"One thing first," Father John interrupted. "No police."

"No police? But if Joy has been a witness . . ."

"No matter," he insisted quietly. "My advice to Joy is to tell the police, but she is too terrified still. She has heard stories of deportations, and that frightens her too. Maybe in a few days, she says. We must respect her wishes. If you can't agree . . . ?"

I sighed, dreading my next meeting with Nicole. But I agreed.

Joy looked up and fixed her eyes on mine. Her lower lid was still in spasm, but I ceased to be aware of it as she spoke. Her words tumbled out, soft and fast and urgent. The need to be understood created a tension in the air, and I had to resist a powerful impulse to cluck and sympathize and soothe, as if her native tongue were my native tongue and not a word escaped me.

At length Father John interceded. He laid a gentle hand on Joy's arm. She was trembling a little with the exertion of her account. She stopped and waited for the priest to interpret. This, more or less, is what he said.

Joy had come into the country with a family from Saudi Arabia. Shortly after her arrival, without explanation, a man took her away. He was rough with her. He forced her to lie down in the back of a van, and he covered her with a blanket. They drove for a long while. Joy was sick more than once on the floor of the van, partly from fear and partly from the jolting. Then they

1 8 3

stopped, and the man got out. After a moment, Joy sat up, terrified. She edged her way toward the front section of the van—there were no windows in the back—and peered out.

When her eyes adjusted to the fluorescent light, Joy could see that the van had been parked inside a building. Ahead of her was a brick wall. Something moved against the wall. Joy jumped back with a start. Then she realized that it was a girl. Here Joy became agitated and joined in with Father John's account, gesturing with her hands to describe how the girl appeared—streaked with dirt and blood, her hair filthy and disarranged, her head drooping on her chest. With a shock, Joy registered that one of the girl's wrists was raised above her shoulder and shackled to the wall, and that part of her finger was missing. She recoiled in horror, and luckily for her she did, because just at that moment the man wrenched open the back door of the van. Joy was sitting up, but she was facing away from the wall on which the girl was chained, and he appeared to believe her when she swore she had seen nothing.

Joy took up the story again. Tears poured down her cheeks now, and she allowed me to hold her hand tightly in mine.

The man in the van was furious. So translated Father John. "What the fuck are you doing?" he snarled. Not loudly, apparently, but all the worse for that. He told Joy that if she didn't lie down again, she would regret it. "You can't even imagine," he spat at her, "how bad things can get."

But of course, he was wrong. She could imagine then, and she hadn't been able since to stop.

The rest of Joy's story—the story of her eventual escape—was poignant in its ordinariness. On a quiet street in Surrey, she was left to live with a couple who looked at her curiously, but asked her few questions. Perhaps they mistook her fear for reticence. Perhaps they didn't care. Joy was terrified that the driver would fulfill his threat and come back for her. She didn't dare to confide in them what she had seen.

"So how did you get away, Joy?" I asked. "How did you come to be here?"

She had waited and watched for her chance. One afternoon, she had brought a tea tray laden with biscuits and scones to the conservatory. She brought the teapot and an extra jug of water, as she had been taught. When her employers were occupied with the refreshments, she picked up her courage and her small bag of possessions and fled.

Father John's translation was so vivid that I could feel some of what Joy had felt. Dangerously conspicuous, running in that quiet suburb where no one ever ran. Confused when she reached the high street, no idea which way to go. She stepped out at the crossing, but when the lights changed, she was dazed by the gunning of engines. She stood in the middle of the crosswalk, clutching her bag and shaking with terror. Cars swept past behind her, cutting off retreat.

Her relief at rescue. A car pulled up behind her and the door on the passenger side opened. A man beckoned. She shrank from him, but he had a kindly face, so she did as she was bid. She couldn't work the seat belt. He fastened it for her. He asked her one or two questions. He let her off in front of a small Catholic church. "Go on, love," he said kindly, "they will take care of you." When he saw that Joy was still too frightened to move, he parked the car and got out stiffly, arthritis dogging every step. He lifted her bag and linked his other arm through hers. He led her up the path to the door of the church and delivered her into their care.

During this long recitation, Joy had never once taken her eyes off my face. Now, as the priest ended his translation, she turned her head in his direction, searching for some sort of authorization.

"It's fine," he murmured gravely. "Just fine."

Joy's eyes darted from the priest's to mine. Her lower eyelid was still at last. The tic had been put to rest.

I turned to Father John. "Can the center find her a job?"

"We are not an employment agency," he said firmly. "But, God willing, something will turn up."

"Be back in five minutes," I promised, and made my way to the main room of the center to check out some of His mysterious ways. Sure enough, there was Sofia, making herself useful. She had a knife in her right hand and an onion in her left.

We climbed over two desks to reach the sofa, where I sat her down and repeated Joy's story. Sofia took it like a woman.

"Are you certain it was my cousin?"

I nodded. "Joy saw the hand that was shackled to the wall. It was Marilou all right."

Sofia wiped her eyes with the backs of her hands, oblivious to the onion smell that clung to her skin. "I'm all right," she said quietly, standing up and climbing off the sofa. "Let's go see Joy."

Joy Escudero was old enough to be, if not Sofia's mother, at least her elder sister. But in the meeting between the two Filipinas, it was Sofia Perez who took control, who reassured, who provided the warmth and protection that she had intended to shower on her little cousin Marilou. And she was practical, too. Sofia rang her employer and then reported that Joy was welcome to stay for a while, until something more permanent could be arranged.

"What are they like?" Joy asked nervously. I heard the American-accented English for the first time.

"My madam is fine. She feeds me well"—Sofia grinned and patted her ample rump—"she pays a decent rate, and she allows me a day and a half off a week. Without fail. She says she doesn't want my mother haunting her dreams if anything happens to me here."

"Like happened to Marilou," Joy whispered. Sofia put her arm around Joy's shoulder and talked to her urgently in Tagalog. I felt about as useful as a pork chop at a vegetarian feast.

It wasn't until moments later that, suddenly, Sofia looked up and acknowledged me with one of her warm smiles. Her red cardigan was damp with Joy's tears.

"Home." Sofia shrugged. "We were talking about home. And about that song that was a hit in the Philippines a few years back. You know, the one with the first line that goes, 'Mama's a maid in London.' "

"Oh." I hadn't heard of it.

"No," said Sofia, teasing me now, "I guess it wouldn't be so popular in England. But I bet it would go down well with the Irish."

There was relief and even something like cheer in the air. Sofia and Joy were linked, obviously, by their common nationality and, less obviously, by a connection to Marilou Flores. Stay for the disco? Father John asked. But Joy wanted to be away. She had last week's wages in her bag and her first priority was to arrange a remittance to the Philippines.

Sofia had the perfect answer. She and Joy would go home via the Filipino Store in Earl's Court. There Joy could use the Peso Express, and at the same time, Sofia would buy what they needed to cook up a feast. The family that employed Sofia was off to visit relatives, so they would have the kitchen to themselves.

And off they went, arm in arm, fears pushed into shadow by the pleasure of each other's company. I walked down the street with them as far as the underground. Sofia was walking with her usual bounce, and Joy wasn't even looking over her shoulder.

17

Joy had provided one stark image—of a girl, almost lifeless, her thin arm clamped to a wall—to flesh out the days before the discovery of Marilou's body in the alley.

But the key issue was still up in the air. Marilou had fled from the Qatari family who had mistreated her; she had stumbled, presumably, through the streets of Kensington, knowing no one, and found refuge at last with the Butlers. But why then did she leave Blenheim after only a few days? If her removal was what it had looked like to Martin Scorsese—abduction—then did the man with the van do it off his own back? And if so, why? Or was he taking orders—from Cracknell, or from Butler himself?

Butler, I kept reminding myself, might be an innocent party in all this. He might have offered the girl shelter, but nothing more. Marilou's disappearance might have shocked him as much as it surprised me.

But this version of events foundered on one logical iceberg: If Butler wasn't involved in the Filipina's disappearance, why would he pretend that he had never seen her in the first place? What would he have to gain by denying her existence?

Well, since the day before, I thought I knew the answer. Now, with Joy Escudero safely tucked away with Sofia Perez, I could focus once again on Thomas Butler.

At last he agreed to meet. In an hour, at his club. The notice was too short, but better short than never.

When I got to Mayfair, however, the man working reception at Butler's club blocked my entry. He had received, he told me in a tone of polite indifference, a call; Mr. Butler had been called away to the country. Mr. Butler regretted that he would be unable to meet me today.

Two can play at that game, I decided. I got a sudden yen to visit the country: Berkshire, to be precise. The University of Reading.

The woman on the telephone in the science-faculty office found me an address for Timothy Butler in no time at all. Full marks for information retrieval. Zero for security. If I had been consulted, I would have insisted that callers produce something more compelling than a vague interest in locating a student before his address could be handed over. Still, what is it they say about a gift horse?

When I found Timothy's address, I considered the possibility that the university official was mistaken as well as indiscreet. This didn't look like a student accommodation. Fronted by a broad lawn edged with low-growing conifers in the American style, it looked, in fact, like a family home in a well-established suburb.

The building was long and low, 1930s in provenance, maybe with a touch of Mies van der Rohe. But leaded windows testified to its English origins, and the laser flash of a burglar alarm spelled affluence.

Luck was with me. There was no answer when I assailed the front door, but while I waited there, I realized that the double garage, imitating the style of the house itself, boasted a flat above. An open staircase ran up the side of the building. And sure enough, when I reached the top step, a white card on the doorframe announced the name of Butler.

All was still and my knock was met with silence. The garage flat, like the house, had an air about it of empty-for-the-day. From my position at the top of the stairs, I could see the trees that formed the back boundary of the garden behind the house. Nothing moved except the branches of a cypress.

Attached to the wall at eye level was a postbox made of the same rough cedar planks that formed the siding on the garage. I lifted the sloping lid and tugged on the piece of string that hung there. I was rewarded with a splinter, not large but painful, and on the end of a long run of twine, a key.

Before I had time to talk myself out of it, I had stepped inside. Just one look, I promised: one chance to assay for myself the character of the boy who, even as a baby, had made Penelope sick.

The garage flat was roomy. There was a high sill, and once you stepped over it and down, the floor was a good two inches lower than the top of the outside staircase. This meant that the ceilings inside were higher, and the room overall—for the flat consisted in essence of one enormous room—managed to be lighter and more airy than the outside of the garage suggested. It was lit inade-

quately by two slanted eaves windows on the front wall
of the garage, and more generously by a row of skylights
edging the peak. The back wall hosted a small shower
room, a WC, a built-in wardrobe, and a bookcase. The
rest of the space was modestly furnished as a study-bed-
sitting-room combination. Pleasant, comfortable, and
clean.

The only thing remarkable about the room was its tidi-
ness. A place for everything, apparently. Certainly everything in its place. Even the books in the bookcase sat
strictly upright, and all protruded to precisely the same
depth. If a party from *Homes and Gardens* should arrive
to do a feature on this flat, the stylist would immediately
set to work to disarrange the room, introducing oblique
lines and curves so that onlookers would no longer feel
that the room, like a toy soldier, was standing to
attention.

The room was so excessively tidy that one might think
it uninhabited. The screen of the computer was protected by a gray cover. The disc box was full—and, as
it turned out, locked—but no discs were lying about.
Nothing else at all was upon the surface of the desk
except for an old instrument box, its lid closed, that
doubled as a pencil case. I glanced inside the desk drawers, relieved to find the usual paraphernalia of Typex
and paper clips, calculator and notepads. All neatly
squared up, but signs, at least, of occupancy.

No dishes were in sight on the worktop, nothing on
the table. The bed was, of course, neatly made. Not just
a duvet shaken over a fitted sheet. No, this bed sported
an old-fashioned coverlet, and under the coverlet were
a quilt, a cellular blanket, and—by now I wasn't surprised—flat sheets with hospital corners. Timothy Butler

didn't gulp down his coffee in the morning and dash for the bus.

I checked outside the door once more, reassured by the continuing stillness, before examining the shower room. A damp towel was in the laundry basket, and the surface of the basin was bone-dry. The only place I had seen that before was in hotels. What sort of person other than a chambermaid—with a supervisor breathing down her neck—wipes the moisture off a basin after it has been used? The wardrobe was organized in the way that used to be recommended by *Just Seventeen:* plastic holdalls for shoes, each with its own see-through compartment; jackets at one end of the rail, trousers next, shirts to follow; jumpers in zip-up bags on the top shelf. When I was a teenager, living in a house with lots of books but not much in the way of cupboard space, I used to think that a wardrobe like this would represent the heights of sophistication. *Sophistication* wasn't the term that came to mind now.

They must have come in while I was inspecting the shower, the noise of the shower door with its metal runners covering the sound of fugitive footsteps. There they stood, side by side, Tweedledum and her unprepossessing chum.

Tweedledum was a woman of late middle age. She was short and round, her abdomen pushing like a balloon against a polyester tunic top. Her hair was coarse and chaotic in shape; her voluptuous lips were painted a shade of cerise slightly darker than the tunic. A dribble of lipstick had escaped onto her cheek.

Tweedledum's chum stood with his hand resting lightly on the back of her arm, as if to turn her away from some potentially corrupting sight.

He was of medium height. His face, like the room,

was modest and tidy, every feature in its place but few signs of being lived in. He was better dressed than the run-of-the-mill undergraduate. His gabardine trousers were clean and freshly pressed, and he sported a jacket and tie.

I stood my ground, smiled, and introduced myself. "I'm looking for Timothy Butler. That must be you."

He didn't move from his poised-for-flight position. He was composed, but not articulate. "People don't usually look for people they don't know inside those people's homes," he pointed out. "How did you get in?"

"The door was open." Behind my back I crossed my fingers, an old habit I've never been able to break. "I thought perhaps you didn't hear the knock."

They didn't believe me. Now that two minutes had passed without mention of the police, I calmed down enough to notice that Timothy Butler was clenching and unclenching his right hand in an effort at self-control.

Tweedledum noticed it too. She rushed to his defense. "You can't do this, you know. Trespass like this. What do you want? Why are you looking for Timothy? Have you come from his father?" Her plump lips moved emphatically as she spoke.

I was longing to ask who she was, but refrained. My mode of entry hardly entitled me to demand information. "No. Not from Thomas Butler. I have come to talk to Timothy of my own accord, before I speak to his father."

Tweedledum looked far from satisfied. "About what?"

"I rather think that's a matter between Timothy and me. I'm a private investigator, you see. I'm looking into a case concerning a young girl, a Filipina, who went missing recently. I know that Timothy can help me. But I fancy he'll wish to speak to me alone, Mrs. . . . ?"

"Carruthers." It's hard to resist. "Carol Carruthers." She loosed her arm from Timothy's grasp and turned him to face her. Her look was full of care. "Do you know what this person is talking about?"

Timothy looked distinctly ill at ease. His composure had crumbled at the mention of a Filipina. His fist still clenched and unclenched in a rhythm of fear, and so, I imagined, did other parts of his body. But when he focused on Carol Carruthers, there was only concern in his face. "It's nothing. But I had better talk to her now. On my own. I won't be long."

Mrs. Carruthers didn't move. She looked from Timothy to me in a weighing-up kind of way, her lips firm against pressure.

"Perhaps," he tried again, looking faintly desperate, "perhaps you could unfreeze a cheesecake? I'm really very hungry."

This did the trick. The woman in cerise squeezed Timothy Butler's hand in a tender gesture and, without glancing further at me, made her surprisingly light-footed way downstairs.

I watched Timothy watch her go. He had the bleak look of someone who had little and was about to lose it all. I waited. Half a minute passed in silence.

"She loves me," he said finally. "Carol thinks I can be the son she never had, the boy that she and her husband longed for. She believes I am good. Like a son should be."

He couldn't avoid a faint emphasis on the word *believes.*

"And are you?"

Timothy sat down heavily on the edge of the bed. His plain face looked vulnerable. He folded his arms across his chest in a self-protective gesture. "I hit her."

"I know."

"I hit her and there was blood all over the place. Even on the mirror. She had a nosebleed."

"Was her nose broken?"

He looked at me as if I had asked an arcane question. "I don't know," he answered, bewildered. Disappointed. It was another defeat. As if he should have known and didn't. "I only saw the blood."

"What happened afterwards? After you hit her?"

"I don't know."

"You must know *something*. What did Marilou do, for instance? Did she scream?"

"She wouldn't stop screaming. My father came in just then. He tried to calm her down. He talked to her and talked to her. He shouted at me to fetch a towel and he held it up to her nose, and then—" He halted in midsentence.

"And then?"

Timothy clasped his arms more tightly than before around his chest, as if to stifle a memory. "And then he sent me away. To my room. Told me to stay there. Just another example, he said it was, of my stupidity."

"Referring to what happened at your school? With the girl from the village?"

Timothy assented mutely. He showed no surprise that I knew about that, as if he assumed that knowledge of his disgrace was universal.

He knew nothing more, he claimed, about the Filipina. He had remained in his room, dulled by shame and tranquilizers. He didn't hear the doorbell, didn't hear anything at all until morning. When his father ordered him back to Reading.

"Tim . . ." He appeared to be retreating to an inner world. "Timothy." At last he looked up at me, his nose damp at the end. "Tell me why. Why you hit her." No response. He looked at me as blankly as if I had addressed him in Swahili.

"Tim. Your sister, Beatrice. Do you hate her?"

Timothy flung his arms outward, baring his chest to my barbs. Astonishment transformed his features, gave them for the first time a spark of vitality. "What has Beatrice to do with this?" This was uttered slowly. "No, I don't hate her. How could I hate her? What a thing to say! She's . . ."

He cast about for words to convey Beatrice's value. "Beatrice is lovely. The loveliest girl in the world. She was a wonderful baby. She was beautiful, she had beautiful fingers and wispy blond hair, just like Mother's."

I took a risk. "But your mother says you hate Beatrice."

"The truth is," Timothy said quietly—almost whispered—"the truth is, my mother hates me. I don't know why. Maybe it's because I don't have her looks. I'm a podge, she says, like my father. Or maybe it's because I'm not very good at things. Father says when I finish university, when I make a success of something, then maybe she'll feel differently." He stood up, calmer now—resigned, perhaps—and walked over to the mirror that hung on the wardrobe door. He stared for a half a minute at the image that confronted him there. At the bland eyes. At the plain features.

"I don't know why I hit the Filipina. She was so thin and frail. Little, like a child. She didn't deserve it."

"Something must have triggered you off."

"When I came downstairs, she was standing by the mirror, in the hallway. Like this," he said as if it were a mere coincidence. "Looking at herself. I wanted to ask her where my father was. I walked up behind her. She didn't hear me coming. I got close behind her, and then I saw her face, in the mirror, as she noticed me. She looked—I don't know, disgusted? Or frightened? I can't remember exactly. She whirled around, and she tried to pull back, but the hall table was in the way. And she began to make a horrible kind of whining noise, and I hit her. I don't know why." Timothy paused, seeing it all again. "And then there was all the blood. On the mirror. On the table. On the post that was sitting there."

He was weeping now, great tears of helplessness that, oddly, gave his features an anguished distinction.

"Do you have any idea what happened to the post?" I asked, thinking of the envelope I had left for Thomas Butler.

"I don't know." The denial was wrenched up from some deeply painful place where far more important problems were being processed.

Enough.

He didn't want me to fetch Carol Carruthers—didn't want her to see him like this. But I couldn't just leave him. I persuaded him that Mrs. Carruthers was distressed, that for her sake he had to offer reassurance.

I walked around to the back of the house. I found Carol Carruthers sitting in a sunny kitchen with colorful cabinets, 1950s style. She sat at a small Formica-topped table. Her lips were cerise no longer. She was steadily eating a portion of Sara Lee cheesecake, forkful after forkful, in a grim parody of the happy consumer.

When I tapped on the window, her face became animated again. I said that Timothy needed her. She needed nothing more. She nodded me a curt good-bye and trotted up the outside staircase to his flat, determination and concern giving spring to her step.

"Good luck, Mrs. Carruthers," I called after her.

She didn't hear me. Or perhaps she was simply too intent on the rescue job ahead to offer me an answer.

The trip to Reading answered some of the remaining questions about Marilou's death, but it did absolutely nothing for my appearance. I stopped at the flat for fifteen minutes—showered, splashed on some scent, put on a black miniskirt and a big linen shirt—then headed out to the office. Sonny and I had arranged to eat out this evening. I suspect that Sonny was hankering after a Big Mac. I was in the mood for something more romantic.

I tripped up the stairs, looking forward to the evening ahead, and entered Aardvark with a smile on my face. But Sonny wasn't there. Stevie was, working still in spite of the hour. She produced a sheaf of messages as long as the proverbial arm.

"Any from Sonny?"

"Two."

"So? Where has the lad got to? We've got a date and I'm very, very hungry."

"About now, he should be enjoying a glass of beer in the Rathausplatz in Vienna. Or perhaps tucking into one of those high-cholesterol meals that the Austrians save for visitors. So if you're hungry, perhaps you had better—"

"What is he doing in Vienna?"

"The usual." Stevie shrugged, passing me a contact sheet. "He'll be back on Saturday. And he says to remind you that Dominic and Daniel will be staying over with you at the flat tomorrow night. The swimming meet begins at seven P.M. and ends at eight-thirty. Don't forget to pick them up. Got that?"

"Got it," I replied, watching Stevie's face. She was looking away.

"And one more thing. Sonny says to give you this."

A theater program? I examined the worn cover with its dramatic illustration for *Without Windows,* the musical that made Thomas Butler a big player in the theatrical world all those years ago. Where did Sonny get his hands on this? And why leave it for me? I flicked through the cast, the advertisers, the reviews, and then at last I saw a single line picked out in italics at the bottom of the page: *Sponsored by: J. L. Irvine and Ahmad Al-Sane.* For all I knew, J. L. Irvine could be the tooth fairy. But Ahmad Al-Sane was an old-timer in the embassy poker school. One of Cracknell's buddies.

Come back, Sonny, all is forgiven.

Stevie, I noticed, was watching me out of the corner of her eye. I gave her a full-frontal inspection and didn't much like what I saw. Stevie was suffering from something that went deeper than the dwindling of a Texan tan.

"Anything wrong, Stevie?"

The phone rang. Stevie's hand shot out. She covered the receiver with her palm and whispered sourly, "Nothing that a lobotomy wouldn't put right." She rescued the receiver. "Aardvark Investigations. . . . Yes, just a moment. Yours."

"Laura Principal here."

It was Inspector Pelletier. I couldn't claim to be surprised. I hadn't responded to her last two messages, and she was bound to catch up with me soon. I took the measure of her mood and decided to meet attack with attack.

"Nicole! I'm on my way. Be with you in half an hour." That took the wind out of her sails.

"You're going out?" Stevie asked. "I thought maybe, since Sonny stood you up, we could have a meal together."

"Love to join you, Stevie, but I'm off to beard the DI in her den. To try to goad her into action, before it's too late."

Stevie looked downcast.

"Tell you what," I offered. "Why don't you drop around and have a drink with me tomorrow evening after I retrieve Dominic and Daniel from swimming. Nine-ish?"

"Agreed." But Stevie didn't look up as I made my way out.

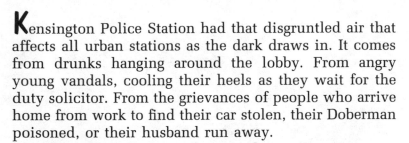

18

Kensington Police Station had that disgruntled air that affects all urban stations as the dark draws in. It comes from drunks hanging around the lobby. From angry young vandals, cooling their heels as they wait for the duty solicitor. From the grievances of people who arrive home from work to find their car stolen, their Doberman poisoned, or their husband run away.

"Inspector Pelletier, please. She's expecting me. Laura Principal."

A constable showed me into the interview room, and Nicole and her boss entered hard on my heels.

DCI Willis was the investigating officer in the murder of Marilou Flores. I had met him at the mortuary when we identified the body. He had left me with an impression of close-cropped gray hair and formidable reserve. DCI Willis, I thought at the time, was a man who kept himself to himself.

Willis elected to sit to one side of the room, his chair tilted back against the wall. Nicole appeared to do the work, but Willis watched. Like a hawk. As they say.

"What have you learned?" I asked.

Nicole snorted. She has always had a way with a snort. In seminars years ago, she used to have the grace to look embarrassed. Now, I suspected, it had become a source of pride.

She leaned her elbows on the table, looked me dead in the eye. "You've been harassing the Butlers." It wasn't a question.

"Harassing?" I was indignant. A little conversation in a garden . . .

"*Harassing* is the word their solicitor used. He tells us you have been to Mrs. Butler's home in Kent. Entered the garden without permission. Accosted the daughter and her friend. All in pursuit, they say, of an imaginary housemaid."

"Housemaid, yes. Imaginary, no. You know as well as I do that the girl at the Butler house—I saw her and Martin Scorsese and Carmen, his housekeeper, saw her too—was Marilou Flores, and you know that she's dead. But Thomas and Penelope Butler continue to lie their heads off about her."

"Marilou Flores *is* dead. And the police are investigating her death. *The police,* not you. Do you know what I think?"

Nicole fixed me with a look she intended, I suppose, to be penetrating. And if I hadn't known her when she burst into tears because Foucault was too difficult, if I hadn't seen her sturdy body wrapped in an outsize Babygro to raise money for the netball team, if I hadn't encountered the smile of relief on her father's face the day she was awarded her B.A. Hons., I might have felt a quiver of anxiety.

As it was, I asked for clarification. "What do *you* think, Nicole?" With the emphasis on the *you,* as in a seminar. That brought the color to her cheeks.

"You know something more. That's what I think. That's why you're staying with the case. And we intend to stay with you—mutual support you could call it— until you tell us precisely what it is."

"Nicole, Nicole," I cajoled, warming to the exchange. "That's fine with me. Listen up and listen tight, because I have a few things—four to be exact—to share with you. But could you send out for a sandwich first? I haven't had supper and I'm starved."

Nicole glanced at Willis. Willis nodded. "Roast beef for me." So the man was human. "And—if they are going past the bakery—three pieces of chocolate fudge cake. And coffees all around." Attaboy.

I wanted to get to bed this evening before my Saab turned into a pumpkin, so I used the minutes while Nicole was on food duty to organize my case. When she returned, I enumerated the four points as persuasively as I could.

First, that a select committee was investigating the legal status and conditions of foreign domestic workers, and that Marilou Flores had an appointment with the committee that she was prevented from attending by her death.

"And where did you come by that little item?" Nicole asked testily. "About the appointment?"

"In Kensington Gardens. I bumped into two Filipinas there who had advised Marilou to contact the committee. Reena Kaur, the committee secretary, confirmed that Marilou had made an appointment. By telephone," I added, heading off the next question. "Ms. Kaur never actually met Marilou Flores."

"Names of these Filipino women?"

I was deciding whether to lie or to stall when Willis saved my bacon. "We'll come back to that." From his manner, he could have been angry. But with someone so controlled, it was difficult to tell. "Roll out number two."

"Two. Only this afternoon I've had a chat with Timothy Butler." I could see Nicole struggling to place the name. Willis didn't twitch. "Yes, I was surprised too. They don't precisely deny his existence, the Butlers— like they do that of Ms. Flores—but they don't advertise it either. He's the lost boy."

"The Butlers have a son?"

I suppressed my "Bravo." Nothing to be gained by infuriating Nicole. "Uh-huh. A chemistry student at Reading University. He lives with a woman named Carol Carruthers, who has become a surrogate mother. And lucky for him that she has, because his own mother has more or less expelled him from the nest."

"So what did you learn from this lost boy?" Nicole was interested, in spite of herself.

"Timothy confirms that Marilou was in the Butlers' house at Palace Gardens Terrace shortly before her death. She was punched, poor girl, in the nose—given a nosebleed, at the least—by Timothy himself."

Nicole was excited now. "He admits assaulting her?"

"He admits it all right. And Thomas Butler—you remember, the man who charges me with harassing his family?—Thomas Butler was there at the time. He sent Timothy to his room. Timothy's involvement with the girl ends there."

"So says Timothy?" asked Nicole with a trace of a

sneer. Police work doesn't develop the trusting side of a person's character.

"I believe him. Unlike his father, Timothy told the truth from the word go. I don't believe he could dissemble. His sense of guilt is on the proportions of the Post Office Tower. Anyway, do you want more about Timothy—I've got a theory—or do you want number three?"

"Number three," Willis cut in. Just the facts, ma'am. "For now."

"Number three," I said, getting down now to the meat of the matter, "is a businessman of sorts named Derek Cracknell, who specializes in sleazy deals with contacts from the Middle East. He negotiates bribes, he provides girls for parties, that sort of thing. I went to Cracknell initially to get his advice about finding a foreign domestic working in London. With his Middle Eastern contacts, I thought he might have some suggestions. But I came away from his office near the Westway with a strong feeling that Cracknell holds the key."

"This feeling," Willis broke in. "Was it based on something more than female intuition?"

Images of Cracknell's soft bulk flashed into my mind. The way his eyes slid away from mine when I mentioned Marilou Flores. The conflict between his claim not to know Butler and the body language that said he did. His inexplicable leave-it-to-me eagerness to help. Maybe Cracknell was just a kindhearted guy, but I didn't think so.

"I prefer to call it observation and experience. And there's two other things you should know about Cracknell. He has had dealings with the family who imported Marilou to London from Qatar; in fact, according to one of Cracknell's poker buddies, he is currently in their bad books. And since they are deal-makers deluxe, being in their bad books is definitely bad for business."

"And?" said Nicole.

"And, Derek Cracknell has an associate named Norberto. A rough diamond, someone Cracknell keeps behind the scenes. I think I've seen him, in the car park beneath Cracknell's office building. He's tall and swarthy. His hairline is retreating from his forehead at a rapid rate, but he tries to compensate for this loss with big black sideburns. And he has a less than gallant way with women. He's a dead ringer, in other words, for the fellow who abducted Marilou Flores from the Butler house."

"Hang on, hang on." Nicole felt rushed. She's a careful girl, likes to get her facts straight before she moves on to the next item. ("Systematic," I wrote in one report about her. "Insists on finishing what she starts, however unproductive the train of thought.")

"Yes? Any sign of that sandwich, by the way?"

She ignored my request. "You say that this Norberto is swarthy?"

"Precisely."

"But Martin Scorsese claimed that the kidnapper was *black,* am I right? Not a dead ringer, then."

"You've met the old guy. He's hardly discriminating when it comes to skin color. He's the old-fashioned kind of racist: anyone who isn't born in England of Anglo-Saxon ancestry is suspect."

"Is this Norberto an employee of Cracknell Associates?"

"Apparently not. Cracknell's assistant feigned ignorance when I mentioned his name. He must be a freelance."

Nicole pressed me for my sources on Cracknell's professional life, and I was foolish enough to mention Stan Porton and Elaine Cracknell.

"So let me get this straight." Nicole then produced a summary that forced me to revise my patronizing assessment. "According to hearsay—some half-drunk hearties at an embassy party and a vindictive ex-wife—Cracknell hangs out with a character called Norberto. In Cracknell's car park, you see a man who is a superficial match for the description Martin Scorsese provided of Marilou's kidnapper. So you conclude—have I got this right?—that the man in Cracknell's car park and the kidnapper and Norberto must be one and the same? And that Cracknell must be behind the murder of Marilou Flores?"

"I'm certain of it," I replied firmly. More firmly than I felt. This girl knows what she's doing, I thought. *Substantial improvement in oral performance this term.*

Willis was sporting the ghost of a smile.

From there, the interview went from bad to worse. I swung on to number four, hoping to regain the initiative. I revealed—to less than wild applause—that Ahmad Al-Sane had backed a play produced by Thomas Butler in the days before Butler acquired his Midas touch. That Al-Sane was chummy with Cracknell, and that—probably—Cracknell had brought the two men together. That, therefore, Cracknell was lying when he said that he didn't know Butler. And that the fact that he lied was further evidence of his guilt.

When I finished number four, there was silence. Not the comfortable kind.

Willis brought the front legs of his chair into contact with the floor. I didn't like his smile. "So," he said in a sparing voice. "What do you make of all that?"

I knew now that it wouldn't get me anywhere, but I

was in a tunnel and there was nowhere to go but straight ahead. So I gave my interpretation, for what little it was worth.

That Thomas Butler knew (as so many people knew) that girls were one of Derek Cracknell's standard commodities for sweetening business deals. Butler wanted to hush up the fact that his son, Timothy, had struck the Filipina. With Timothy's past record, Thomas couldn't risk a police complaint. And, maybe at that point, Thomas hoped to conceal Timothy's involvement from Penelope. So Butler arranged with Derek Cracknell to have Marilou removed from his home in Palace Gardens Terrace.

That Cracknell had jumped at a chance to do a favor for Butler. He may even have intended to return Marilou to the family from Qatar. If they were outraged at the fact she had run away, what better way to get back again into their good books?

That Norberto was the go-between, engaged to remove Marilou from the Butlers' house. For reasons as yet unclear (I ignored Nicole's skeptical glance) Norberto took Marilou to a garage somewhere and restrained her by shackling her to a wall. She might have been killed to prevent her speaking to the committee, since Cracknell was already skating on thin ice with some of his clients and might be keen to avoid any more scandal. Or, more likely, Marilou's death was an accident. Perhaps at some point during the abduction she resisted. Everything we knew of Marilou suggested a girl who was bold in standing up for herself, but against a man the size of Norberto, that frail little body, however bold, would have had very little chance.

I added that, in my view, the police investigating team should concentrate on tightening the net around Cracknell. Before, I emphasized, *before* Cracknell got the wind up and left Britain permanently for the Middle East.

Willis stood up. "Inspector?" he invited.

"Well, sir, a word with this Derek Cracknell would be in order. But if you ask me"—Willis was of course asking Nicole, so this was purely for my benefit—"the Butlers are higher on the agenda. Thomas, Penelope, *and* Timothy."

"You're not persuaded that Cracknell is involved?" Willis asked.

"The way I see it, the evidence linking Cracknell to the dead girl wouldn't convince Fred Flintstone, let alone the DPP. But a boy like Timothy Butler who already admits to assaulting the Filipino girl may have much darker secrets to reveal."

Willis, the man of few words, gave her a thumbs-up and stuck his head out of the door. "Sandwiches are here," he said, picking up a tray. "Perhaps you would like to eat, Ms. Principal, while you give Inspector Pelletier a few more details. For the record."

So I did, on both counts. I offered descriptions (no names—I didn't know the names, did I?) of my informants in Kensington Gardens. The descriptions were accurate without being definitive. Nicole wasn't overly insistent. She was glowing with the thumbs-up from her governor and ready to indulge me a little.

Until, that is, I told her about Joy Escudero, and how she had been a witness to Marilou's confinement. She demanded to know Joy's whereabouts. I refused. I explained the fear among the Filipinas about speaking to the police. She wasn't moved. She sent for Willis. He listened. He demanded to see Joy. I promised to do my best to persuade Joy to be interviewed when she had recovered from the immediate impact of her ordeal.

In the end, Willis compromised: "You've got twenty-four hours to bring this Joy Escudero here, to the station. If she needs support, bring a solicitor. Bring someone from—what's that place?—the crisis center for Filipino migrant workers. I don't care. But have her here. Or else."

And somehow, when Chief Inspector Willis said "or else," it didn't sound silly.

Sonny's flat was dark and cold when I finally tumbled through the door. I had a warm shower just to cheer myself up and dug a sweat suit out of the bottom drawer. If I had to sleep without Sonny curled around me, I could at least be cozy.

I also poured a large whiskey. And that made me think of Stevie, who had looked earlier in the day as if she had downed too many whiskeys. And as if she had had far too good a reason for doing so.

She answered on the second ring.

"You awake?"

"Am now." She pooh-poohed my apology.

"Look, Stevie, did you say you're having an office day tomorrow?"

"Sure am. My client is spending the day at a health farm where bodyguards are not part of the regimen. So it's a paperwork bonanza for me."

"Well, could you leave the paperwork for another time? There's something important I'd like you to do. Do you remember me mentioning a sleazy businessman called Derek Cracknell? Who has some connection with the Filipina whose body turned up near the cinema?"

She did—Stevie doesn't forget that kind of detail. I asked her to locate him and to keep him under surveillance.

"Shouldn't the police be doing that?"

"Tell me about it." She heard my tone and didn't inquire further. "I want to know where he is and what he's up to. And I especially want a warning if he shows any sign of hightailing it out of the country. Can you handle that?"

It was a stupid question, of course.

"Can" as in "will"? At Wildfell, we're pals. But in Aardvark, Stevie—nominally at least—works for Sonny and me.

"Can" as in "able"? Stevie is a whiz at surveillance. She could track the third man through the sewers of Vienna and he'd never smell a rat.

I had the kind of sleep that night—blank and timeless—that is usually reserved for periods of jet lag, and I awoke with the illusion that I had only just closed my eyes. Then the sun slashing through the slats in the blinds told me it was morning. More than morning. Judging by the way the beams struck the top of the chest of drawers, I would have said we were heading toward noon.

I made some coffee and returned to bed, dreaming up schemes to pin Cracknell down and wondering whether the police had managed to crack Thomas Butler's shell.

I rang Nicole's extension. Willis answered. He recognized my voice and promised me a wealth of unwelcome experience if I didn't bring Joy Escudero to the station by the end of the day.

Once he had got that off his chest, he passed me on to Nicole. She waited until he'd left the room. Then she confirmed that Thomas Butler and Penelope Butler were both in Kent, and yes, they had been interviewed again that morning. With their solicitor present.

Nicole described a couple with arms linked, meta-phorically speaking. Funny what adversity can do. Now that the Timothy card was on the table, the Butlers no longer denied knowing the Filipino housemaid. They admitted having hired her, and they admitted (with much tutting) that Timothy had hit her. A tap on the nose, the lawyer interrupted, not a serious assault.

Side by side, like a Greek chorus, Thomas and Penelope proclaimed their horror at the death of Marilou Flores. They professed to be sick with grief. And with even more vehemence, they insisted they were in no way implicated in her death. We tried to help her, they said: We took her in, we bought her clothes, we did everything we could. But, they complained—after all we did for her—the child ran away. What happened after that is not our responsibility.

Not in the least, said the lawyer: no responsibility, no complicity, no liability, no culpability. No concern.

"And are they sick with grief?" I inquired. Nicole's a good judge of this sort of thing.

"Sick." She didn't elaborate. But she did say that the Butlers were coming in to the station on Ladbroke Grove later in the afternoon. And that she and Willis were looking forward to another little chat.

A couple of hours later, I received the call from Father John. His voice was still soft, but what I had taken for a built-in chuckle had disappeared.

"Something wrong, Father?"

Some simple phrases are, in a particular context, redolent with dread. Like the order, delivered by a stranger in a dark place, "Don't move!" Or from a police officer, on your doorstep, late at night: "Are you the mother of———?"

Father John produced such a phrase. The resulting rush of adrenaline took my breath away.

"Laura, have you got Sofia Perez and Joy Escudero with you?"

"No." Not with me. No, no, no.

Father John had just been rung by Sofia's employer. The family had returned from an overnight visit to relatives and were alarmed to find no trace of the two Filipinas. Joy's room—the one that Sofia was supposed to prepare for her—was uninhabited. No sheets on the bed. No clothes in the wardrobe. No Joy.

"Has she contacted the police?"

"Of course. She spoke to a desk sergeant at Kensington Station who was blandly reassuring—Filipino maids often run away, nothing to worry about, call us again if need be in a couple of days. Not good enough, really. So the employer got in touch with me, and I—well. What can we do?"

"I'll have to try to track them down, Father. Retrace their steps. I'll ring you the minute there's news."

The Filipino Store was crammed with shoppers. I had to flatten myself against the shelves of tinned goods to allow two tiny women to squeeze past on their way to the checkout counter. I picked up a bottle of annatto seeds and waited in the queue. When I reached the cash register, the man with the YANKEES T-shirt reached for my purchase without making eye contact. "Just a minute," I said, and described Sofia and Joy. "Have you seen them? It's very important."

He shook his head, again extended his hand. "You do speak English?" He shrugged. "The manager. I need to speak to the manager." His eyes flicked toward the back of the shop, but he didn't move. That's when I spotted the receipt book. I snatched it up. If there hadn't been a counter between us, he would probably have tried physically to restrain me. He shouted at me first in Tagalog and then—fluently—in English.

"The remittance book is not for customers!"

From the back of the shop, passing under the shrine of the Virgin Mary, the manager scuttled out, small and quick and neat. Her exchange with the man behind the counter took only a few seconds. With dignity, she turned to me. I explained. She reached out her hand and I relinquished the receipt book.

"Yesterday?" she checked. "Joy Escudero? Remittance to Manila, here it is."

So they had been here.

The manager questioned the shop assistant, who added—with a sullen glance at me—that Joy Escudero and Sofia Perez had left the shop at about 3 P.M. and set off toward the tube station. He was very definite about the direction.

When I left the shop, without the annatto seeds, I hesitated. Of course, I would have to inquire at the tube station, but I knew full well what the response would be. Two foreign girls? In Earl's Court? Yesterday afternoon? Fat chance.

On spec, I entered the little restaurant across the street where Sofia and I had eaten pan-fried roast pork. The waitress remembered me. And did she recall my companion? The Filipina with a red cardigan?

"Yes. Very attractive," she said, capturing Sofia in her memory.

"And," I asked, holding my breath, "has she been in here since? Yesterday, perhaps?"

Her "No" was definite and I was not surprised. Sofia would not, I think, have dreamed of eating in a restaurant if she hadn't been my guest. I stood up to take my leave.

"But," the waitress added, pleased to be of help, "I saw this Sofia outside, on Kenway Road. Going off with her driver, in a van."

I sat down with a whoosh on the plastic seat. With a nice eye for detail, the waitress described Norberto. He had come into the Filipino restaurant yesterday and had stayed for hours. He had ordered coffee from time to time, but mostly, he just sat and stared at the Filipino Store.

In the afternoon Norberto had received a telephone call. The caller simply said—in English—that he wanted to speak to the man in the restaurant.

"There was only one," she added doubtfully, as if she might have done something wrong.

"No, no that's fine," I assured her quickly. "And what did they talk about? You must have heard some of their conversation."

She shook her head. "There *was* no conversation." Norberto had listened for a few seconds, then left money on the table to pay his bill and rushed out. Intrigued, the waitress had hurried to the window.

And what she saw then was Sofia Perez, clutching a bag of groceries, in animated conversation with an older woman (Joy Escudero) near the corner of Kenway Road. The man with the sideburns took his van from its parking spot, drove it up behind them, and jumped out. He grabbed Sofia by the arm. She dropped her groceries all over the pavement. And Joy just stared at him then, sort of quietly, the waitress said.

"Did he have a weapon?"

The waitress couldn't see. The van had partially blocked her vision. But she did see how brutally he had shoved the two women into the back of the van. And when she opened the door of the restaurant, concerned for their safety—seconds before he drove off—she thought she heard a scream.

"You must have been concerned. But you didn't ring the police?"

No, she had sought help more directly. When the shop assistant came out of the Filipino Store to pick up the groceries that were scattered on the pavement, she had rushed across the street and told him exactly what she'd seen. Nothing to worry about, he'd soothed. The man with the sideburns was merely their driver, instructed by the madam to give her two maids a lift home.

Well, I decided, the shop assistant could be dealt with later, by the police. For now, I had my mind set not on vengeance, but on finding the two women alive.

My brain rehearsed the possibilities. Only a few days had elapsed between Marilou Flores's forcible removal from Palace Gardens Terrace and the discovery of her battered body. If, as it seemed, Norberto had abducted Joy and Sofia, and if, as was likely, he intended to prevent Joy from linking him to Marilou's murder, then Joy and Sofia could be killed at any moment.

I rang Kensington Police Station. Neither Nicole nor DCI Willis was available, and the officer who took my call was distinctly cool. I couldn't afford—Joy Escudero and Sofia Perez couldn't afford—to wait upon the whim of the police.

19

There was only one place to look.

Portobello Road stretches from Notting Hill Gate into North Kensington, and for much of its length, the street is submerged by one of the liveliest markets in London.

I made my way on foot from the southern end, cutting a swath through the categories of people who cluster around the market: the browsers, the strollers, the bargain hunters, the photographers. The militant pedestrians, assertively staking a claim to the road. The lovers, savoring the sensation of being alone in a crowd. The thieves, expecting rich pickings. And maybe even—who's to say?—a murderer or two.

I arrived at a stretch of the road with the darker hue, the autumnal colors, of secondhand clothing and antique goods. I selected a stall with clothes that were cheap but not cheerful, and considerably more second-hand than antique.

My first object of desire was a threadbare woolen over-coat. Then I seized upon a rough belt; wound around my waist twice, it held the coat in place and added to my appearance a certain je ne sais quoi. I pulled on a pair of men's work socks with a built-in-slouch and exchanged my shoes for trainers that slopped in the heel.

The stall holder, who was preparing to close for the night, passed me a speckled mirror and I inspected the result. Suitably comic. A pair of cotton gloves and a knitted object with a bauble on the peak, more tea cozy than hat, completed the ensemble. The tea cozy made me itchy, so I consigned it to my pocket for later. Hats off, I thought, for Portobello Market. Where else could you acquire a new outfit for less than the price of a lunch? And where else could you deck yourself out like a bag lady and not raise even a smile from the seen-it-all-before stall holder?

"Considered a trilby?" she asked when the tea cozy came off my head.

"Not my style," I replied, and stuffed my leather shoes into a bag and continued on my way. The new trainers produced a scuffling noise, and for a second—until I took myself in hand—I thought I was being followed.

I had only one real lead to work on. I stood at the mouth of Clydesdale Mews, closed my eyes, and re-called the evening when Norberto's Jaguar had pulled away from me. It had moved slowly down the rutted surface of the mews, bouncing to the right as the wheels hit the central depression that served as a drain. The glow of the taillights had been amplified in the restricted space. I visualized the depth that the Jaguar had reached before I had been forced to move away: exactly opposite the apron that divided the brick warehouse from the well-fenced vacant lot. I pulled on my tea cozy, scratched once, and headed for that point. My trainers squeaked absurdly, but no matter. In this outfit, I wouldn't need the element of surprise. Bag ladies aren't high on the list of things that keep bad guys awake at night.

Joy Escudero had seen for only a moment the rough room where Marilou had been kept prisoner, but this fleeting image was all I had to go on. I looked afresh at the mewshouses. They retained their demure and modest charm, but I was struck now by the fact that, being mewshouses, they featured as many double doors as ordinary entrances. One of them might have had bare brick walls inside and fluorescent light and space to park an indigo van. If Norberto was lodged behind one of those entrances with Sofia and Joy, I didn't fancy my chances of finding him unaided.

I put the vacant lot to one side, metaphorically speaking. The extravagant security was intriguing, but you'd have been unlikely to get a van inside the pint size prefab that was the only building on the lot.

For now, I targeted the warehouse. I bumbled along the street, making a closer inspection of its bulk. The wall that loomed along Clydesdale Mews from the Portobello Road to the apron had two pairs of wooden doors cut into it, both of them added within the past thirty or forty years. One door was punctured by a letterbox some ten inches above ground level. It was also fitted with a telephone cable. As good a place as any to make a start.

I stumbled conspicuously and fell with a thump to the ground. Clutching my ankle, I rolled toward the doors and leaned against them, resting my forehead on the letterbox. It was quiet inside. With one hand, I pushed open the flap. Nothing moved; but then it was too dark to see anyway. I leaned against the door with my eyes closed, allowing them to adjust to blackness, then tried again. This time, I could discern the outlines of a modestly furnished office. Some sort of mail-order business, probably, or a telephone-sales franchise. The absence of any outward attempt to notify of its where-abouts was curious; surely even a mail-order business needed deliveries? But since there was no space on the walls for an iron ring, nothing like the barren jail that Joy had glimpsed, I scrambled to my feet and pushed on.

By now, fairly certain that I wasn't being watched, I dropped the playacting. I put my ear to the second pair of doors in the side wall of the warehouse. I could hear the ticking of an electronic clock, but apart from that, the inside seemed as quiet as the grave.

The end wall of the warehouse yielded directly onto the apron, which must have served, at some period, as a loading bay. This end wall was painted knock-your-eye-out blue, a legacy presumably from squatters of ear-lier years. The warehouse wasn't squatted now. Its broad blue wooden doors, secured with a recently installed Yale lock, were firmly shut. The area of the wall that might have afforded access through windows was sur-faced with corrugated tin. Above that, at third-floor level, vicious shards of glass remained affixed to broken windows, but no light trickled through. On the top floor, opening out into thin air, was a door where goods had once been lowered up and down. In the faded glare from an old metal streetlamp, I could see that it was nailed shut. In short, no sign of life. Unless, of course, you count as life the notice spray-painted over the corru-gated tin that Jason R was a wanker.

As I stepped onto the apron, I heard a swishing noise. It reminded me of sweeping, but I couldn't figure out whether the source was human or mechanical. It seemed to issue from behind the blue doors.

Quietly, I turned my attention to the rubbish bins. Poised between disgust and fascination, and very glad of my cotton gloves, I worked resolutely through the debris. The archaeologist in me rose to the surface, and I pondered the significance of junk mail and broken jewelry, cat litter and beach toys, and enough packaging materials to make a cosmic dent in the ozone layer. Heaven help the academic who would try to reconstruct the lives of the 1990s from rubbish such as this. Or do I mean, heaven help the men and women who live these lives?

Many things in the bins were of interest, some of them even potentially criminal. But there were no indications that Sofia Perez or Joy Escudero might have been held here at that moment or that Marilou might have been captive in the past. I began the tedious job of returning the rubbish to its bins. It's one thing to be a bag lady, another to be a litterbug.

The footsteps were almost on me by the time I noticed them. Two men treading firmly, coming from the direction of the snicket. Taking a shortcut through to the Portobello Road. I didn't have time to disappear behind the trolleys. Only one thing to do. I snatched an empty vodka bottle off the ground and lay down right where I was, amidst the mess. I rolled onto my stomach and put my hands in a position where they could, if necessary, protect my head.

There was a fifty-fifty chance that the men would stroll right past without a glance in my direction, but I'm glad I didn't place a bet. They spotted me right away. That much was obvious from their startled curses. One stepped forward cautiously, peered at me without getting too close.

"It's a woman. And she's breathing." He pushed the vodka bottle with the toe of his sneakers. "Look." The fear in his voice changed to contempt. He kicked my arm, the one holding the bottle, but he was wearing soft shoes and it didn't really hurt. "Silly old cow." With a burst of relieved laughter, they moved off down the alley, the apparent drinking of a homeless woman dissolving the hook of responsibility.

With this incident, I became disenchanted with playacting and longingly aware of the alternative attractions of a shower and a glass of Sonny's Chilean chardonnay. But I thought of the one thing that had to be done to complete my archaeological excavation, and my obsessive streak won through.

I took a closer look at the three bins that were, apparently, empty. I hefted each in turn above my head and shook. From the first, there tumbled out a sauce bottle and some wood shavings; from the second, a carton that had once contained spring rolls; and from the third, there fluttered fragments of glossy paper, patterned in tones of black and gray and white.

I scooped the largest fragment off the ground. It was the size of a matchbook. And there on its surface were eyes berry bright behind wire-rimmed spectacles, small neat teeth, and an unforgettable heart-shaped face. In the dark I could almost see her foot resting provocatively on the balustrade of the railway bridge. Could almost hear her mother's voice, rising toward panic. "Claire! Get down immediately." And see the ghost of a wink that followed, because of course her mother's alarm had always been half the fun.

Snick: I scarcely registered the sound. I collected the remaining fragments of the photograph and slid them into the pocket of my shirt, next to my heart. Intent on Claire—on Marilou, on Sofia, on Joy—I examined the bin again. There was no number, nothing to link it with one address in Clydesdale Mews rather than another. I was no more than ten feet away from the blue wooden doors that gave access to the warehouse when the snick repeated, and then—too late I glanced up—the bolt that fastened the doors from the inside shot back with an aggressive clunk.

"Fool!" I berated myself, and worse. I threw myself once again to the ground, banging my shoulder on the edge of a market stall and letting out an involuntary moan.

He would have seen me anyway. The glare from the streetlamp revealed me as a lump of shadows, a living collection of rags. I repeated the moan, giving it a sing-song ending. If you can't hide, you had best convey the impression that you have no interest in doing so. My hand scrabbled surreptiously in the muck under the trolley and came up with a soda bottle. Not convincing as a source of alcohol, but it would do at a pinch as a weapon. I was facing away from the warehouse. Behind me, I could sense, one of the doors stood open. But I didn't hear a sound. The swishing noise that I had noticed earlier was gone.

Then he was on me. For his size, he moved quietly. He bent over, picked me up by the shoulders of my greatcoat, and looked for an instant at the profile of my face. I prayed that the dirt on my face was as disfiguring as it felt. No way did the whites of my eyes or my teeth look like those of a drunk, and although the effort of keeping the scream in my throat made me gag, I pressed my eyes shut and my lips closed. When he shoved me again to the ground, I rolled over and secured my head in my arms. He didn't go for my head. He contented himself instead with two hard kicks to my lower body. One landed on my hip and the other on my leg. The shattering feel of a steel-toed boot connecting with the power of a sixteen-stone man on the center of my shin is not an experience I want to repeat. I almost wished I *had* been drinking.

"Get the fuck out of here," he muttered viciously. I snatched a glimpse. It was Norberto all right. He towered above me, looking like one of the ogres of childhood fantasy. For a fraction of a second, I had the illusion that he was going to leap in the air and come down, all six feet of him, on my stomach. Or my head. So when he merely kicked me again, I felt almost grateful. I did as I was bid. Scrambling to my feet, it was Laura Principal, not the bag lady, who was trembling. I staggered out of the courtyard toward the Portobello Road.

Willis wasn't available when I rang Kensington Police from the British Telecom kiosk in Colville Square. "I think I've found Joy Escudero," I told Nicole. "You can have her now. But bring some officers with you."

"What?" Nicole sneered. "This little Filipina has turned desperado? She's going to offer resistance?"

"No. But you just might get some resistance from the man who abducted her and her companion. The same man who killed Marilou Flores."

Who would have thought that Nicole could move so fast? She picked me up near the telephone kiosk minutes later. I had wanted to limp back to the mews, but Nicole was in charge now, and she wouldn't hear of it.

"In the middle," Nicole ordered, positioning me in

the back of the car so that I was flanked on one side by a detective constable and on the other by a uniformed man. We shot off around the corner.

"No siren?" I inquired.

"Hah hah," responded Nicole. Ever the charmer. "Why tell him we're coming?"

At the head of the mews, two uniformed men were waiting. We all piled out of the car. Nicole gave the order to proceed to the apron—*proceed* was her word, not mine—on foot. Two officers were stationed on the Portobello Road and one near the snicket to deflect civilians away. It is at moments like that that I envy the police. If Stevie and I diverted local traffic in the interests of surveillance, we'd get our faces rearranged.

At the courtyard, Nicole pointed people into position. Her arm—that arm that used to tremble slightly when she did a seminar presentation—was now completely at home with authority. She allowed me to watch, but that was all. "Behind him," she insisted, indicating the most junior uniform in the group. I slunk into position.

Our brief was to wait. At least until DCI Willis showed up, and maybe longer. Even though Sofia Perez and Joy Escudero were in danger; even though Norberto had been involved (said I) in one murder already; even though Marilou had been fettered in a building not unlike this one and her body dumped in an alley nearby.

In spite of all this, Nicole was adamant that the police would lie low until someone came out (barring, of course, immediate signs of trouble). The waiting game has been one of the triumphs of the British police: no shoot-'em-out-and-shoot-'em-up, no Rambo to the rescue, no ending of sieges in a chaos of bullets that brings death to perpetrator and victim alike. The courage just to wait. And when they come out, as of course they will, insist they disarm, and when they disarm, caution them, and when they have been cautioned, cart them off to prison. Civilized and sensible and safe.

But civilization breeds its own discontents. The silence from inside the workshop made my flesh creep. If there were three people in there—Norberto and the two Filipinas—why was there no sound?

And the occasional noises didn't help. A tremor of metal, that swishing noise (again), a soft shuffle. What did these discreet sounds signify against the background of the murder of Marilou? I thought at one point I picked up a quiet sob, a sound so desperate that the dozen or so watchers gathered around the warehouse caught their breaths. It wasn't repeated. I didn't know which frightened me more, the noises or the stillness. The metallic tremor reminded me of an image of shackles. But some instruments of execution—a blow to the head, for instance, from a sixteen-stone man—could kill and kill again and never even disturb the sounds of silence.

I stepped forward gingerly and placed my hand on Nicole's shoulder. "Nicole, we have to—"

"Shut it," she snapped, and I did, as I too heard the bolt retract. The wooden door opened a meter's width. A boot delivered a searing kick and an enormous rubbish bag rolled onto the cobbled apron. Then, leading with his left shoulder, Norberto swung himself through the open door, picked up the bag, and hefted it over his shoulder.

Like a diver breaking the surface of the water, I drew in a huge breath. The man was big. But he wasn't that big. Not big enough to swing over his shoulder in that effortless way a bag that was weighed down by the body of a woman.

Nicole pointed and several uniformed officers descended on the man. When Nicole stepped up to Norberto, he didn't even blink. He replaced the black bag on the ground with a movement that was slow and careful—suggesting he knew the form—and remained standing, looking toward the vacant lot, while Nicole cautioned him. His indifference was unnerving. As if he hardly noticed we were there.

I slipped past the knot of people who had swooped on the suspect and edged between the doors into the workshop. The room was—as Joy Escudero had said it would be—dirty and dank. The brick walls were filthy. But someone—Norberto presumably—had swept up. No scattering of debris disguised the dark brown stains that discolored the concrete floor.

But of course all this was merely background. Background for the eyes that locked on mine across fifteen feet of room: large, dark, sunken, and nothing short of terrified. Sofia was alive.

Nicole's voice blurted out, "Don't touch her!"

I didn't. In truth, couldn't. Couldn't move. Sofia was alive, yes, but something was desperately wrong. On her face there was no relief, no sign that she knew she had been rescued. Only terror so raw that I feared that some part of her as precious as her body was dead. But she did recognize me, or I think she did. And I tried to will into her the strength to take note, once again, of reality. With our eyes only we communicated, my message one of safety, hers a searing plea. Let it not be true, her eyes screamed. I scarcely noticed the broad strip of tape that sealed her mouth and disfigured her cheek. I barely registered the policewoman who knelt by Sofia's side, speaking gentle words of comfort, calling her back. All I could see were her eyes.

And then, at last, she blinked. The horrible knowledge

that had seemed to fill Sofia's universe began to recede, began to take its place in the past. My face flooded with tears.

And flooded is not a mere figure of speech. Salty tears washed down my cheeks in sheets, like a river overflowing its banks. Washing away the landscape of fear.

20

The indigo van was parked inside the warehouse, and Joy was found in the back. She was trussed and gagged and suffering from abdominal bruising—Norberto had no scruples about hitting a woman—but she was at least alive.

The doctors at St. Mary's Hospital could see no signs of permanent damage, but insisted nonetheless that both women be kept in overnight. We were ordered off the ward, but not before Sofia sketched the outline of their abduction.

As the waitress had said, Norberto had taken them by surprise as they stood outside the Filipino Store in Kenway Road. He used a knife to force them into the van. Joy's previous ordeal had imbued her not with caution but with terror; she panicked and tried to escape. Enraged by opposition, Norberto pushed Joy back into the van, grabbed her by the hair, and delivered two sharp blows to her abdomen—so hard, Sofia whispered, that Joy passed out from the pain. Norberto drove them to the warehouse, tied and gagged Joy on the floor of the van where she lay, and pinned Sofia's wrist in the same manacle that had held Marilou's. There they remained, helpless, until Nicole's officers secured their release.

The police didn't get Cracknell's name from Norberto, at least not at first. And I kept to myself—quietly savored—the knowledge that all that day, Stevie had held Derek Cracknell in her sights. But it didn't take the police long to learn that Cracknell Associates held the lease on the warehouse in Clydesdale Mews, and to confirm—as I'd known since the embassy party—that Norberto was Cracknell's backstage boy.

If Norberto was shy initially of implicating Cracknell, the Butlers had lost all such inhibitions. They admitted at last that the dead girl had not run away from Blenheim of her own accord. Thomas Butler and Derek Cracknell had conspired to have Marilou forcibly removed. The night that Marilou escaped from her Qatari employers, she had headed through Holland Park and east with no clear idea where to go. She had a vague notion, she told Penelope Butler, of appealing for help from the committee, which she knew only was located at the House of Commons. But the distances and the cold confounded her, and by the time she arrived at Palace Gardens Terrace, she was exhausted and disoriented. Penelope found the girl at daybreak, crouching in the doorway of their cellar. She took her in, rang Thomas at his club—interrupting my meeting with him—and offered Marilou a job. At last, Penelope had the help she desired.

Nicole thought that Penelope Butler's initial urge to protect the girl, though bolstered by self-interest, was probably sincere. But that was before poor disturbed Timothy Butler gave Marilou a nosebleed. When there emerged the possibility of public scandal—even, given Timothy's record, of a criminal conviction—the protective inclination faded. Penelope despised Timothy, but she wouldn't allow the family name to be dragged through the mud.

Inconvenient. That's the word Butler had used, apparently, when he asked Cracknell to take the Filipina off his hands. To return her to the Qatari family from whom she had fled. *Inconvenient.* Did this word describe Marilou's presence at Blenheim? I wondered. Or did it describe the girl herself?

And Cracknell's part in this? Unless Norberto opens up, Nicole warned, we'll have to wait until we get our hands on Cracknell to finish the story. To know for sure why Cracknell was willing to arrange the girl's removal. And to know why, instead of returning her to the Qataris, he allowed her to be taken to his warehouse off the Portobello Road.

"I can make some suggestions," I said. "First, you might say that the packaging of girls is Derek Cracknell's speciality. He did it in the Middle East years ago, supplying British nurses for parties, and he does it in England now, using Filipinas to sweeten business deals. One of his contacts from the Gulf, someone who wants to do business, will bring in a girl as part of his household. Then Norberto will shift her from that household to another, where her arrival may help to clinch a deal." In a city like London where, so they say, it is difficult to get decent help, Cracknell's ability to produce a pliable housekeeper—educated, soft-spoken, willing to work long hours, and likely to stay for years—could be very persuasive.

"But," I continued, "Cracknell had nothing to do with placing Marilou Flores. She entered the UK quite legitimately, with the Qatari family, on what's known as a Home Office concession. When she found that her employers were cheating her—weren't remitting money home to her family—she ran away, off her own determined little back. Nevertheless, when Thomas Butler rang to ask Cracknell to remove Marilou from Palace Gardens Terrace, Cracknell did have a pressing reason to comply." And I recounted for Nicole's benefit the relevant parts of my exchanges at the Kuwaiti embassy with Elaine Cracknell and Stan Porton. About the fragility of Cracknell's finances. About his falling out with the Qatari family—and presumably, since they brokered a lot of the trade between Britain and the Middle East, Cracknell's need to win them back.

"So you reckon," Nicole checked, "that when Thomas Butler asked Cracknell to take Marilou off his hands—and when Cracknell learned that this skinny kid had run away, leaving the Qatari family furious—Cracknell saw her return as a route back into their affections?"

"You got it. Cracknell instructed Norberto to take his indigo van to Palace Gardens Terrace, to remove the girl, and to rendezvous in Holland Park. There Cracknell intended to hand Marilou over in triumph—that's my bet—to her appropriately grateful Middle Eastern employer."

Nicole was not yet convinced. "Why then did he change his mind? What would Cracknell have to gain by keeping Marilou shackled to a wall in a warehouse instead?"

"Simple," I said, striving for modesty. "If Cracknell had intended to win the gratitude of the Qatari household by returning to them a contrite and cowed Marilou Flores, his plan came up against a colossal hitch."

I rehearsed for Nicole the things that had been said to me—spat at me—by Marilou's first employer, the Qatari madam who had shaken her gold rings in my face. That, for example, the family had been packing to go skiing when, *just like that,* little Marilou—*that good-for-nothing girl*—had run away. When Cracknell and Norberto rendezvoused at their prosperous front door with Marilou in tow, they found nothing active but the burglar alarm. The members of the Qatari household were out on the piste.

"So you think that Cracknell was looking for a quick fix for his damaged reputation," Nicole concluded. "But instead, he and Norberto found themselves bang in the middle of Holland Park with an indignant teenager, a none-too-pliable Filipina, on their hands."

"Bingo," I said. "In which case, confinement to the warehouse might have been Cracknell's only chance of keeping Marilou under control until the Qataris returned from the slopes."

"Not bad," said Nicole. Grudging, but better than nothing.

So now it was all-cars-on-the-lookout for Cracknell. There was a very real danger that the police might lose him, permanently. Here was a man who had spent years overseas; who had no close family in Britain; whose contacts in the Middle East were well-established; and who would undoubtedly have a valid passport and liquid assets in hand. Why would he wait around to be presented with a murder charge?

In short, I argued, the sooner we could lay our hands on Cracknell, the better. Willis didn't doubt it. So while Norberto cooled his heels in the cells, and while the smooth edge of his silence began to fray, Nicole sent her men and women scurrying here and there with instructions to bring Cracknell in.

One by one the units of the investigating team radioed back. Not at the office: Cracknell Associates was locked and unlit. Not at home: neighbors, titillated by the taint of scandal, claimed nevertheless to know little about his comings and goings.

I waited for the right moment. Discovered that my mobile phone wouldn't work in the station house. Nipped down the corridor to the public telephone.

It's just as well that I was out of earshot of the duty sergeant when I found that Stevie was not at her post, because the oath that escaped my lips would have offended even his seasoned ears.

"Cracknell was at his office until seven-fifteen," I told Nicole.

"How the hell do you know that?" Ungrateful woman. Not a word of appreciation for my efforts.

"Yesterday, after you and Willis had pooh-poohed the idea of closing in on Cracknell, I arranged for my associate to keep him in her sights. Or thought I did."

Nicole ignored the criticism and went on the attack. "She's not watching him now?"

I shook my head, trying to cover how angry I was with Stevie at that moment. "The message on the office answerphone just says she had to go at seven-fifteen, leaving the target working in his office."

Nicole shrugged in irritation and tugged her skirt

down roughly, as if her hemline were the one thing she could control. I stopped her as she turned away.

"Got it."

"What?" Her exasperation was like an exclamation mark. "What?" She all but shook me.

"I know"—I spoke slowly, relishing the sense of power for a few seconds longer—"where Cracknell has got to." I grinned.

Nicole had to react, of course. She flustered and blustered, threatened an obstruction charge, and only calmed down when she realized that my plan was a workable one.

We agreed that a few hours spent rolling among the rubbish had done little for my image. We also agreed that the bag-lady look was not the most effective one for the job I had in mind. She gave me five minutes to make myself look like someone in the mainstream of society: a face wash, moisturizer, lipstick, hair brushed and up, and a straightening of the clothes was all I could manage, but at the end I looked almost as smart as I felt. Which wasn't saying a lot. Nicole, meanwhile, had persuaded Willis of the wisdom of our course and we were off.

People get it all wrong about foreign embassies and the law. While police have no power of entry into a foreign embassy, they may of course knock on the door in the pursuit of their duty. If they are invited in, they could ask to speak to someone inside, and to discuss with them questions of intention and alibi, innocence and guilt. But every senior police officer knows that if you upset the applecart unnecessarily—if you embarrass the visitors and trigger a complaint to the Foreign Office—your reputation as an officer of tact and discretion will suffer. And tact and discretion are as important as intelligence and courage when it comes to promotion to top jobs.

Nicole isn't in line for assistant commissioner. Not yet, not by a long chalk. But she works for a man who works for a man who works for a man who might be. So it's her handsome backside on the line where something like this is involved. If I messed up, she warned me, she would make my life hell. I didn't doubt it for a minute.

This time there was no doorman. The VIP entrance of the Kuwaiti embassy on Queen's Gate was decisively closed. I made my way around to the side door, stepped through the metal detector, smiled into the video cameras, and waited. Eventually a security man rose from his cubicle and asked me my business. I replied that I had an urgent message for Derek Cracknell.

No sign of recognition.

I gave him some help. "Mr. Cracknell is not a member of the embassy staff, but I know that he's playing poker here this evening. It's important that I speak to him."

The porter gave a barely perceptible bow, but left me standing outside still while he used the telephone.

A moment later, he admitted me into the entrance hall. "You are right, madam. Derek Cracknell is in the embassy this evening." His tone was distinctly more genial now. "I shall be happy to convey your message to him. Or," he added, seeing my hesitation, "you may prefer to write your message down and give it to me to deliver."

"I would prefer"—here I smiled, the kind of smile used in Miss Congeniality competitions—"to speak to Mr. Cracknell myself. What I have to say is best said face-to-face." Before he could demur, I continued,

"Please tell him that I've learned something of signifi-cance about the missing girl. About Marilou Flores."

He did so, I guess, because he returned from the phone a moment later and with a prim smile informed me that Mr. Cracknell could spare me five minutes. I followed demurely up the staircase and along carpeted corridors until we reached a comfortable room furnished with cream-colored sofas.

Derek Cracknell was standing in the middle of the room. Even in a dinner jacket, he still looked every inch a rugby player. I half-expected him to pluck off his bow tie and run with the ball.

"Refreshments, sir?" asked the security man.

Cracknell began to shake his head, then looked at me. "You?" From his sour expression, he seemed to have forgotten that manners are about putting people at their ease.

I ran through the drinks on offer while Cracknell fid-dled with his shirt cuffs. He looked nervous. He looked guilty as sin.

I settled for a cup of Kuwaiti tea.

The porter made a speedy return with a demitasse of a syrupy, amber liquid. "Perhaps we could get on with it," Cracknell suggested. He waited, I noticed, until the porter was out of earshot.

I took a seat in the corner of one of the sofas. Cracknell placed himself in an armchair at right angles to me. He wasn't trying to get closer to me now.

I began in a tone of mild inquiry. "When you were a teenager, did you ever have a close friend? The kind who knows you inside out, maybe better than your mother knows you? Who understands the things you re-ally care about?"

"The point! What is the point of all this? I'm up by

two thousand pounds, and if you throw me off my winning streak, I swear I'll . . ."

"You're off your winning streak already." That quieted him down. "Listen, I'm getting to the point. I had a friend like that. My friend Claire. I had a single photo of Claire, of a brilliant day together long ago. And I had a telephone number that represented my one chance to meet her again—this week—after nine long years. But I left the photo and the telephone number with Butler's Filipino housekeeper. Marilou Flores. And when Marilou disappeared, my links with Claire disappeared too."

I paused. "And then, Marilou turned up dead. But you knew that. Didn't you?"

A telephone rang forlornly. Neither of us moved. I finished my cup of tea. It was refreshing and light, but in the end it tasted bitter.

"And do you know where I found the photo? At your warehouse, the one you lease in Clydesdale Mews. Where, I guess, you held Marilou before she was killed. The point is, Mr. Cracknell . . . The point is, I'm very upset. And I want you to give me one good reason why I shouldn't go to the police with what I know."

Cracknell's breathing was shallow. "The police?" In spite of his sun-pinked skin he went very very pale. "One good reason? There's no need to go to the police. I can give you a good reason. Cash," he said, biting the bait as I knew he would. "Enough cash to help you get over missing your friend. I can get it for you from my office. First thing tomorrow."

I set my teacup on the side table. "Now. I can't wait until tomorrow."

Cracknell smiled, with relief and something else, and it didn't make me feel safe. He excused himself for a moment and left the room, ostensibly to fetch his coat. To ring Norberto, I bet. Let him try: His backstage boy was no longer waiting in the wings.

We left the embassy by the side door and walked round the corner toward Baden Powell House where my car was parked. As I fumbled with the key, Nicole and Willis and two uniformed officers approached Cracknell from behind.

"Derek Cracknell?" Willis asked. "Well, well, well," he chuckled. Proving that the CID does have a sense of humor. "Just the bloke we wanted to see."

Cracknell looked confused, like an opportunistic thief who having hot-wired a sports car suddenly finds himself at the head of a procession. But turmoil rapidly resolved itself into something more like fury.

"You lied!" he shouted, shaking his fist near my face.

"Most of what I told you was the gospel truth."

Cracknell didn't look impressed by my claims to veracity. I suspected that I had just been wiped off his party list.

Oh, well. When you're in my line of business, you have to be prepared to make sacrifices.

There are occasions in life when the momentum of doing what you're doing—of scanning and evaluating, acting and reacting—is so strong that you barrel along from one maneuver to the next with hardly a pause for breath. When your brain is buzzing and decisions flow from somewhere inside you that has never known fear. When you just can't stop.

I should have been tired from the long day, exhausted from the tension, bruised from Norberto's kicks. But as Nicole and Willis drove off with Cracknell in tow, I had energy to burn. My mother has a phrase for it: all dressed up and nowhere to go.

St. Mary's Hospital again, maybe? To check on Joy and Sofia?

I glanced at my watch. And stopped. Dead. The energy drained away in an instant; its place was supplanted by dread.

Almost nine o'clock. At eight-thirty Dominic and Daniel's swimming meet had ended. I should have been there at seven, to catch the tryouts and cheer the boys on. But the absolute deadline was half-past eight. If I can't make it to the tryouts, I had assured them. I'll definitely be waiting when you come out of the changing rooms. We'll go for a pizza, you can tell me all about it.

And now it was almost nine o'clock. Dominic and Daniel must have been shivering there in the lobby of the pool for half an hour, with the draft from the glass doors tracing icicles through their wet hair. They must have been hungry—no, ravenous after swimming—and thirsty and tired. Had they any money to buy something from the machines? Had they stayed safely inside? Had they tried to locate me, tried desperately to phone? My mobile phone hadn't worked in the police station, and when I left for the embassy, I had abandoned it there. I wasn't sure that the boys had my mobile number anyway.

When I try to rush, my driving deteriorates, but I had no choice. I drove like a maniac. The journey seemed to take forever, and when I parked in front of the pool, I realized with a shock worse than the initial shock of forgetting that the swimming pool was closed. Fast-food containers rattled disconsolately across the forecourt, which was chillingly dark and empty. And Dominic and

Daniel, Sonny's little boys, were all alone somewhere in the night in the city.

After a moment of sheer panic—a moment in which the description of Marilou's body lying in the alley blended hideously with visions of Dominic and Daniel— I found a public telephone that worked and rang the flat. The phone was answered by the chirpy voice of Daniel.

"You're home!" I burst out.

"I did it! I got on the team!" he reported, blissfully ignorant of the thudding of my heart.

"That's great, Daniel. And Dominic?" A reserve apparently. And happy enough with that. Swimming was a minor interest of Dominic's, something he did to keep company with his friends. "Haven't you two done well," I responded warmly. "I'm very sorry that I couldn't get to the pool on time. How did you manage to get home? Did you take a taxi?"

"Uh-uh. Stevie picked us up. But we didn't get our pizza. She's making hamburgers instead. With real chips. I'm helping."

"Put her on, will you, Dan?" Here I was worried sick about the boys, and they were playing Delia Smith with Stevie.

Stevie was brusque. "You've got two minutes, Laura. I don't want the chip pan to go up in smoke."

She could tell from my voice that I couldn't figure it, and she provided the all-too-simple explanation. Stevie had been keeping watch on Cracknell. He had disappeared into his office at half-past six, so she'd parked herself where she could keep an eye on things. She rang the police station to remind me about the swimming tryouts, learned that I had gone out with Willis and Pelletier, and figured straightaway that I had forgotten Sonny's injunction to pick up the boys. She couldn't raise me on my mobile phone, thought about the boys alone at the pool, decided she couldn't take the risk.

I felt guilty: for having forgotten the boys, exposed them to risk; and for having been angry with Stevie for abandoning the surveillance.

I felt grateful.

And I felt lucky to have a friend like Stevie. Who instead of rehearsing my failures, simply recalled me to responsibilities in the present.

"Dominic and Daniel are waiting to tell you about the tryouts," was all she said.

So I went home.

They were bickering, mildly. Something about whose turn it was to choose a video. Daniel had a chip—one of Stevie's glistening, fresh, homemade chips—inserted in his left nostril. *A Fish Called Wanda* has a lot to answer for.

"Hi, guys."

Dominic returned my greeting in an indifferent way, his eyes glued on the telly.

Daniel pointed his nose-chip at me and waited for a reaction. "You look like a walrus. Or maybe half a walrus. Daniel, I'm so pleased you made the team. Well done."

He took the chip out of his nose and grinned at me. "My time was almost as good as Jonathan's," he boasted, bouncing over to offer me his yogurt. I returned it to him. Much as he might like to, he can't survive on chips alone.

"And Dom?" I was only too aware that Dominic hadn't so much as glanced in my direction since I entered the room. "You made the reserves, Dom? That's terrific. What was your time?" No answer. "Dominic? Were you pleased with your time?"

243

"Umm. It was okay." He looked at me for the first time. Right at me. "I wish Dad had been there."

I scooped him up off the sofa into my arms—no mean feat at his size—and he snuggled his head against my shoulder for the barest warmest moment. "I know, Dom." Then he uncoiled himself and popped down, picked up his plate off the coffee table, and dashed out to the kitchen.

Stevie called out, "Laura, you want me to save some of these chips for you?"

"Let the boys have them," I replied, feeling full of fortune.

21

Helen rang the next morning—her day off—with a welcome suggestion. Since I was so busy in London, she said, she would have to come to me.

We met at Joe Allen's in Covent Garden and treated ourselves to a proper dry martini, American style, before lunch. We sat up at the bar. Helen wiped the traces of olive from her fingers and showed me, one by one, the fruits of her morning's shopping. I saluted the washbag from Muji and cooed over the black beret she had bought for Ginny at a stall. We collapsed into giggles trying to re-create the look of a Chaplinesque clown who had been meandering through the market and, at a reproving glance from the barman, arranged ourselves more decorously on our stools.

"Act your age," we ordered one another, and fell about laughing again.

But when the food was ready, and we had shifted to a table, the mood shifted too. "Laura," Helen said, "it's time you told me how that case turned out. Your slip of a girl."

I recounted the basics, glad to clear it from my head by sharing it with a friend. At the end of my synopsis, Helen moved into question mode.

"There's the family from Qatar who brought Marilou Flores into the country—under the Home Office concession—and treated her like a slave. There's the Butlers, who took her in when she escaped. What I'm not clear on is exactly how Derek Cracknell and this thug you call the backstage boy—"

"Norberto."

"Cracknell and Norberto"—Helen nodded, prodding her monkfish with a fork—"became involved." She tucked into her fish, leaving me to fill in the gaps.

"Butler knew Cracknell from the past, when Cracknell had arranged a Kuwaiti backer for one of his plays. He also knew that Cracknell operated an under-the-table trade in Filipinas. So Cracknell was the one Butler turned to when he needed to off-load a little girl whose presence threatened to embarrass him—threatened, more importantly, to embarrass the imperious Penelope. But Cracknell had his own reason for wanting to get involved in the case of Marilou Flores."

"The Qatari family? Go on, Laura, eat your carbonara," Helen urged, but she didn't give me time.

"Quite. Marilou had the misfortune to be recruited by a family who were rich and influential. Hardly any big deals take place between London and the Gulf without their approval. Only a couple of months ago, Cracknell had acted as go-between for a construction project in Qatar, but the deal fell through when someone in the chain was exposed as a fraud. The tabloids got wind of the story and created a storm of anti-Arab publicity, implying that the Qatari family had been in on the con. They were understandably furious. Bad publicity was not the sort of thing for which they paid the likes of Cracknell, and he found himself shouldered out of future deals."

Helen saw how it worked. "So when Butler asked Cracknell to rid him of this girl, Cracknell jumped at the chance to reestablish himself as persona grata."

"You got it. But when he took Marilou to Holland Park, the Qatari family were away and Cracknell had to improvise." I paused in the telling of the tale for a moment, so that I could catch up with Helen. She had finished her monkfish. I was only halfway through my pasta. I diverted her attention to the puddings section of the menu while I polished off the salad.

"No dessert for you, Laura?"

"I'm resting. Just a cappuccino."

"You're not resting yet. Why in the world was she killed?"

I skated over the scene in the warehouse, reconstructed for Nicole by Cracknell and for me by Nicole, as quickly as Helen's curiosity would allow. Cracknell's decision to hold Marilou quietly chained up in his warehouse until the Qataris returned. His alarm when Marilou's indignation continued to mount. None of his threats (more to the point, none of Norberto's) worked. My slip of a girl was mentally tough, and she insisted that she would report every detail of the bad treatment she had received—from the Qataris, from Timothy, from Norberto, from Cracknell—at the first opportunity. To the chairman, she said stoutly, of the Home Affairs Select Committee, who was already expecting her visit.

The mention of the committee was what did it for Cracknell. His aim had been to worm his way back into the good books of the Qataris, to overcome their displeasure at the bad publicity they had suffered before. And here was this girl threatening to expose them all—including the Qataris—to the hostile glare of an inquiry.

"Shut her up," Cracknell shouted.

Meaning, his barrister would insist later in court, something like, "Ask her to desist."

Meaning, Norberto's barrister would claim, deliver her a blow that will prevent her talking.

It would be up to the jury to decide. Either way, Norberto hit her. Marilou, frightened but not cowed, was treating them both to a stream of indignation, daring them to detain her a moment longer, when the punch landed on her temple. She stopped speaking then. Her head snapped back, smashed against the bolt that protruded from the brick wall. She lost consciousness only briefly. But she certainly shut up.

She was alive for days, confused, increasingly in pain, as the seepage of blood inside her skull—relatively quick for this kind of injury, the pathologist said—gradually crushed her brain.

"It was an accident," Norberto insisted. He didn't mean to kill her.

True? Helen asked. Probable, I replied. But they left her without medical help, even though they knew she was severely injured. Cracknell and Norberto had conspired to let Marilou's young life slip away, and they would be charged.

"And what about Joy Escudero and Sofia Perez?" Helen asked. "What was it that made Norberto go after them?"

"Joy Escudero was the only witness to Marilou's imprisonment, the person who could establish beyond a doubt Norberto's—and Cracknell's—key role in her death. That didn't worry Cracknell as long as Joy was silent in suburbia where no one would listen to her tale. But when he heard that she had fled, he ordered Norberto to find her. Norberto bribed the man at the Filipino Store, waited in the restaurant, and finally forced the two women—since Sofia was there, he had to take her too—into the van at knifepoint. He drove them to Clydesdale Mews, made a naive attempt to clear the warehouse of evidence—that must have been the sweeping noise I'd heard—and kept Sofia and Joy imprisoned while Cracknell made arrangements to spirit them out of the country, fast, before they spoke to the police."

"Cracknell didn't intend to kill them?"

"It wasn't softness on his part, it was self-preservation. When Marilou died, Cracknell and Norberto moved her body to the alley beside the cinema, convinced it would never even be identified, let alone traced to them. The slip of a girl who came to Britain on a Home Office concession would simply be forgotten, they assumed. Just another TNT—"

"A what?"

"There's a phrase in Tagalog to describe the girls who are forced to leave their employers. The initials are TNT. The meaning is *hide-and-hide.*"

"So," Helen said, piecing it together, "covering up the death was trickier than they had expected."

"Exactly. Cracknell had a shock when I came to his office looking for Marilou Flores. He had even more of a shock when her body was identified. He learned the hard way that it is difficult to dispose safely of a body. That's why he decided that the disappearance of Joy—

and of her companion, Sofia—would suit his purpose better than their deaths."

I finished, as all good storytellers should, with the happy ending. With Sofia Perez on the road to emotional recovery. With Joy Escudero secure and well.

"But not Marilou Flores," Helen reminded me.

No. No happy ending for her.

And no happy ending for me and Claire, either. "I couldn't piece together the telephone number from the fragments of photograph," I said, shrugging in answer to Helen's inquiry.

"Is there no way—?" Helen stopped short. She knew as well as I that a million people pass through Heathrow every week. That London's a big place. That without a point of contact, not even V. I. Warshawski would have a hope in hell of meeting up with Claire.

"I'll just have to wait," I said, trying to look nonchalant, "for another nine years."

That's when Helen—moved by friendship, I'm sure— put the screws on. Come to Wildfell. Spend August there, with me and Ginny and Stevie. Bring the saxophone and we'll get the band going again. And so on.

It should have helped, but what with my exhaustion and the fact that Sonny was pushing for a decision on Provence, it felt like pressure. I switched the subject. "Speaking of Stevie, have you winkled out an identity yet for the new lover? She was grinning like the Cheshire cat when she came back from Texas."

Helen looked at me oddly.

"What? Is it a secret, then?"

"Didn't you know? The lover was a helicopter pilot from the Scottish oil rigs, on holiday in Texas. But when it seemed on return to Britain that this relationship was getting serious, the pilot pleaded heavy workload and winged away."

I dropped my spoon. The waiter, thinking I needed something, tilted toward our table. I waved him off. Oh, Stevie, I thought; the lover's come and gone. That's why those grins have been thin on the ground.

"We were scheduled for a heart-to-heart after the swimming meet," I explained, "but in all the excitement about the boys and the swimming meet and Norberto's and Cracknell's arrests, we didn't get around to it."

And anyway, I realized with a start, I wasn't used to thinking much about Stevie's feelings. "She seems so self-sufficient," I said, wondering.

"You don't really *believe* that," Helen said, and consoled me with the final spoonful of her crème brûlée.

I got up early the day my Saab was booked in for repair. Not a moment too soon. On the journey to Cherry Hinton, on the outskirts of Cambridge, the car balked at every sudden pressure on the accelerator, making me the target of pitying looks from other drivers. Not a pretty thought.

Abandoning the car on the forecourt, I entered the working area. Two cars were already up on the lifts, and to my unpracticed eye the mechanics looked to be hard at work. Or most of them did. The bold young man who had got up my nose last time managed to get up my nose once again. He swung past me with a cocky gait, opened the door of the Saab, and lifted my overnight bag out of the passenger seat. I hadn't asked him to do this. He set the bag down in front of me.

"Yours?" he asked with a knowing smile.

"Thanks."

"Going anywhere nice?"

"If you call Glasgow nice, yes." I shrugged. "Personally, I like the town, even if its regeneration has been overhyped." He had no reply to make. I carried my case into the office and handed my key ring to the receptionist. She suspended the ring from the end of one manicured finger while entering the details in her logbook with the other hand.

"I'll pick it up late tomorrow afternoon, okay? Assuming that my plane gets in on time. Otherwise . . ."

"The office closes at six o'clock," she said primly. It was not a point of negotiation.

"That should be all right. Would you mind"—I smiled sweetly, enjoying her resistance to these opening words—"would you mind ringing for a cab to take me to Stansted?"

I waited outside. When the cab finally showed up, I climbed in and asked the friendly driver to take me first to Newnham.

"What happened to Stansted?" he asked, less friendly now.

I touched his shoulder with a twenty-pound note.

"I've always liked Newnham," he chirped. "You live there?"

At Helen's house, or more specifically under the rhododendron bush in her garden, I retrieved the spare set of keys that were hidden there. I stocked up at the deli on the way past. And finally, after checking that the coast was clear outside my own house, I paid my friendly driver, including the voluntary surcharge, and exited the cab.

It was dim and cool inside my house, the curtains closed, the central heating off. I didn't change a thing—except, that is, in the bedroom. There I set up a convector heater, expensive but quiet to run. Arranged a picnic of *ciabatta* bread and olives and sun-dried tomatoes. Angled a Victorian gooseneck lamp so that the light flooded the armchair in the corner of the room. Placed the telephone within reach. Took off my shoes and settled down at last for a comfortable read. I thought wistfully of my CDs, but suppressed the idea of Alberta Hunter as unprofessional. After this heretical moment, I was away, immersed in Robertson Davies and—I had to admit—quite keen on the peace and quiet.

As a writer, Robertson Davies has a lot to answer for. So enthralling was the presentation of Mary-Jacobine at court that I noticed nothing until there were footsteps, downstairs, in my sitting room. I lifted the telephone receiver, punched the first digit of 999, and listened with shock to the echo of a dead line.

With a finely poised pressure, ready to retreat from the movement at any moment, I depressed the switch on the gooseneck lamp. The bedroom withdrew into sullen darkness. I stood perfectly still while my eyes adjusted to the absence of light, urging myself all the time out of the grip of passive fear.

I crossed the room with swift steps and positioned myself behind the door. Strained to hear, to track the sounds in the sitting room, the thumps and the clunks, of drawers sliding open, of objects being moved. Whatever my man was doing down there, he was not particularly concerned about noise.

Under my sweaty left palm, the handle of the bedroom door felt stiff and uncompromising, as if a sharp wrench might be required to make it open. But no, it yielded smoothly. I retreated with a start. A shadow crossed the gap, indicating that someone was on the upstairs landing. One man I could handle. I hadn't counted on two.

Before I could curse myself for carelessness, the door

was flung open. I retreated toward the wardrobe, caught the heel of my boot on the kilim, and fell backward with a crash. In grammar school, my one dramatic triumph was the scene where Rosalind faints in *As You Like It*. This time as I fell, I composed my face, closed my eyes, and prayed for good reviews. If I couldn't see the intruders, then I couldn't recognize them, and the impulse to silence me with force might conceivably be softened.

Someone crept toward me. From my position on the floor, I could feel him coming. He leaned over me. To lay motionless as a thug bends low, when you can feel his shallow breath on your eyelids, smell the residue of cigarette smoke, hear the creak of denim, takes greater reserves of acting ability than I knew I had. I thought desperately of Mrs. Perry, our drama coach. Break a leg, Laura, she would say. I did my best.

My performance must have been passable. The intruder moved away and called in a low voice, "She's out cold. Hit her head on the edge of the wardrobe. If she identifies us, we're done. Let's get out of here."

The voice of the other man came from a spot near me. I hadn't heard him enter the room. "So," he said, his voice insinuating and sly. "It *is* her. But what's she doing here?"

"What do you mean?" the first fellow demanded, fired by nerves. "She lives here! What are you talking about?"

"Yeah, but she's supposed to be in Glasgow. What does that suggest to you?"

His brain was working overtime and in directions I didn't particularly like. But he moved to the chest of drawers on the other side of the room, and I heard furious sounds of searching. Did I dare to open my eyes? I allowed myself a glimpse of a male back striped by my own eyelashes. The other back, and the man attached to it, had returned, I hoped, to the sitting room.

Before my fall, my rush toward the wardrobe hadn't been for nothing. Nestled there inside my loafer, where I had placed it two hours ago, just in case, was my gun. If only it could be reached. I felt for the soft fabric of the shoe with my left hand, grabbed for the handgun, pushing myself to a crouching position. I wasn't sure yet that I could stand. My faint was faked, but my fall was genuine. And to follow a bang on the head by lying prone with your eyes closed doesn't do a lot for your balance.

"Hold it," I said, the warning intended in small part to steady myself.

The gun was clutched in both my hands, arms outstretched in front of me. I pressed my back against the wall and slowly straightened my knees. He turned around.

I didn't like him any better now than I had at the garage. He wasn't wearing those designer clothes that had first made me wonder how he managed on a mechanic's wage. He was dressed in a working overall, his hands encased in surgical gloves. But Harding still had that cocky air, that gimme-gimme-always-gets that had got, all right, right up my nose.

Trouble is, he hadn't lost that look now. There I was with a gun trained on him, and he looked too comfortable by half. I glanced across and saw the gangly manager bearing down on me from the side.

"Not another inch," I barked. Well, I tried for a bark. It came out like a seal with laryngitis. Mrs. Perry's lessons couldn't help with the effects of fear.

Mr. Cocky kept his eyes on my face. "It's empty," he told his companion. "Nobody keeps a loaded gun in their closet. Not even customers who lie when they say they are going to Glasgow."

"Like hell it is," I hissed.

"Empty. No ammunition. No bullets. Just an empty little handgun, too small to be effective even as a club. Whereas this," he said confidently, picking up the stone carving that Sonny had fetched me back from Zimbabwe, hefting it in his hands, "with this or with that"— he pointed his companion toward my baseball bat just inside the wardrobe—"with this or with that, we could bash her brains in." He smiled.

I swallowed. For once my voice came out as I had intended, strong and sure. "Just try it."

It gave him pause. But not enough to prevent him from risking his accomplice. "Go for it, Mick."

But Mick, bless his chicken little heart, was wavering. "Look, maybe we should just get out of here. Run for it. We don't want to hurt anybody."

Harding didn't look as if he considered himself part of that "we." He had been thwarted. And for someone like him, being thwarted would often provoke an attack. When gimme-gimme doesn't get . . .

They had me awkwardly positioned, at the point of an equilateral triangle. I couldn't cover them both at once.

I glanced at Mick to make certain that the baseball bat hadn't entered his repetoire. Harding raised the stone carving and charged. I aimed at his knee and pulled the trigger. Aiming for the legs is always risky; they are slender targets and they don't stay in one place. But I knew I couldn't bring myself to discharge a bullet at his chest. There's a western from my childhood where the hero asked of the gunslinger, "How many lives do you figure yours is worth?" I had never worked out an answer to that question.

The bullet hit his thigh. He doubled up, the carving just missing my skull as the folding of his body pulled his arm down. He hit the floor with a thunk. I leaned over him, snatched the carving, tossed it on the bed, and ordered him to roll over on his stomach. This time he didn't claim that I was having him on. With a silk scarf, I secured his hands behind him. Then I sat him in a chair and ordered Mick to use a clean pillowcase to staunch the flow of blood. I winced at the blood that puddled on the kilim, but otherwise felt a guilty surge of pride at the careful placing of the wound.

By the time the local police and the ambulance arrived, Harding was trussed and bandaged. Mick sat disconsolate on a stool, like a homesick camper waiting for his parents to fetch him away, and I—in an action that owed nothing to Mrs. Perry and everything to the aftereffects of excitement and shock—collapsed on the bed, scarcely able to keep my eyes open.

But the sleep that I longed for was long in coming. The police were waiting for me down at Parkside Station. They wanted not only a statement, but also to discuss—late into the evening—the delicate issue of my having a loaded handgun in the house.

And after that I had to keep my promise to ring Sonny in Vienna. I took the mobile phone into the bathroom along with a bottle of cold white wine and lowered my aching body gingerly into a bathtub full of warm water spiked with tea rose oil. By the time I emerged from the bathtub, fragrant and dripping and ever so slightly tipsy, the worst was over. Sonny knew about my temporary forgetting of Dominic and Daniel, and about the shooting that had ended the Cambridge case. We had quarreled and made it up again, and I fell, steeped in the aura of tea rose, into a deep and contented sleep.

22

Two out of three passengers off the morning flight from Vienna were businessmen, well-fed and bleak-eyed. The third, tall and lean with a smile that would melt your heart—did still after all these years melt mine—was Sonny.

He smiled. "I didn't expect you," he said, stating the obvious. Obviously pleased.

"Surprise." I kissed him. We stood there, in the middle of the gangway, while emerging passengers flowed around us and the bleak-eyed businessmen tried not to stare.

"I've missed you, Laura," Sonny said at last, pulling away, "but I've got an appointment in town."

"Me too," I agreed, on both counts. "So when will we two meet again?"

"Tonight, if I haven't got my dates wrong, we're off to the theater, aren't we?"

We swapped news on the way back into town. Sonny couldn't wait to tell me about a terrific blues club he'd discovered.

"Blues? In Vienna?" I asked in mock horror. "Whatever happened to Strauss, Mozart, Beethoven? Even Schoenberg?"

"Still available, as far as I know. But I made do—quite comfortably—with Otis Rush."

And I managed to get in a selective summary of the Cambridge case, ignoring the shooting, and going straight to the police, so to speak. How they had a lead on Marcia's paintings from an antiques warehouse in Ipswich; they were pretty sure of recovering the pictures before they were shipped to Japan. How, once I had planted the suggestion that the poorly dressed manager hankered after his receptionist, they had found pieces—such as Marcia Shields's missing bracelet—in her jewelry box that linked Harding and Mick to five other burglaries. How the police had located Harding's watch, not on his wrist where you might think to find it, but in the repair shop nearby, where it had been left to be fitted with a new crown shortly after Marcia Shields's paintings were stolen.

Sonny looked blank. Had to be reminded of the little pin I had found beneath Marcia's skirting board. "Not just a pretty face," he said in a teasing tone. "But what made you so damn sure it was Harding?"

"The Saab garage interested me from the beginning. They knew, after all, that Marcia would be away. The question of access was a puzzle, but once I was certain that all the legitimate keys were accounted for, my interest grew. Then there were Harding's clothes—no one makes that kind of money fixing carburetors. But to tell you the truth, I didn't forge the final link until after

Harding broke into my house. Then I recalled that the shop on Gwydir Street where Petersee had seen one of the stolen paintings belonged in fact to Harding and Callow, Dealers in Objets d'Art."

"Husband and wife?"

"Sister and brother. They inherited the antiques business from their father, but Harding Jr. had no talent for selling, so he concentrated on the acquisition side instead. And persuaded the garage manager to join him."

"And getting back to the question of access. You obligingly left them your keys?" Sonny said, his question colored by a hint of disapproval.

"Of course. I wanted to make damn sure that they didn't demolish my doorframe."

"That's you. But what about Marcia Shields? Wasn't she adamant that her housekeys were in her handbag all weekend?"

"She was. And they were. Except for four or five minutes. They had a nice little system going at the Saab garage. Harding met Marcia, took her key pouch, and parked her car, while the gangly manager engaged her in discussion."

"You're not suggesting," Sonny asked dryly, "that their chat lasted long enough for Harding to get from Cherry Hinton to Lyndewode Road, lift the paintings, and drive back?"

"You're right. I'm not. What I'm saying is that Harding nipped to the kiosk that adjoined the garage, where a key was speedily cut for Marcia's front door."

"So," Sonny asked as I let him off near Baker Street, "you can chalk up another satisfied Cambridge customer, then?"

"I guess you could put it like that. Marcia Shields is happy on three counts. About the imminent return of her paintings. About the return to domestic harmony now that the cloud of suspicion over Layla has been lifted. And about the fact that my visit to the Mertons precipitated a marital breakup. Kay got the wrong end of the stick, assumed that I was another of her husband's paramours, and during the rows that followed, apparently, she agreed at last to a divorce. Terry and Marcia's long affair can now be out in the open. And Marcia is absurdly grateful, believing it was all down to me."

"So. Everyone wins, huh?"

"I don't know about that." I blew him a kiss. I had an uncomfortable flash of Kay Merton's miserable face. "More like winners and losers, I guess. See you tonight."

We linked up with the rest of our party that evening in the crowded foyer of the Duke of Leicester. Sofia Perez had been to a matinee before, but *Inside Sherwood Forest* was her first evening performance, and her employer, protective after recent events, had assigned a driver to see her safely there and back. Her eyes sparkled—and as ever, heads turned—when she bounced into the theater. Hugo and Justine were close behind. To my chagrin, they had the talkative Sarah in tow, their neighbor whose reference to a man who knew *everyone who was anyone* in the Gulf had first alerted me to Derek Cracknell. What Justine finds to like in Sarah I shall never understand; as far as I'm concerned, if there had been more Sarahs around in the 1970s, the concept of sisterhood would never even have got a look-in.

I was queuing for the loo when Sarah pounced, her voice husky with excitement. "Did you really shoot a man?"

And I had thought I could put it all behind me. "Yes. In the leg."

And then I told her the truth. That the whole thing was a cock-up. That I had had no intention of shooting anyone. That I had dialed 999 expecting the police at Parkside to stampede to my rescue, but was stymied because the telephone wires had been cut; Mick may have looked dim, but he had an instinct for self-preservation. That there had been two bad guys instead of one. That I had tripped on my way across the room and lost the initiative. And that I had been convinced Harding was going to kill me. Using my gun, I said, was a surefire admission of failure.

I kept to myself that there would be an inquiry into the shooting. That the police had revoked my firearms license. That Sonny had called me an idiot and worse, and that my mother was insisting on visiting from Bristol to check that I was okay.

The sour taste of success.

And though I managed to distance myself from both Sarah and the Cambridge case for the rest of the evening, the mood of melancholy persisted. The act 1 monologue about living on the margins triggered a stream of associations that I would have preferred to do without. Sonny put his finger on it. Doesn't it feel strange, he whispered as the interval curtain came down, being in the audience when you have all this inside information about the producer?

Well, yes, it did feel strange. The Butlers—Thomas, Penelope, and the unfortunate Tim—had been interviewed by the police to little avail. Timothy confessed to making Marilou's nose bleed and was prepared (accident or not) to take the punishment that he assumed was his due. But the director of public prosecutions would not be interested in a mere assault case when she had a couple of killers to hand.

And Thomas and Penelope? Their intentions in turning Marilou over to Cracknell and his henchman were a
matter of great interest to the police. But the Butlers
presented themselves as the victims of misunder-
standing, and there was little chance of proving otherwise. They had to send Marilou away, they claimed, to
avoid embarrassment for Timothy. Of course, I knew—
and they knew—that it was not care for Timothy that
was foremost in this decision; Timothy's welfare had
long ago been sacrificed. Foremost in this decision was
care for the Butler reputation. For the liberal reputation,
on his side. For the ladylike, on hers.

But that's not a crime. No charges have been laid
against Thomas and Penelope Butler. And none will be.

"What else could I do? Under the circumstances?"
Thomas Butler had asked, his words for the police, but
his eyes on his wife.

Plenty, Nicole responded. You knew that Cracknell
planned to return Marilou forcibly to the household
where she had been treated like a slave. You could have
bought her legal advice. You could have honored your
offer of protection, kept her with you until a genuinely
safe haven was found. You could have treated Marilou
Flores as a human being with the same right to personal
security—to freedom—as yourself.

Enough, said DCI Willis. But he didn't contradict her.

We spotted them at the other end of the bar, at a large
table set aside for the producer. Penelope looked stun-
ning, her hair and body gracefully arranged. She was
conversing with an elderly man, and her head was tilted
in a evocation of attentiveness. But I'm certain she
didn't hear a word he said. Her perfect eyes looked perfectly vacant to me.

Thomas Butler on the other hand was glowing. The prepreview reviews (or rave-views, as one tabloid called them) guaranteed a hit. And Butler's reputation as the daring producer, the social conscience of the West End, was assured. "Some people won't like it!" critics warned, referring to the biting social criticism.

Of course they would. They would be moved by the script, impressed by the playing, and convinced—for the moment—by the issues. They would adjust their bow ties, drink another glass of bubbly, and go home. They'd discuss it with their friends and find a way to neutralize the call to action while remaining thrilled by the art.

That's entertainment.

My round. Cynicism didn't become me, and I needed a stiff drink to shake it off. I collected orders and joined the warm mass of theatergoers clustered around the bar. And just as I got the drinks and fought free of the crowd, Thomas Butler detached himself from his coterie and made his way toward me.

"Miss Principal," he said in his attractive voice. Once again the easy charm. "Could we have a moment?"

"Hope you haven't had any more trouble with missing items backstage," I said, as if I cared.

"The thefts did stop after all—when Liam O'Laughlin's mother left London. But that's not why I wanted a word."

And while I watched the fizzle subside in Sofia's mineral water, he told me how sorry he was for everything. How he would give his right arm—funny saying, that, and hardly the issue—to bring her back again. And he was sorry also to have given me the runaround. If there was ever anything he could do for me . . .

No time to be coy. "There is one thing," I said. True

to his word, he agreed to send around by courier tomorrow one of the photographs from his office wall.

When Thomas Butler left, Sarah—the loquacious Sarah, Ms. Foot-in-the-Mouth—came rushing over. "The interval's almost over," she exclaimed. "Wasn't that Thomas Butler himself? Is he pleased with the play? Isn't he just wonderful?"

I answered her curtly. Yes. Yes. And no.

My mind was cleft by the memory of two children.

On the one hand, Thomas's daughter, Beatrice, secure in her laughter, pacing her pony around a paddock in Kent.

And on the other, a clever girl from the Philippines who was christened Maria Luisa Flores, the passionate hope of parents far away. Who had sought shelter with the Butlers and who, when her presence became inconvenient, had been delivered to her death.

In the taxi on the way home, I was melancholy still. "Come on, sweetie, out with it," Sonny urged. "Why so pensive? Is this lovesickness—are you yearning after Liam O'Laughlin, like the preteens in the audience? Or guilt—do you feel bad at last that you used your gun on that poor young Cambridge lad? Or are you regretting that you didn't wait for me to rescue you?"

I tossed him a look of mock outrage and laid my head on his shoulder.

"I wish you were always there to protect me," I said, half in jest.

"Me too." The other half. And he waited for my real answer.

"Tell you in the morning. Promise."

The boys had guaranteed us breakfast in bed, and breakfast in bed we got. Charred croissants, lukewarm instant coffee, a tulip in a jam jar, and Dominic and Daniel, bouncing on the bed, full of beans.

Later, they linked up with friends for a trip to the cinema. Sonny set to work sorting out receipts in preparation for a meeting with his accountant. I should have got down to work too, but I had a better idea.

I whispered in Sonny's ear, "Let's have breakfast in bed all over again." He looked startled, his finger still tracing a line down an invoice. I repeated the suggestion, embellished it a little.

"What if I'm not hungry?"

But he was. Something along the lines of a full English breakfast.

After a while, we opened the blinds and lay curled around one another, the pressure of the past weeks washing away. I felt happy for the first time in ages.

"Will it be like this in Provence, do you think?" I mused. "I can imagine the sun flaming down outside, and us lying cool and relaxed in a big shady bedroom, listening to the cicadas. Or strolling down the lane to the village, with nothing at all on our agenda but to buy and prepare the tastiest chicken, the most succulent vegetables in all of France. And to drink the best wine."

Sonny picked up the thread. "Or swimming in the stream—naked if it's private enough—and laying ourselves out in the sun to dry. But more likely," he teased, "we'll succumb to pressure from Dominic and Daniel and spend our time in search of municipal swimming pools and McDonald's."

What can you do with a man like that? I tickled him until he promised a united front against Ronald McD.

"You've decided then." Sonny looked triumphant. "You're coming to Provence."

I pretended there had never been an issue. "Wouldn't

miss it for the world. We're going to have the best two weeks of our life together. Our life so far, that is."

Sonny rose up on one elbow. "The farmhouse is rented by the month," he challenged.

"I can think of lots of friends who would be glad to join a party in Provence for the other two weeks." I had thought this through. "We'll have a splendid fortnight there, with Hugo and Justine and the children. And then I'll have another fortnight on my own turf. At Wildfell."

I dared him to object. Sonny brushed his thick blond hair off his forehead. "Is this a case, Laura," he asked with a flick of annoyance, "of trying to have your cake and eat it too?"

"More a case of learning—as you said I should—to compromise." I watched his face, lovingly, anxiously. "Tell me you understand."

Sonny put his arms around me and snuggled his face into my neck. Then he pulled back and looked at me a long time. "I understand." And he grinned. "But what if you like it so much in France that you can't bear to say au revoir?"

Stevie didn't show up for work the next day. There was no phone call, no explanation in the diary, no apology. Just the briefest of notes, skewered to her desk with a letter opener. *Gone fishing.*

Well, Stevie has a lot of eccentric habits, but fishing wasn't—as far as I knew—one of them. The note meant something else. The note meant that Stevie had given up on anything resembling support from me and had retreated to Wildfell to lick her wounds. Alone.

I dragged Desiree out of bed and down to the office. It would be a quiet day, I promised (as if I could). All she had to do was keep things ticking over and fill in for me on a couple of appointments.

"Where you off to?" she asked. She didn't have the dog with her. Apparently, they had successfully bonded at last, so the director had allowed her to relinquish Fifi's company.

"To spend some time with a friend. To Wildfell."

Once out of London it was easy. I had an exceptional run and arrived in Burnham St. Stephens just as the church clock should have been striking noon. The clock was silent, of course, as it has been for years. The vicar insists—and who can argue—that the roof has priority over the clock, and the overseas aid fund has priority over the roof. I know this because Helen is a sucker for church fetes and always returns with some sturdy item of village information.

It was good to be back.

I found Stevie crouched beside the stream. She was completely still, gazing at the swans on the bank opposite, and all she said when I swished toward her was, "Ssh." Suspended next to her was a long flexible fishing rod. The ensemble was completed by a bag of gear and a plastic tub containing—one glance was enough for me—live maggots.

I plumped down on a damp clump of grass next to her. "I didn't know you liked to fish."

Stevie looked at me flat-eyed. "Lots of things you don't know."

"True. And that's why I'm here. Tell me about this helicopter pilot."

"It's over." Stevie shrugged her shoulders. As if it didn't matter.

"Not until you've told me."

So with only a little more persuasion, she did. About

excitement and hope and disappointment, and about having to reevaluate some of the important things in life. We talked until the weather changed, until the surface of the stream was pocked with rain.

Then we collected up the fishing gear—Stevie carried the maggots—deposited it in the shed, and strolled along to the Unicorn. They were still serving lunch. The captain's chairs by the fireside were free and mussels were on the menu, freshly delivered from the coast. So Stevie and I stretched out our legs toward the fire and shared a massive bowl of steamed mussels and—unusually for the time of day—a bottle of white wine.

"How decadent is this on a scale of one to ten?" Stevie asked, and I was pleased to see that her old grin had resurfaced. "After all, it's not even the weekend."

But I took this as my cue and explained that today wasn't just any old weekday. Today was the day—overdue—when I would tell her how much I valued what she had done for Dominic and Daniel at the swimming pool. And what she had done, on this as on many other occasions, for me.

Stevie was embarrassed and bent her head over the last stubborn shell; but she looked nonetheless as if she had needed this acknowledgment.

I didn't stop there. I went on to tell Stevie how glad I was that she had joined Helen and me at Wildfell. "We need you here. You really make a difference."

Stevie fetched some more of the landlady's homemade bread to mop up the last of the garlicky juice. She glanced at me shyly. But then, since I was coming clean, she followed my example. "A couple of weeks ago, you know—when you were so anxious about Claire—I got the idea that you might have resented me being here in the face of Claire's absence. After all, I've only known you for a comparatively short time. And well—Claire sounds so extraordinary."

"Even if she had shown up, even if Claire had asked to move back in with us at Wildfell, one thing is for sure. Old friends don't chase out new."

Stevie hadn't forgotten that the whole thing had begun with a letter and a black-and-white image from my childhood. She looked at me squarely now, her confidence restored. "Tell me honestly, are you still upset about that photograph?"

"Nope. Not much." I linked my arm through hers. "Why cry over a photograph of friendship when you can have the real thing?"

EPILOGUE

But some people live their lives through pictures. For them, a photograph may make all the difference.

I had told Martin Scorsese to expect me—didn't want to arrive in the middle of a video—but I hadn't told him why. I refused offers of refreshment from him and Carmen—coffee on the one hand, tea on the other, the skirmish raging still—and simply presented the old man with a parcel. For the fun of it, I had encased the package from Butler's office in knock-your-eye-out wrapping paper and topped it off with a big red bow.

"A gift?" His eyes glinted. He ripped the paper off like a toddler searching for sweets.

And like a toddler receiving sweets, he was delighted.

"Robert De Niro! Signed! 'With best wishes!' Now how did you get that?"

I spun him a story, a pack of lies about wild times and wilder coincidences on the mean streets of London. The old guy likes stories. He knew it wasn't true, but that's hardly the point.